Daniel took a step closer.

"Let's do each other a favor, Sarah. You stay the hell away from me, and I'll keep my mouth shut. Will that satisfy you?"

Sarah nodded, but made no move to go.

Daniel sighed. "Answer me one question—is the law after you?"

"Of course not!" She shouldn't have been surprised by the question, considering what he thought of her.

"Of course not," he mumbled.

At the sarcasm in his tone, she turned to him. "Daniel, let me explain."

"Listen! You had a chance to explain in court. My name is River now, and I don't know you. Can you remember that? If it's all the same with you, I'd just as soon these people didn't know what a fool you made of me six years ago...."

Dear Reader,

Cassandra Austin's first book, the poignant
Wait for the Sunrise, was published as part of our
Western Skies promotion in September 1993, and was very
well received. Since then, we have been eagerly awaiting
her next title, and this month we are delighted to be able to
bring it to you. *Trusting Sarah* is the story of a young
woman who heads west on a wagon train, trying to escape
her past, only to run headlong into it again, in the form
of the man who wrongly sent her to jail years before.
Trusting Sarah is our featured Women of the West title
for August and we hope you enjoy it.

And from gifted author Laurel Ames comes her fourth
book, *Playing To Win,* a Regency about a young wife who
is willing to do anything to win the love of her husband, a
rakish duke with an uncanny conscience.

Our titles this month also include *The Magician's Quest,*
Claire Delacroix's sequel to *Honeyed Lies,* the tale of a
man who must come to terms with the legacy left him by
his father, and his love for a woman of questionable virtue.
And from talented medieval author Catherine Archer, her
latest delightful story, *Velvet Bond.*

Whatever your taste in historical reading, we hope you'll
enjoy all four titles, available wherever Harlequin
Historicals are sold.

Sincerely,

Tracy Farrell
Senior Editor

Please address questions and book requests to:
Harlequin Reader Service
U.S.: 3010 Walden Ave., P.O. Box 1325, Buffalo, NY 14269
Canadian: P.O. Box 609, Fort Erie, Ont. L2A 5X3

CASSANDRA AUSTIN

TRUSTING SARAH

Harlequin Books

TORONTO • NEW YORK • LONDON
AMSTERDAM • PARIS • SYDNEY • HAMBURG
STOCKHOLM • ATHENS • TOKYO • MILAN
MADRID • WARSAW • BUDAPEST • AUCKLAND

ISBN 0-373-28879-4

TRUSTING SARAH

Copyright © 1995 by Sandra Detrixhe.

This edition published by arrangement with Harlequin Books S.A.

® and TM are trademarks of the publisher. Trademarks indicated with
® are registered in the United States Patent and Trademark Office, the
Canadian Trade Marks Office and in other countries.

Printed in U.S.A.

CASSANDRA AUSTIN

has always lived in north central Kansas, and was raised on museums and arrowhead hunts; when she began writing, America's Old West seemed the natural setting. Now she writes between—and sometimes during—4H, school events and the various activities of her three children. Her husband farms, and they live in the house where he grew up.

To Janet and Aggie

Prologue

Albany, New York—1853

Sarah Tanton shivered. The thin shawl around her shoulders did little to ward off the chill of the courtroom, and nothing to stop the dread that turned her blood to ice.

Her attorney had told her what to expect, had told her in essence what Daniel would say, but, as she watched him walk confidently toward the stand, she didn't want to believe it. He looked the same as always, wonderfully tall and handsome, dressed in a well-tailored suit, new for the occasion.

"State your name." The bailiff's voice rang in the silence.

"Daniel Harrison." With one hand raised and the other on a Bible, he swore to tell the truth.

"It was late Saturday night, close to midnight. My father had a large amount of money at the store. The other employees and I were to take turns guarding it until the bank opened on Monday morning."

Sarah knew she should listen carefully to the words, not just the reassuring sound of his voice. Surely he would explain. He would put an end to this terrible misunderstanding.

"I remember feeling a little uneasy as I came through the alley, like someone was watching me, but I can't say I heard or saw anything then. The back door was supposed to be locked, but it wasn't even closed. I took a couple steps inside and found Frank. Frank Abernathy, I mean. He had the shift just before mine. I knew he was hurt, and I was kneeling down to help him when I heard a sound in the alley. I rushed to the door, and that's when I saw her running away."

"Is the person you saw in this courtroom?"

Sarah had been gazing at the familiar face, willing the blue eyes to turn in her direction. Now, suddenly, they did.

"Yes. That's her."

It took Sarah a full minute to understand. Her mind screamed, "Why, Daniel? I thought you loved me! What happened to all our plans?"

Of course she didn't speak aloud but stared into his cool blue eyes in frozen silence. He was the first to turn away.

She sat through another hour of testimony, thinking the pain would crush her at any moment. Finally, she stood with the rest, and the jailer took her arm to lead her out of the courtroom. As usual, her attorney joined them for the walk back to her cell.

The scene from the large window at the landing between the second and third floors had become Sarah's only view of the outside world, and the jailer routinely gave her a moment there, "to catch her breath." It was at this window that Sarah managed to find her voice. "Tell Daniel I want to see him."

The attorney turned away from her, gazing out the dirty window. "I don't believe that would be a good idea, Miss Tanton," he said after a moment.

"Please," she begged, "I have to see him!"

The man's expression didn't change. "As you wish, miss." He turned to descend the stairs without another glance at her. She and the jailer continued their quiet walk to the jail.

Sarah paced the cell for what seemed like hours. She had imagined Daniel hurrying to her. The longer she waited, the more she dreaded his explanation. Finally she heard voices and the jingle of keys as the outer door was unlocked. The jailer and her attorney came down the short hall to her cell.

She barely dared to whisper, "Daniel?"

"He refuses to come, Miss Tanton. You better get some sleep." With these words, the attorney turned and left the cell block, the jailer close behind.

Sarah found his advice impossible to follow. She entered the courtroom the next morning, hollow-eyed and trembling. The attorney barely acknowledged her as she took her place beside him.

"All rise." The bailiff's clear voice brought everyone to their feet. Sarah watched the judge enter and take his place. She sat with the others, and the bailiff spoke. "The defendant will rise."

The attorney's hand on her elbow urged her up again.

"Sarah Tanton, you have been found guilty of robbery and assault. Do you have anything to say?"

Sarah swallowed. She couldn't have spoken if she had wanted to. She shook her head.

The judge frowned. "You have been uncommonly stubborn, young woman. In light of your total lack of remorse, I have little choice but to sentence you to twenty years in Auburn Prison. If, at some future time, your cooperation leads to the recovery of Mr. Harrison's money, this court will reconsider the sentence. Court is adjourned."

The judge's gavel struck the block, and Sarah cringed.

"All rise," the bailiff said.

Sarah turned toward the spectators in the courtroom, needing to see Daniel again, to plead with him to help her. The jailer took her arm and pulled her away even as she found him. His back to her, he was walking away. She tried to call to him, but his name came out a whisper. "Daniel."

He turned then and their eyes locked. His face was unreadable.

The tightened grip on her arm made her realize she was struggling. "Daniel!" The cry lodged in her throat as she was pulled from the room.

Chapter One

Outside Fort Leavenworth
Kansas Territory—1859

The wagon master sat at his plank-and-barrel desk, tapping the end of the pencil against his gray mustache, and studied the young woman. While she wasn't tall, she stood so straight with her head erect that it kept her from looking tiny. Her straight hair was a chestnut brown, red where the sun caught it, and smoothed back from a gentle face that seemed somehow at odds with her stiff bearing. Her soft brown eyes made him want to help her.

She turned to watch a flock of blackbirds, her face registering such delight the man glanced at the birds himself before eyeing her curiously. Why would a flock of noisy birds be so entertaining?

Pete Milburn considered himself a good judge of character, and this Miss Sarah Tanton looked like a stayer. He was sure she would make her request of other trains if he turned her down.

She brushed a strand of hair away from her cheek as she turned back to face him. "Well, Mr. Milburn?"

Milburn took a deep breath and let it out slowly. "Miss Tanton, let me be honest. I'm afraid I will be shorthanded, but what I need is someone to drive the supply wagon. I got Rice pulling double duty till River catches up. Can you handle an ox team, Miss Tanton?"

Sarah didn't miss the hopeful note in the question. She looked toward the grassy riverbank where the gentle beasts were grazing. They looked massive, and Sarah's confidence slipped. "I don't know, sir. That's why I didn't purchase a wagon and team. All I'll need . . ."

"Are the supplies to cross the continent. Miss Tanton, this isn't a passenger train."

"Perhaps I could learn to drive a wagon, sir." Her eyes were silently pleading.

Milburn sighed again. He adjusted the pencil and studied the ledger in front of him. Carefully he wrote "Sarah Tanton—May 3, 1859" on the topmost vacant line. Under the amounts paid by the other travelers, he wrote "Hired."

"Mr. Milburn, I—" she began.

"Rice!" he yelled over his shoulder, startling her into silence. In a softer voice he asked, "Where are your things?"

Before Sarah could do more than stammer and point, a gangling young man, barely in his teens, hurried up to his boss.

"Rice, this is Sarah Tanton. She's going to be helping Eli. Find room for her things in the lead wagon."

"Helping Eli?" Rice glanced at Sarah before tilting his blond head toward Milburn. "But Eli—"

"Don't argue, boy!" Milburn rose from his seat, smiling at Sarah. "If you'll excuse me, miss, there's a fella coming I need to talk to." He tipped his hat and left them.

Rice stared dubiously after his boss, and Sarah felt apprehensive. "I only have one trunk," she said.

Earlier, Sarah had caught a ride out from town. Now she found the trunk where the driver had left it. Rice was stronger than he looked, and the two of them had little trouble carrying it to the lead wagon.

"Thank you for helping me, Mr. Rice," Sarah said.

"Shucks, ma'am. I ain't no Mr. Rice. I'm just plain Rice."

"Don't you have a first name?" she asked, smiling.

"Yes, ma'am." He blushed. "I'll make room for this." He scrambled over the tailboard so quickly he nearly fell in.

Sarah smiled after him. She sat down on her little wooden trunk. Everything she owned was inside. Somehow it seemed appropriate to perch herself on top of it. *Here sits Sarah Tanton on all her worldly goods, in the middle of a meadow where the East ends and the West begins.* She might have added, "where the past meets the future," but her thoughts were interrupted.

An old man rounded the wagon and stopped in surprise when he saw her. "What are ya doin' here?"

Sarah came to her feet as the man went to the wagon demanding, "What's goin' on in here?"

"Oh, Eli," Rice mumbled. After some scraping and shuffling, Rice stuck his head out the back of the wagon. "Eli, this is Miss Tanton. Miss Tanton, this here's Eli." The boy grinned broadly at his display of proper manners.

"That don't tell me nothin'," declared the old man.

"Oh." Rice sobered. "Mr. Milburn, he hired her to... uh... to help you." His smile was more hopeful than happy.

Eli looked Sarah up and down. "We'll see about that. Don't ya move nothin' in that wagon till I get back!" He hurried toward the supply wagon and Milburn's makeshift office.

Sarah looked after him in horror. She hadn't had a chance to say a word. He would never allow her to work with him. She turned to thank Rice for trying to help.

Rice hopped out of the wagon and unhooked the hinged tailboard. "Eli ain't so bad." He grabbed her trunk and hoisted it into the wagon.

"What are you doing? You'll get yourself in trouble."

"No, ma'am. Mr. Milburn's boss. Eli, well…he's Eli." Rice nodded to punctuate his explanation. "Eli's just Eli."

Sarah was not reassured. "What does Eli do?"

"Whatever Mr. Milburn needs done," was the boy's reply. Perhaps realizing that was an inadequate explanation, he added, "Cooking mostly. Helping with breakdowns, stuff like that."

Eli returned, obviously displeased. He told Rice to build a fire and stood by until the rocks and wood were placed to his satisfaction. Dismissed, Rice waved and trotted away. Sarah waved back, then turned to find Eli scowling at her.

"I guess Pete hired ya, a'right," he said. "Ya ain't what I had in mind when I said I wanted better help 'an that boy."

Sarah found herself tongue-tied again.

Eli lifted the tailboard parallel to the ground and fastened it to chains on the side of the wagon. Using it as a table, he took tins and utensils from a small cupboard that faced outward. "I guess I'm stuck with ya, long as ya last. We always meet a few wagons goin' back. When ya give it up, ya can get a ride with one a them."

Sarah felt she should say something. "Mr. Eli—"

"I ain't gonna call ya Miss Tanton, so there ain't no use callin' me Mr. Eli," he interrupted. "I'm Eli, and yer Sarie. If ya don't like it, you best answer to it anyhow."

"Fine, sir," she lied. Sarie! It sounded terrible. "What would you like me to do?"

"Do? Don't do nothin'. Just stay outta my way."

Sarah watched his agile movements, wondering if he was younger than she had first thought. What hair she could see under the brim of his black slouch hat was dark, but his face was lined and tanned until it resembled leather. His gray eyes were clear and ageless.

The ingredients in his bowl had become a stiff dough. He stirred it vigorously with a wooden spoon. "Some city gal decides to go west, and Pete gets soft." He shaped handfuls of dough into biscuits and crowded them into a heavy iron skillet. "Softheaded, if ya ask me. Stubborn as an old mule, and I ain't got *no* use for mules!" His words faded to unintelligible grumbles.

Slamming an iron lid on the skillet, he shoved it directly into the fire. "Ya didn't think I could just pop 'em in an oven, did ya?" He was obviously hoping to have shocked her, and expressed his disappointment at her calm gaze by muttering again.

Eli added spices to his kettle and set tin bowls and cups out on the tailboard. First Rice then Milburn joined them. Sarah noticed other groups around other fires, taking their evening meal. A few had tables and camp stools, but most sat near their fires, balancing plates on their laps.

Sarah took her portion and sat on a crate near Rice. The stew was hearty, with a meat she couldn't identify. She didn't consider asking about it. The biscuit was a little heavy, but she wouldn't mention that, either. She ate slowly, not wanting to show how hungry she was.

Rice had no such concern; he ate twice as much as anybody else in half the time. Eli had evidently come to expect it. "This is my third trip west, Miss Tanton," the boy announced between servings.

"Don't go bragging about it," Eli scolded. "Ya ain't no old hand, by a long shot."

Sarah smiled at the youth, and he beamed back. "I'm gonna be one day, Eli. I'll be a scout like River. River says we're leaving in the morning. That right, Mr. Milburn?"

Milburn grinned at the boy. "There's grass enough to support the stock. We'll pull out tomorrow."

Rice's delight was too great to hold inside, and he whooped for joy. Milburn laughed. "Help me tell the others."

The boy rose eagerly, setting his bowl aside. "River says he ain't leaving with us. That right, too, Mr. Milburn?"

"We'll wait for him at Fort Kearny, if he hasn't caught up by then." He put an arm across the boy's shoulders. "I can count on you to fill the gap, can't I, son?"

"Yes, sir!" he responded.

Eli grumbled something about fool boys.

As Sarah helped Eli clean the dishes and put them away, she began to feel uneasy. After tomorrow, there would be no turning back. She silently scolded herself. The things she had kept from Milburn shouldn't matter anymore.

Eli spoke, causing her to jump. "Ya don't talk much, do ya?"

Sarah had to take a slow breath so her voice wouldn't shake. "I'm used to working in silence." At his curious look she amended, "Working alone." Eli went on with the cleaning, but she knew he watched her.

"I don't guess ya come prepared with blankets and such," he commented as he closed the door on the last of the dishes.

"I have blankets in my trunk," she said.

Eli frowned. "Ya can sleep in the wagon. Better turn in. Day don't start at noon out here like in the city."

As he sauntered away, she almost laughed. When had she slept past daybreak? Suddenly she remembered the parties, the nightlife of Albany, and Daniel. How could she have forgotten? Still, it seemed like a different lifetime, a different Sarah. She shuddered and climbed into the wagon. She wouldn't think about Daniel.

The interior of the wagon seemed dim and gray. There were boxes and crates neatly stacked and a canvas cover overhead. The canvas was equipped with pucker strings that could close the ends completely. She moved forward in the wagon and loosened the strings as much as possible.

Finding her trunk in the settling darkness, she removed her little jewelry box and let her fingers trace the flower carved in the walnut surface. This was her most treasured possession, a gift from Daniel years ago. Disgusted with herself for becoming melancholy, she opened the box and dropped the hairpins in as she removed them from her hair. She needed to separate the happy memories from the sad, she decided, or not think about Daniel at all.

Her blankets spread on the floor between the piles of crates, Sarah listened to the sounds outside, trying to let the soft voices reassure her. She willed herself to relax on her hard bed but found herself gripping the blankets so tightly her fingers hurt. The images that intruded were too vivid. Knowing them for what they were made little difference. She crawled to the rear of the wagon and breathed in the fresh cool air.

She didn't know how long she sat there, but the camp grew still, and the fires died. Quietly, afraid of disturbing the others, she took her blankets a short distance from the wagons. The ground was no harder than the wagon, and the stars overhead brought her a peace the gray wagon had not.

Activity in the camp awakened her. Though it was still dark, men were bringing in teams and meals were being prepared. Their own fire had been rekindled, and Eli hovered near it. She stretched stiff muscles and, gathering up her blankets, hurried to put them away and tend to herself.

When she returned, Eli eyed her sourly. "Ain't much left for ya to do."

Sarah wondered if he had let her sleep in order to confirm his own assessment of her. Breakfast did seem to be nearly ready. A coffeepot sat on a grate above the fire, and Eli held the long handle of a skillet in which bacon hissed and crackled.

After setting out the tin plates and cups, she moved near the fire, letting its warmth ease the morning chill. Breathing in the smell of wood smoke, bacon and brewing coffee, she felt an unexpected sense of freedom. She wished she had Rice's lack of inhibitions and could throw back her head and whoop. She could imagine what Eli would think of her then.

Rice brought the teams in, and Milburn came to help hitch them up. Sarah wondered if she should offer to help or take over the breakfast so Eli could. She wished someone would tell her what she was expected to do. Questions formed in her mind, but Eli's closed expression kept them there.

When Milburn and Rice came to the fire, Eli served their breakfast. "Can Miss Sarah ride with me?" Rice asked, passing his plate for more.

Milburn laughed. "I imagine Eli wants to talk to her about her duties, Rice. Maybe another day."

Sarah glanced from Rice's frown to Eli's scowl and felt as bad as Rice. She tried to be more careful not to show it.

It was more than an hour, however, before she had to climb onto the wagon seat with Eli. Milburn called a meeting to explain the route by army road to Fort Kearny and announce the order of wagons, describing the rotation system that would keep any one person from always having the dusty rear position.

He introduced the Reverend Fleenor, a young man with an unruly shock of dark hair who invited everyone to worship services on Sundays.

"Hold on a minute!" A hard-faced, stocky man pushed his way through the crowd. "I don't got time to waste while the Reverend prays for our souls. I say we move as far and fast as we can."

There was a murmur in the crowd, of assent or dissent, it was hard to tell. Milburn raised his hand. "We'll avoid longer delays if we keep wagons and harnesses in good condition. Besides, both man and beast need rest. We'll stop on Sundays if we can."

The authority in his voice made the man back down. Sarah watched him join two other hard cases. The youngest sported a black eye. From a brawl, she imagined.

Finally, Eli helped Sarah onto the lead wagon. He seated himself beside her and waited. It wasn't long before Milburn waved his hat in the air. Eli hollered at the oxen, cracking a whip above their backs, and the wagon moved forward.

Off to their right, another train was preparing to pull out. A lone wagon was already ahead of them. Sarah breathed deeply, taking in the crisp spring morning. Birds were singing, and an occasional wildflower peeked among the prairie grasses.

She was leaving the states behind. Leaning out the wagon to look behind them, she could see Fort Leavenworth, with its flag catching the breeze, and the town across the river. There were clusters of wagons still behind them and thirty-six wagons following Milburn into the unknown.

"Ya wishin' ya'd stayed back there?" Eli asked.

"No. I just want to remember."

Eli glanced at the pretty face and frowned. In spite of himself, he was curious. Why was she going west, and how did she come to be all alone? The way women liked to talk, he'd bet his back teeth he'd know all about it by the end of the day.

As the sun rose higher, Sarah donned the sunbonnet she had been holding in her lap. It restricted her view but protected her skin and hair from the relentless rays. It also, she discovered, offered some protection from Eli's curious glances.

At midday, Milburn signaled for a stop. Eli angled his wagon off the main track, and Rice pulled his up beside it. The others did the same. They ate a cold meal, checked stock and harnesses and were on their way again in less than an hour.

Back in the wagon seat, Sarah wondered if she should ask Eli about her duties. She was afraid he would tell her she was useless. She was planning her defense when he broke the silence. "Sarie, what do ya 'spect Pete hired ya for?"

She decided not to answer directly. "I intend to earn my keep, but I'll have to be told what to do."

Eli grunted. "Ya think ya know how to take orders, huh?"

It sounded more like a challenge than a question. She couldn't imagine anything he could tell her to do that would bother her, except handle the oxen. Their yokes and harnesses looked too complicated to ever understand, and the beasts themselves seemed enormous. Eli watched her, probably taking her silence as hesitation. "Try giving a few orders, sir," she said.

Her answer seemed to satisfy him; at least he said nothing more. Sarah was free to enjoy the countryside and think about her future. But the future was too uncertain, and the past always hovered in her mind.

The past seemed to consist only of Daniel Harrison. She wondered how six years had changed him. No one back home would tell her where he had gone, but then few had been willing to tell her much of anything. Her former jailer had had some information, even some newspapers, but had been quiet about Daniel. That was probably the way his family wanted it.

She guessed he was doing well. With his father's money it would be hard not to. Perhaps he was running a branch store or had found something else to interest him, with Papa's approval.

She watched storm clouds gather in the southwest, their changing shapes fascinating her. They rolled over one another much as her own memories did. Soon they would become too full of anger and pain to hold it inside any longer.

She quickly shook off the illusion. She couldn't start to cry now, not while she sat beside Eli!

Near a deep ravine where a spring-fed creek watered a stand of cottonwoods, Milburn gave the signal to stop. Eli turned his team in a wide arc and pulled up behind the last wagon, turning again at the last moment to put the oxen outside the circle.

Eli sent Sarah to gather firewood. She had found only a few skinny sticks when a woman near her gave a cry of alarm. She had tried to balance too much wood in her small arms and was now clutching at the pieces as they tumbled out of her grasp. She stomped her foot in exasperation and threw one last stick after the rest.

"Let me help you," Sarah offered.

The woman brushed at the bits of dirt and bark that clung to her sleeves. The thin fabric of the much mended dress stretched tightly across her round middle. She bent awkwardly to retrieve her load, and Sarah knelt beside her. "Such little pieces of wood will burn quickly, and I didn't want to make two trips." When her arms were full and Sarah had helped her to her feet, she added, "I'm Martha Williams."

"Sarah Tanton."

"I wish I could help *you* now," she said as Sarah began to gather sticks for herself.

Sarah smiled. "I can manage."

"I'm just glad there's wood. I've heard out on the prairie we'll have to burn—" Martha leaned closer, whispering "—buffalo dung." She wrinkled her nose.

Sarah eyed her skeptically. They walked back together, parting at the supply wagon.

"Took ya long enough." Eli was directly behind her.

Sarah jumped and dropped the wood, her reaction startling Eli into a hasty step backward. As she gathered the sticks, she stammered, "I'm s-sorry." She was too embarrassed to look at him.

"There you go, Eli, frightening women and children again." Milburn put a hand on her elbow, helping her to her feet.

"Thank you," she murmured, and hurried to put the wood where Eli had told her. She wished she had more control over her reactions, but Eli's tone had sounded too familiar.

The next morning the camp woke to a cold drizzle. Sarah wrapped her blanket around her shoulders and helped Eli begin breakfast. Several of the emigrants had hung tentlike structures from their wagons to shelter their fires. Eli scoffed, saying he would save his for a real rain.

When breakfast was finished and the wagons hitched, Rice asked, "Miss Sarah can ride with me today, can't she, Eli?"

Eli shoved the iron skillet into its place at the back of the wagon and scowled at the grinning boy. "Well now, I guess so. That is if she wants to ride with a no-account boy."

Neither the tone nor the words dampened Rice's spirits. "You do want to ride with me, don't you, Miss Sarah?"

Sarah was delighted but tried not to show it for fear of insulting Eli. "I think that would be nice," she said.

Milburn rode toward them and drew up near Eli. "No hurry," he said. "Half the train's not ready yet."

"I'd give 'em five minutes," Eli declared.

"Eli, if it was up to you, you'd leave the whole dad-gum train back in Missouri."

Eli chuckled as Milburn rode away.

Even before Milburn gave the signal, Sarah was enjoying the pleasant company. Rice told her about Milburn's organization of guards and hunters, and how he was the best person to travel west with. "He even tries to see that there's a doctor with us," he told her. "That's why River's going to meet us at Fort Kearny. Mr. Milburn heard from a doctor wantin' to go, but he hadn't showed up yet, so Riv-

er's gonna wait for him. River's another reason this
here's the best train. He's worked for the army and
for a stagecoach line and knows all about Indians.
He's gonna get me a rattlesnake skin for a hatband.
I'm his best friend.''

Sarah smiled at the boy's enthusiasm. ''You're
part of Mr. Milburn's team, too. How did he find
you?''

Rice grinned proudly. ''I'm an orphan, but Mr.
Milburn and my grandpa were real good friends.
When I lost everybody, Mr. Milburn came. He was
going to put me in some sort of school, but I knew
all kinds a stories about Mr. Milburn and Grandpa
in the war with Mexico, and in the mountains, and I
reminded Mr. Milburn about all them times.'' He
grinned again, and Sarah could imagine how he
convinced Mr. Milburn.

''Anyway, I got to call him Mr. Milburn and do
my job the best I can, or he'll send me off to that
school.''

Sarah looked at the earnest face. ''I don't think
you have to worry,'' she said.

That evening, while Sarah was peeling potatoes for
the stew, a loud voice announced, ''I'm Amy. I'm
four years old!''

A little girl with dark curls working their way free
from short little braids was standing in front of her.
''My mommy's peeling 'tatoes, too. Do you have any
candy?''

Sarah smiled. "I'm afraid not, but friends are almost as good, Amy. I'm Sarah. Won't your mommy be worried?"

"No," she said simply.

Sarah set aside her knife and, wiping her hands on her apron, got to her feet. "I think we better tell her where you are, anyway." She took the little girl's hand and let her lead the way to her wagon. Stirring a pot at the fire was the woman Sarah had met gathering wood. "Hello again," Sarah greeted her.

"I see you've met Amy," Martha said.

"See? She's not worried. I'm big." Amy skipped to a wooden box and cooed to its contents.

This earned a quick response from the mother. "Amy! Don't wake the baby." With a sigh she turned back to Sarah. "I'll have to have Tom fix a harness for her, too." She nodded toward a small boy on the ground, a leather harness and string keeping him within three feet of the wagon wheel.

Sarah assured her that Amy was welcome to visit anytime but reminded the little girl to tell her mother first. After saying goodbye, she returned to her own wagon.

"While ya was off socializin' I had to finish the taters." Eli kept his eyes on the pot as he spoke.

Protests formed in Sarah's mind, but they all sounded like excuses. "I'm sorry," she said.

Eli scowled at her. She had already turned and was unpacking the tin bowls. There was something peculiar about a woman who hardly talked at all, especially when she had an opportunity to argue.

"It's just perfect 'cause there was more rain here and it's early in the season and we're one of the first trains," Rice reported in one breath. They always rode together now, except for two or three times a day when they would walk, with Rice driving the team from near the rear left ox's shoulder. The days with the exuberant Rice made up for the evenings with Eli.

"Rice, what are you talking about?" Sarah asked, smiling.

"This is Saturday!" Rice explained. At Sarah's puzzled expression, he continued more slowly. "If there's enough grass to feed the stock a whole day, we'll rest tomorrow. Mr. Milburn said we oughta make it to Walnut Creek early. When we camp early, especially on Saturday, there's a dance!"

Sarah could tell he thought she was extremely slow, but he had gone from rain to dance in one leap of logic. "Is there one girl in particular you're hoping to dance with?" she asked.

He grinned at her. "Naw. I dance with all the girls. I'm good at it. River taught me. He dances with all the girls, too. Can you dance, Miss Sarah?"

"I used to, but your dancing tonight might be different."

Rice shrugged, and Sarah tried to keep her mind from recalling the dances of her past and Daniel's warm arms around her.

As Rice had hoped, it was early when Milburn led the train to a grassy area near a creek. As soon as the livestock was turned loose, banjos and fiddles were unpacked, and a small band was formed.

The dancing began almost immediately. Rice left Eli to grumble over the meal preparations. "Weren't you ever young, Eli?" Milburn asked.

"I can't say as I was," Eli replied.

Sarah watched the dancers. The twirling calico dresses looked like elegant gowns in the waning light. Daniel had loved to dance and had bought her pretty dresses to dance in.

Milburn pointed a finger at Sarah. "Don't think you're going to be left out. There's always more men than women, and someone will come get you sooner or later."

It turned out to be sooner. A man whose wife was already in a round needed a partner and, seeing Sarah, hurried over. While Eli tried to protest, Milburn waved her away.

The dance sent everyone spinning from one partner to the next with a momentum greater than the music warranted. The music grew louder as the dance brought Sarah closer to the players and faded at the other end of the circle. The campfires seemed to flash by. When she came to Rice, he grinned and whirled her into the arms of her next partner.

When the music stopped, Sarah found herself standing next to her last partner. "My name's Gaines," he said, taking her elbow and pulling her out of the crowd. He was of less than average height but broad and heavily muscled. "Folks call me Bull." He drew himself up in a way calculated to impress her.

"Sarah Tanton," she said. Even in the uncertain light she recognized him as the man who had objected to stopping on Sundays. It was silly since she had just danced with him, but she didn't want to shake his hand.

The musicians started again, and he reached out to pull her into the dance. She stepped away. "I have to get back."

"Anyone that wants you will know where to find you, missy." He caught her arm and forced her toward him.

The tune had no established steps, leaving the dancers free to improvise. Bull kept Sarah on the edge of the crowd. "You traveling with Milburn's bunch?" If it was a question, he didn't wait for an answer. "I seen you with him and that old man." He was leaning closer to be sure she could hear, and Sarah drew away. "You that old man's daughter or somethin'?"

Sarah thought of saying she was his wife. It wasn't natural for her to lie, however, and she told him Milburn had hired her. Seeing his leering face in the light of one of the fires, she regretted her honesty.

When the dance was over, she stepped away. "I have to get back." She wanted to run, but hesitated. The dancing had ruined her sense of direction.

"I'll walk you to your wagon, missy," he said. Again he didn't wait for a reply but took her elbow and started away. "I'm traveling with my friend, Herman Kirby," he told her. "Him and my brother's boy, Nathan. He's alone now 'cept for me." He led her slowly around the circle of wagons, tipping his hat to the folks they passed. "We're gonna take land in Oregon," he went on. "Each of us will take a piece, but I'll have to run it all, 'cause they ain't exactly up to it."

Sarah gave no answer, but he didn't seem to expect one. "That's my wagon," she said when she saw Eli. She was actually glad to see the grumpy old man. Without looking back for fear Bull would take it as encouragement, she went directly to the wagon and climbed inside.

"Who's that?" she heard Eli ask in his usual gruff tone.

"Oh, his name's Gaines," Milburn said. "He's a little hard to get along with, but I guess he's all right."

In a few minutes Sarah climbed out carrying her sewing basket. She wouldn't have time to do any mending until after supper, but getting it was an excuse for hiding in the wagon.

"I don't like his looks," Eli said, scowling at Sarah.

Sarah stared. How could he blame her?

"Well, Eli," said Milburn, "I don't reckon he likes your looks, neither."

Chapter Two

"We thank the Lord for leading us to this grassy meadow," Reverend Fleenor shouted with outstretched arms. "As long as we are faithful, He will lead us safely to our new homes."

The dance floor of Saturday night had become the church of Sunday morning. Nearly all the travelers had left their work to listen to the reverend and add their voices to the hymns.

"Chances are I'll hear it all from here," Eli had said. "But ya go on, Sarie, if ya want."

Noticing the disdain in his voice and certain his humor would be even worse if he had to do the baking alone, she decided to stay and help. He turned out to be right; they didn't miss a word. The effect of the sermon was somewhat changed, however, by Eli's continual comments.

He thought, for instance, that Milburn should receive the credit for leading them to the meadow. When Sarah pointed out that Milburn had found it, not made it, Eli grunted and told her to knead the dough.

Emotion made Fleenor's voice crack. "Everything, from the fall of a leaf to the birth of a child, is God's will."

"I reckon ya go along with that, too," Eli said, reaching for the flour to mix up a second batch.

"I guess so." How had she gotten herself into this kind of discussion, and, more important, how could she get herself out before she made Eli impossibly angry? She had been working for Eli for five days, and this was the first time she had dared to disagree with him.

"Ya guess so," Eli repeated slowly. He slammed his spoon into the dough. "What about death?"

"Every sorrow," Fleenor said, as if in anticipation of Eli's argument, "is God's will."

Eli grunted. "Then He wills more pain than He's worth."

Sarah looked at Eli, shocked by what he had said and by the fact that he had said it so loudly. She didn't have the nerve to see if anyone else might have heard.

"Let me ask ya this," Eli went on, trading the dough he had finished mixing for what Sarah had kneaded and motioning her to continue. "Yer life weren't all parlor games and gay-las back home or ya wouldn't be moving west. Am I right?"

Sarah was sure her expression held a mixture of disbelief and fear. She quickly looked away.

Whatever Eli read in her expression didn't discourage him. "Well, do ya think ya deserved whatever it was that made ya want to start over?"

The reverend's shout seemed to be directed at her alone. "God punishes us for our sins. If we did not sin, there would be no sorrow." She swallowed but couldn't make her voice work. Finally she nodded.

Eli grunted in disgust. "Well, too often the sorrow goes to someone other than the fella committin' the sin."

When both batches of dough were shaped in cloth-covered pans and set in the sun to rise, Eli found other work for Sarah, all of which kept her near the wagon where he could bait her with questions she couldn't answer.

When he finally sent her to the creek with a bag of clothes to wash, she wanted to run. Sheltered by the trees, she dropped the bag on the ground. How had Eli guessed she was running away? What could he further guess from what she had said? Nothing, she hoped.

When she heard a twig snap, she jumped. Grabbing the laundry, she tried to look busy. In a moment Martha Williams joined her.

"I saw you come this way and thought it would be more fun to do this with a little company," she said. She upended her basket, letting the clothes spill to the ground. Kneeling on the bank, Martha wet the first garment and rubbed it with her cake of soap.

Sarah followed her example. "You look kind of pale, dear. Are you feeling all right?"

"I'm fine," Sarah said, afraid to look at her companion.

"Please don't worry," Martha said. "You can talk to me. I saw how that old man made you work all morning and miss the service."

This time Sarah did look up. Would deception be this easy? Letting Eli take the blame for her uneasiness wasn't a lie, anyway. "It doesn't matter," she said, realizing how easily the quiver in her voice could be misinterpreted.

Martha looked sympathetic. "Where you from, honey?"

"New York." Sarah braced herself for more questions, but Martha just wanted an opening to talk about herself.

"We're from Tennessee," she began. "We're moving west because Tom's afraid there's going to be a war. Tom says with the three babies, and one more on the way . . ." She stopped working long enough to pat her damp waist with an even damper hand. A dreamy smile formed on her face before she continued, "Tom didn't want to risk leaving us alone if he had to fight."

"Surely they wouldn't take young fathers." Sarah had heard talk, but it had seemed far away from her and her own problems.

"To tell you the truth," Martha confided, "he's wanted to go west for a long time. Now he can say he's protecting his family instead of endangering us with the trip."

The two women finished their washing and walked back to the camp together. Sarah imagined Eli waiting to pounce on her, having spent her absence thinking of new ways to upset her.

"Got a string twixt the wagons for the clothes," Eli said.

Sarah eyed him suspiciously; he sounded almost pleasant.

"The hunters came in whilst ya was gone," he said. "Got us a big chunk of deer to roast for dinner."

Sarah offered no reply.

Around the circle, several wood-burning stoves had been unloaded. Their owners were doing a brisk business renting them to travelers who hadn't brought their own. Eli, however, was baking his bread in a Dutch oven in the fire. "I've seen a lot a stoves just like 'em," he said when he noticed what Sarah was watching. "Most was lying along the trail farther west."

The recollection made Eli happy. When he smiled, his face looked like the cracked leather cover on her grandmother's Bible. *What would Eli think of that image?* she wondered.

Secretly, she thought the stoves would come in handy when the families built their new homes. She kept quiet while she helped Eli rig the spit for the venison, peeled potatoes and sliced a loaf of the fresh bread. She was glad when she saw Milburn and Rice coming.

Rice found a place to sit near the wagon. His hair was mussed more than usual. He had a smear of axle grease on his cheek and another on his shirt, which Sarah realized she would be expected to wash out. "That smells good, Eli," he said.

"Ya think any food smells good," Eli grumbled.

Rice turned to Sarah. "If River'd been here last night, he wouldn't'a let that Gaines fella walk you home."

"Now, it's none of yer affair who walks Sarie anywheres, boy," Eli scolded.

Rice continued as if he hadn't heard. "Me and Mr. Milburn helped everybody check their wagons, and Gaines didn't let us check his. He—"

"Ya needn't tell everything that happens," Eli interrupted.

"Aw, the boy's not talking to you," Milburn said. "Rice saw Sarah and Gaines last night, and he wants to tell her what he knows about him."

"I guess I don't like him much myself," Eli conceded.

"River wouldn't like him, either, Eli," Rice insisted. "He's mean and grumpy, and he called me a 'no-account boy.'"

Eli took a thin knife and tested the potatoes. "I call ya a no-account boy all the time."

"But he ain't got no right to," Rice said reasonably.

Milburn laughed. "Go wash your face, boy."

"Yes, sir." Rice cast Sarah a questioning look. She gave him her most reassuring smile and was rewarded with a grin.

Milburn took off his hat and rubbed his sleeve across his forehead. "I best join Rice and get cleaned up for supper."

Eli was watching Rice walk toward the creek. "Funny to see that kid wantin' to look after somebody else, ain't it, Pete?"

Milburn studied Eli for a long moment. "I don't know what's gotten into you, Eli. You're almost cheerful. Did you find someone willing to fight with you all day?"

"Oh, just get outta here." Eli threatened Milburn with the knife. He glanced at Sarah before becoming busy at the fire.

Five days later, the wagons stopped at a clear stream some sixty yards wide, by far the largest they had crossed. "That's the Big Blue," Rice told Sarah. He had proudly shared all the place names with her. "Mr. Milburn's makin' sure it's safe. If River was with us, he woulda done it."

Sarah clung to the seat as the wagon rocked down the ford into the water. Rice didn't seem nervous. "We're real close to a trail crossing," he told her. "There'll be wagons all over and not near as much grass. We might see Indians, too." He looked at Sarah with childish anticipation. "You don't need to worry about them, though. These around here ain't much trouble, and by the time we get to where the bad ones are, River'll be with us."

Sarah smiled at the boy's attempt at reassurance.

The wagon rocked again as it climbed onto dry land. "You're the best guide anybody could hope for, Rice. You're willing to explain things everybody else thinks I should already know."

"That's just 'cause I only learned it a while ago, and I know how you feel," he said, blushing at the compliment.

"Sort of like repeating a lesson," Sarah suggested.

Rice wrinkled his nose, and she laughed.

"Breakdown! Breakdown!" Milburn brought the word to the front of the line. Rice set the brake and jumped down, craning his neck to see where Milburn had headed as he helped Sarah. By the time her feet were on the ground, Eli had joined them.

"Will we circle and stop here?" the boy asked. Sarah didn't miss the hopeful note in the young voice.

"You don't have to tell *me* it's Saturday," Eli responded.

A large crowd had gathered around a wagon halfway down the line. As Eli elbowed his way through, Rice and Sarah followed in his wake. "It's not too bad, but we'll have to remove the wheel to fix it," Milburn was saying. "Another hour and a half and the sun'll set. Let's circle up. It'll be a hike to the creek, but we can manage one night."

When the teams were unhitched, Eli took the heavy jack and went to help Milburn. As Sarah started a fire with wood from the possum belly, a sling that hung under each wagon, Rice began the quarter-mile walk to the creek to replenish the supply.

A shout of alarm caught Sarah's attention. People ran toward the broken wagon, and Sarah found herself moving with them. Over their heads, she could see the top of the wagon, twisted at an awkward angle. Pushing through the last of the crowd, she found Milburn on the ground, Eli kneeling beside him. Sarah's mind rebelled, and she looked away, seeing instead the smashed jack under the corner of the tipped wagon box. She turned from that, as well; it looked too much like Milburn's legs.

"I sent a couple fellas to unload the supply wagon," Eli said.

Sarah watched a distant figure move toward them for a full minute before recognition penetrated her foggy brain. "Rice!"

"Don't let him see Pete till he's under a blanket."

Sarah nodded and started across the prairie. Rice's long legs carried him toward her with alarming speed. She walked slowly, stalling, if only a few minutes.

"Hey, Miss Sarah, what are you doing out here?"

"I have to talk to you," she said.

"Sure," he replied, expecting her to follow as he continued toward the wagons. When she didn't, he stopped. "What's wrong?"

"Rice," Sarah began. "There's been an accident." She had to tell him; blunt seemed the best way. "Mr. Milburn was hurt."

The boy stared at her, his mouth shaping his boss's name. Suddenly he dropped the wood and turned to run. Sarah caught his arm, aware that manners stopped him, not the strength of her hand.

"Give Eli some time to make him comfortable."

Face white with horror, the boy whispered, "How bad?"

Sarah swallowed. "Bad."

"He'll want to see me," he said.

"Of course, but give him a few minutes. And we'll still need the wood." Together they gathered up the sticks and walked silently to camp.

Reverend Fleenor and Mr. Williams were climbing out of the supply wagon as they approached. Nodding to Sarah and Rice, the reverend said, "We moved Mr. Millburn inside. Mr. Eli is with him now."

His grim face wasn't encouraging.

"Better call out before you go in," Sarah said, nudging Rice forward.

She watched Rice make his way through the clutter of unloaded supplies and turned her attention to the meal she had started, not so long ago. She wished Eli would come and scold her for spoiling the supper, tell her there wasn't enough wood, anything to make things seem normal again.

Rice came out and sat by the fire. At her questioning look, he shook his head. Supper was ready, but neither wanted to eat. The camp was as quiet as midnight by the time it was fully dark.

Finally Eli left the wagon. He went directly to the fire and dipped up a bowl of stew. "Eat," he said, handing the bowl to Rice. "Both a ya." He didn't speak again until they had begun to eat. "I give him some laudanum, and he's asleep. Soon as ya finish eatin', turn in. Ya'll be walkin' back and forth to that crick most all day."

"Yes, sir," Rice responded between mouthfuls.

When Sarah began to clean up after the meal, Eli told her to leave the coffeepot and went to check on Milburn. He returned in a few minutes and refilled his cup. When the rest of the dishes were put away and Rice had fallen asleep under the wagon, Eli suggested Sarah turn in, as well.

"It's your chance to sleep while Milburn does," Sarah said. "I can wake you if he stirs."

Eli shook his head. "I wouldn't sleep." Sarah knew he spoke for her, as well. Silence stretched between them before Eli spoke again. "He won't make it, ya know."

Sarah glanced at the shadow where she knew Rice slept.

"Ol' Pete's been a friend long as I can remember," Eli continued softly. "If I cut off his legs he

might live, but probably not. I ain't got the heart to
do it.''

Sarah didn't trust her voice. Eli didn't seem to expect an answer anyway.

With the first dim light of dawn, Sarah watched
the camp come slowly back to life. Eli returned from
one of his frequent trips to the supply wagon and
made a fresh pot of coffee. Rice awakened and was
sent to the creek for wood. Sarah tried to concentrate on breakfast preparations.

Shortly after breakfast, Reverend Fleenor came,
but Eli's scowl discouraged him from asking to see
Milburn. He mumbled his concern and hurried away.
Sarah watched him try to get a gathering for Sunday
service, but several families were slower than usual
with their morning chores. Also, the pastor had
competition. "What's going on?" Sarah asked Eli,
tilting her head toward a knot of travelers.

Eli studied them with narrowed eyes and grunted.
''I reckon they'll be letting us know soon enough.''
He sent Rice for water and went to the supply wagon.
Sarah could only wonder if he knew something she
didn't.

She had the first batch of bread mixed when Eli
sent her to find Rice. Wiping her hands on her apron,
Sarah ran to the creek. Rice barely gave her time to
explain before he headed for the wagon.

Sarah returned to camp just as Fleenor started his
service. There were fewer attending than the week

before. The reverend's words didn't carry so well this morning, and Sarah hoped Eli wouldn't comment on what little they could hear. The other gathering, whose purpose was still a mystery, had grown during the few minutes she had been gone.

At the fire, Eli sat watching this latter group. A deep scowl creased his leather face. He showed no sign of noticing her presence so she didn't speak. She kneaded the bread, her mind following the words of the hymn.

"Wouldn't take no more of the laudanum," Eli said abruptly. "Didn't want to sleep through what was left of his life." Eli glanced toward the supply wagon. "I suspect once he's had his talk with the boy he'll take some."

Presently, Rice came out of the wagon, pale and shaken. He seemed to want to say something to Eli, but the old man only clapped him on the shoulder as he hurried past.

Sarah had quit working to watch him, and Rice took it as an invitation to join her. "He says he's gonna die," Rice said.

Sarah slowly nodded and turned to her baking. She didn't want Rice to see how much her heart ached for him.

Rice paced near the wagons, squatting occasionally by the fire or standing close to watch her work. He came to quick attention when Eli climbed out of the supply wagon.

"He's asleep" was Eli's reply to their unspoken question. He took the seat he had vacated a few minutes before and went back to staring at the travelers across the camp. When the benediction was pronounced, the group, swelled by a few of the worshipers, made its way toward them, Bull Gaines in the lead.

"Say what ya come to say." Eli stood like a watchdog prepared to protect its master.

"We're moving out in the morning." Gaines put his hands on his hips, and Sarah understood how he got his name.

"But, Bull, I ain't so sure." A man tugged at his sleeve.

"Shut up, Herman. You ain't never been sure about nothin'!"

Herman looked hurt. The poor man was clearly slow-witted. Sarah wondered how he had gotten mixed up with Bull Gaines.

"This wagon ain't movin' till I say so," said Eli.

"I don't care about that wagon. It's mine I'm thinkin' of. And these folks', too," he added as an afterthought.

Eli spoke to the crowd instead of to Bull. "Ya all paid yer money for a guide west. In a day or so, River'll catch up. He'll guide ya on. Ain't no need to go strikin' out on yer own."

"Well, I ain't worried about a guide." Bull raised his voice. "It's the time we're wasting that worries me. That man could linger for weeks. We gonna sit here that long?''

A murmur rose from the crowd.

"It won't be weeks," Eli said. "But if it is, we'll sit."

The murmur grew louder, and Bull smirked. "You'd risk trapping us in the mountains rather than pull out? Now that don't make sense. A lot of trains elect their own captains and travel without a guide. Just give back the money to those of us what want to pull out."

"Can't," said Eli. "It's been spent on extra supplies." Everyone but Eli glanced at the crates scattered haphazardly around the supply wagon. "Ya wanna take yer money in supplies, won't bother me to see ya go." He stalked to the back of the lead wagon, removing a metal box. Setting it on a stack of crates, he unlocked and opened it. He lifted out Milburn's book, found the page and scowled at the crowd. Several people looked away, unwilling to be the first to abandon the train.

Bull Gaines hesitated only a moment. "You'd overload our wagons with supplies we don't need. I want mine in cash."

Eli's scowl deepened. With a muttered oath, he lifted a leather wallet from the box. "It's my own savings, but it's worth it to get rid of ya," he said.

While Gaines pocketed the money, another man took a place behind him and a line formed, most willing to take their pay in blankets, flour and the like. Gaines approached Sarah. "You best come with me, missy," he said. Sarah was too startled to speak. He took it as indecision. "That's Herman and my nephew." He indicated his companions at the edge of the crowd. "You'd be safer with us than that old man and his dying friend."

"No," Sarah said, barely able to find her voice.

Bull grinned, stepping closer. "You wanna come but can't say so in front of the boss's boy." He touched her cheek with his rough knuckles. "You'll wish you'd spoke up."

Sarah drew away, but Gaines only laughed and joined his friends. Sarah wiped at her cheek with her apron.

The next morning, Rice pointed to each of the wagons scattered on the prairie. "That's the preacher fella, Fleenor," he began, "and you know Tom Williams and his family. That one way out there's the Hess family." Rice indicated the wagon with the broken wheel. "And next to it is Old Man Daugherty and his wife." His eyes seemed to brighten as he came to the last wagon. "Them's the von Schiller family. They don't hardly speak no English, but the girls are learning a little."

Sarah smiled ruefully, realizing it was Rice's version of English they were learning. Even from this distance, Sarah could see that the girls were young women. Rice waved and beamed when the girls waved back.

"Any change?" Sarah asked when Eli joined them.

Eli shook his head. "Tell the folks to bring the wagons in," he said to Rice. "Let's make a circle again. And count the men. We need to set up guards for the stock."

"Yes, sir," Rice murmured and started away.

"Rice—" Eli stopped him "—find out who has a jack. We still got a wagon to fix."

Sarah saw Rice hesitate before turning to do as he was told.

The day seemed to go on forever. Sarah divided her time between what mending or cooking tasks she could think of and watching the crippled wagon through the gap in the shrunken circle. She checked on Milburn often, but he was always asleep.

By midafternoon the Hess wagon was hitched and pulled into the circle with the rest. Sarah relaxed a little, realizing she had been worried someone else would get hurt.

Sarah fixed supper for the three of them, which they ate without comment. When the dishes were put away, she decided to turn in. Eli was with Milburn, and she was sure he wouldn't let her take his place.

She slept with the wagon flap tied open and her head where she could see the stars. Some small sound awakened her. She stuck her head out the wagon and saw Eli sitting near the fire, shoulders slumped and head bowed. He heard her behind him and straightened, waiting until she had found a place to sit before he spoke, then he simply said, "He's gone."

The next morning, Sarah repacked the supply wagon. Tom Williams had lifted the heaviest crates to the tailboard while Rice and Eli finished at the grave. They had had a simple service at dawn and everyone was eager to pull out.

Sarah was trying to remember all of Eli's rules for loading a wagon when she heard Rice shout. Leaning out of the wagon, she saw a rider coming and Rice waving at him excitedly. The white-and-brown horse picked up speed until it was running directly for the boy, the space between them shrinking at an alarming pace. The fringe on the rider's buckskin jacket danced to the rhythm of the horse's gait. In seconds, Rice caught the man's arm, leaping up behind him, and they galloped away.

Sarah put her hand to her heart to try to slow its rapid beating as the horse and riders made a wide circle in the prairie. In a short time, the horse was walking toward the wagons. This, she decided, must be River.

She had just finished the packing when she heard Eli's voice. "So I give 'em supplies in place of their money and promised the ones what stayed that ya'd lead the wagons."

"You promised them what?" came the reply, and Sarah jumped.

"I woulda promised to do it myself, but I'm an old man, River. Nobody's gonna listen to me," Eli replied.

"You're no older than Milburn."

"Don't matter. They'll trust ya."

"They don't even know me."

Eli's voice changed slightly. "It was his last wish."

"It was what!"

Sarah didn't hear the rest; the blood pounding in her ears had reached a pitch that drowned out the voices. She had turned hot, then cold, and found herself sitting on one of the crates. Her hands were shaking, and she clasped them tightly in her lap. She had to calm down and listen; she must be sure.

Carefully, she moved to the back of the wagon. Holding her breath, she pulled the canvas aside. Eli and River walked past as they talked. The two men stopped and turned to face each other. River was a full head taller than Eli. His hat was encircled by a snakeskin, as Rice had mentioned, with a menacing rattle dangling over the edge of the brim. Long muscular legs were encased in brown twill trousers that disappeared into the tops of knee-high boots. A sheath stitched onto the thigh of the pants held a bone-handled knife. Sarah almost laughed in relief. Her mind was playing tricks on her.

"I'll bring in the Carroll wagons," River said.

"We'll be ready to pull on out when you get back."

The men shook hands, and River turned in her direction. She jumped back, pressing her face against the cool wagon cover. She hadn't been mistaken! The new arrival was Daniel!

Sarah waited until Daniel had ridden away before daring to venture out of the wagon. It would only delay the inevitable, but she didn't want him to see her. How could she have thought she had escaped her past?

But how could she have imagined Daniel Harrison on this train? Rice's talk of River hadn't sounded anything like Daniel. And why was he using this strange name?

She finished the preparations for travel out of habit, aware only of the fact that Daniel was here. She realized she wanted desperately to see him but at the same time she was terrified. She had gone back to Albany after her release to talk to him, but that was before she had put her past behind her. Nobody here knew anything about her, and she had thought she was safe. Now Daniel was here, and he would ruin everything.

She climbed onto the wagon seat and donned the sunbonnet. She usually went without it as long as the wagon cover offered her shade. If Rice noticed anything unusual, he didn't mention it. But he was wrapped up in his own thoughts about Milburn's death and River's arrival. Daniel's arrival.

She sighed. What was she going to do? Could she go to him and beg him to keep quiet? Six years ago he hadn't given her a chance to explain, let alone beg. Why should she expect things to be different now?

She imagined a desperate escape from the train, but here in the middle of nowhere, that was pure foolishness. Rescue by another train would lead to more questions than she could expect from this one.

Rice leaned over the side of the wagon to look behind him. "Here comes River!" he called, straightening in the seat without noticing Sarah jump. "I can call him over so you can meet him."

"No," Sarah said too quickly. "He's busy. I can meet him tonight."

Sarah watched him gallop past and pull up beside Eli's wagon. A moment later it started forward. Daniel wheeled the horse and galloped toward the two new wagons. Sarah breathed a sigh of relief as Rice called to his team, and they started after Eli. She had been afraid Daniel would come to talk to Rice, but she had been right, he was busy. She could postpone for a little longer the meeting and the painful scene that would follow.

In truth, she had no choice. She had to accept the fact that her charade was over. She would have to live with the shame the truth would cause. But Daniel hadn't seen her yet. He had ridden away and given her one more day to enjoy her friendship with Rice before that, too, was over.

Chapter Three

River rode away from the wagons to the little rise where he had watched the funeral. He hadn't known then that it was his friend being buried, that the seven wagons were all that was left of Milburn's train.

Now he watched the circle of wagons work its way into a straight line, move back onto what the army called a road and head out once again, toward Fort Kearny. The Carroll and Ortman wagons came toward the others and neatly added themselves to the end of the train. That was the first time those two had managed to do anything right.

Dr. Carroll and his brother-in-law had shown up in Leavenworth the night before Milburn had pulled out. Both men and the doctor's wife had marched right into the saloon to find him, scaring away the girl he had been talking to. When he thought of Prudence Carroll, he wondered why he hadn't run, himself. She was large and imposing, her eyes condemning him for being where he was, even though she was in the place, too.

Her brother, Ernest Ortman, was tall and as skinny as she was fat. He had tried to match his sister's glower, but that was a tall order. Dr. Carroll was plain and quiet, everything about him seemed average, at least in contrast to the company he kept.

River would have gladly turned them over to Milburn if they hadn't been the worst-prepared emigrants he hoped he would ever see. He had spent an entire day helping them buy their supplies, while Ernest Ortman argued with every statement he made. In spite of his good intentions, everything he said or did offended Prudence and Ernest.

"Damn," he muttered, and the pinto twitched its ears. "I was really looking forward to turning those folks over to Milburn."

River rode down as the dust settled on the abandoned camp and grave. *No marker,* he thought. *And nobody here to visit it on Sundays. Why mark what no one's ever going to try to find?*

He dismounted at the site. Eli had carefully replaced the sod so it barely looked like a grave. A few of the wagons had even rolled across it, further obscuring its presence. There would be no Indians digging up this grave for clothes.

"Sorry I wasn't here, boss," he said, playing with the reins in his hands. "Sure hate to think of you going like that." He pressed a loose piece of sod into place with a booted toe and looked across the prairie at the receding wagons. "But that was one dirty trick, leaving me in charge. I'm a good scout but a sorry captain."

Sarah went about the meal preparations, telling herself she should feel lucky for every minute but knowing the waiting was making her tense and jumpy. Eli had startled her twice, though that had happened often enough before tonight.

"If ya'd take off that silly bonnet, a body couldn't sneak up on ya so easy," he had said the last time.

But she didn't want to take it off. She wore it until the sun was sinking beneath the horizon and she could no longer claim she needed it for shade. Finally, she tossed it into the wagon, glad to be free of it but missing the illusion of safety it had given her.

She set out the last of the dishes and tried to come to a decision. She could plead an upset stomach and refuse supper. It was tempting to go to bed, but she slept in the wagon where all the dishes were kept and the tailboard served as a table. Perhaps she could visit Martha and Amy, tell Eli she had been asked to watch the children for a while.

That seemed like her best choice, and she decided to tell Eli at once. She spun around and gasped. There he stood, leaning against the supply wagon, watching her. His arms were folded across his chest, his hat pushed to the back of his head. One ankle had been casually thrown across the other. He had been there long enough to make himself comfortable.

The sight of him did alarming things to her pulse. *He startled me!* she thought, but deep inside, she knew it was more than that.

While Sarah was still trying to catch her breath, he spoke. "Sarah Tanton." It wasn't a question.

Sarah didn't know what to say. She took a step backward and steadied herself against the tailboard. It was Daniel, but he looked so different. Maybe it was the buckskin jacket, but his shoulders seemed broader than she remembered. His dark blond hair was longer and sun-streaked. In spite of a few days' growth of sandy beard, he was at least as handsome as he had been six years ago. It seemed a most inappropriate thought. She tried to ignore it and continue her study of this familiar stranger.

Six years had added some lines at the corners of his eyes, and the sun had darkened his skin, but little else had changed. No, the biggest differences she could find were his clothes and this unusual name, River.

His blue eyes, which she had so often seen dance with mischief, watched her curiously. She still hadn't found her voice. Her mind seemed to want her to gaze at him forever.

"Rice has been telling me a lot about you," he said. He pushed away from the wagon and closed the distance between them. She leaned back, bending over the tailboard as he grew nearer, too confused to think of stepping out of his way. He stopped mere inches from her.

"You're the last person I ever expected to see," he said in a low voice. "I'd like to know how you managed to be here. But we'll talk some other time." He reached around her, lifted a plate from the stack and turned to go.

"Daniel." She barely breathed his name.

He faced her again. What had she wanted to say? That he was wrong about her? That she could explain? That she still loved him and was ready to forgive him? In the end, she said nothing, and he walked away.

It was then she discovered Eli watching her. She had been so intent on Daniel she had not seen him. Perhaps Daniel had. Had his whispered comment meant he would give her a chance to talk this time? Perhaps it wasn't too late. Perhaps he hadn't yet said anything to Rice or the others. Could it be that Daniel didn't want his friends knowing about their former association any more than she did?

She realized she had been staring at Eli without seeing him. He looked from her to Daniel and back, and Sarah quickly turned away. She wanted to run, but Rice was beside her.

"Did you meet River?" he asked cheerfully, grabbing two plates and shoving one into Sarah's hands. "What's to eat? I'm starved." He headed toward Eli and the cooking pot, and Sarah didn't know what to do but follow. She filled her plate, sitting a little away from the others.

"How far are we from Fort Kearny?" Rice asked, finding a place close to River and to the food.

"Around a hundred twenty…maybe forty miles," answered River, smiling at the boy. "Take about a week, I think."

"There's a little store near here. That right, River?" Rice glanced at Sarah to see if she was listening. She smiled to let him know she was impressed by his knowledge.

"At the Cottonwood Creek crossing. At least it was there last year. We ought to be going by sometime in the morning."

"We gonna stop?"

Eli leaned to the side, making a big show of looking at the side of Rice's leg. The boy looked at Eli, down at his pants and back at Eli. "What?"

"Don't see no smoke, but them coins von Schiller give ya must be gettin' mighty hot by now."

River laughed. The sound brought back so many memories, Sarah found herself staring at him again. It was hard not to picture the same handsome face in different surroundings, different circumstances.

River turned his easy smile on Rice and said, "Some of the folks will need things, and the rest'll want to see what it's like. I reckon we'll stop."

"I reckon" was not something Sarah would have expected Daniel to say. Maybe the changes went deeper than she had first thought. Of course they did, she realized, if the reckless storekeeper was now a respected scout. He caught her watching him, and she looked quickly at her plate.

"I'm taking the first watch," he said. "Thanks for dinner." He carried his plate to the tailboard and walked away without another glance in Sarah's direction.

She tried not to gaze after him; she needed to act as if nothing were amiss. Rising to scrape her half-finished plate of food into the fire, she noticed Eli studying her. He would start asking questions if she continued like this, and until things were settled between her and Daniel, she wouldn't be able to relax. She would have to talk to Daniel tonight.

River tried to make himself comfortable. The most he could hope for on guard duty was something to lean against, and he had found it tonight in the form of a boulder on a hillside. From here he could look down on both the train and the herd of cattle a short distance away. The horses were picketed near the wagons. He cradled the rifle in his arms and watched the sky darken until all he could make out of the train was the silhouette against a few flickering fires.

How in all the world did she end up out here, on my train? he asked himself. *Could she have wanted to find me?*

When Rice had first mentioned her name, he had been surprised but honestly thought he didn't care. She could do whatever she pleased as long as she stayed away from him. But seeing her had changed that. There were too many memories between them and the wounds weren't as healed as he had thought.

Damn her! What can she want now? Her frightened little-girl act wasn't going to fool him. He *knew* her! She had used him, betrayed him! What was she planning now?

River laughed at himself. What could she do on this train that could possibly compare with what she had done six years ago? Since then, he had tried not to think about Sarah Tanton. As he sat in the lonely meadow, he let the memories come back. He told himself he had to remember so he would be prepared for what she did next, but he knew he couldn't have stopped the memories if he had tried.

Six years ago, he had been working for his father. Sarah was a local girl he had known all his life. He smiled slightly at the memory. She had been a little wild but lots of fun. His folks hadn't liked her, but mostly he had done what he pleased in those days.

He couldn't even remember which of his father's many enterprises had generated the money that was to be in the store overnight. It had arrived in town on Sunday, and rather than calling attention to it by asking the bank to open, the old man decided to keep it in the store until Monday morning. He often had someone stay at the store at night, so a guard on duty didn't seem unusual. Hardly anyone knew about the money. But River had known, and he had told Sarah.

River shook his head as he remembered. He had wanted to impress her. As if she had been hard to impress! He had been a complete fool, and she had used the information to rob his father.

Damn her! If anyone else had claimed to have seen her running from the scene, he would have called him a liar and stood by his Sarah to the end. His Sarah? Honest to God, that was how he had thought of her. But *he* had been the one and only witness, and he had found no choice but to turn her in. How could he help but recognize her? She had even been wearing the red dress he had bought for her.

River sighed and tried to bring his thoughts back to the wagons and the stock. They were peaceful and couldn't hold his attention. Sarah had been arrested that very night. He hadn't seen her again except briefly at her trial.

But he had tried. Fool that he was, he had gone every day and asked to see her. The jailer consistently reported that she did not want to see him. He had even begged her attorney to get him in. Again he had been refused. He had been slow to believe that she had betrayed him.

"Why, Sarah?" he murmured under his breath. "Why did you do it, and why are you here?"

At her trial, she had denied everything, pretended she couldn't understand what was going on. She had been sent to prison, supposedly for twenty years. But he was sure his father would have been willing to work for her release in exchange for the money, and his father usually got what he worked for. Something like that must have taken place after he had left New York.

The law might have forgiven her, but he hadn't. She had pretended to love him when all along it had been his money she wanted. When she realized the old man would never allow her into his family, she had found another way to use him. Well, he wasn't such a fool now; she wouldn't use him again.

The moon was making a feeble attempt to light the sky, and River could make out the wagons more clearly. As he watched, one shadow broke away from the others and moved toward the stock.

Sarah slipped out of the wagon after moonrise. She wasn't sure how to find Daniel, but she had to try. She was equally unsure of what she would say to him.

The guard was supposed to watch the stock to see that nothing frightened them. Therefore, that was the direction she headed. Moving about in the pale moonlight was more difficult than she had anticipated. The tall grass and brush tugged at her long skirts and made her afraid of stumbling.

She walked what seemed to be a long way from the wagon but saw no sign of River. *This was a stupid idea,* she told herself. But how else could she talk to him with no danger of being overheard? When she stumbled over a loose stone and came close to crying out, she decided she was never going to find Daniel out here in the dark. If he was any kind of guard he would have found her by now! In frustration, she turned toward the wagons.

One step was all she took. A strong hand fell across her mouth, forcing her head against a hard shoulder while another arm went around her waist, lifting her off the ground. Long quick strides carried her farther from the wagons.

Sarah was horrified! She had wandered away from the wagons and was being carried off by an Indian! That was, she had learned, the worst fear of all the women on the train. She had thought it was foolish. Now she was paying for her disbelief. In her horror she imagined Daniel witnessing her capture and not bothering to come to her rescue.

When her feet were on the ground again, her knees were too weak to hold her weight, and she found herself leaning against the man who still held her. A voice near her ear spoke as the hands slipped away from her. "What do you think you're doing out here?"

"Daniel," she breathed, weak with relief and thrown off-balance as he drew away.

He saw her sway and caught her shoulders, turning her to face him. "So far, that's all I've heard you say."

She pretended a courage she didn't feel. She could barely make out his features in the dark, and his voice hadn't given much away. "I have to talk to you," she said, surprising herself with the coolness in her voice.

Feeling the narrow shoulders straighten, River slowly dropped his hands. "There are a few answers I'd like myself."

Now was her chance, but she still didn't know what to say. How could she make him listen long enough to explain everything? She wasn't even sure where to start, and he might walk away at any moment. "I just want to start over," she blurted.

"Not with me!"

She was taken aback by the force of the statement. "No," she whispered. "Of course not."

River wanted to pace. His arm could still feel the softness of her body; he absently rubbed the spot on his shoulder where her head had rested. "How did you find me?"

"You found me."

"I don't mean tonight. I mean the train. How did you know to ask for Milburn's train?"

"I didn't. I didn't even know you had come west." She took a step toward him. "I went home to find you, but no one would tell me where you had gone."

"It's just bad luck then," he said.

Sarah tried not to be hurt by his words. She had seen his arrival that morning as a stroke of bad luck, as well.

River sighed. "Once you decided to come west, I guess it isn't that surprising that we'd meet. There are only about three major jumping-off points, and Leavenworth seems to be the most popular this season. Milburn's is the largest and best-equipped train. Was," he added almost under his breath.

They watched each other while an owl called its question to the night. Sarah shivered and finally spoke. "No one knows. I don't want them to know."

Daniel took a step closer. "Let's do each other a favor. You stay the hell away from me, and I'll keep my mouth shut. Will that satisfy you?"

Sarah nodded.

"Can you make it back to the wagons?"

"I think so," she said, but made no move to go.

River sighed. "I'll walk you partway." He took her arm and led her back the way she had come. "Answer me one question," he said. "Is the law after you?"

"Of course not!" She shouldn't have been surprised by the question, considering what he thought of her.

"Of course not," he mumbled.

At the sarcasm in his tone, she turned to him. "Daniel, let me explain."

"Listen! You had a chance to explain in court," he said, holding her at arm's length. "My name is River, and I don't know you. Can you remember that? You see, I'd just as soon these people didn't know what a fool you made of me six years ago."

Sarah slowly nodded. He walked with her until they were some fifty yards from the wagons, then his hand left her arm, and he slipped away.

* * *

The next morning in the wagon seat beside Rice, Sarah tried to pretend that this was the same as any other morning. It seemed, however, that everything had changed. Milburn was dead. Daniel was here. Somehow neither seemed quite real.

She tried to sort out her feelings about last night. She should be grateful for Daniel's promise. River's. She must remember to think of him as River. That had been a condition of his promise. She didn't know him; he didn't know her. If she called him River, her secret was safe.

Wasn't his silence all she had wanted from him? He had promised that much, and she should be relieved. Why had she found herself crying when she returned to the wagon? Why had her mind been full of questions about him and his life these past years? She wished she had plied Rice with questions about his friend during that first week and a half of travel. Now she was afraid to ask.

At midmorning they came to the trail crossing and could see wagons coming from the southeast and more ahead of them. The wheels stirred up a fine dust, and Sarah, holding a small white handkerchief over her nose, wished for a large bandanna to tie about her face. For the first time she understood what the passengers in the rear wagons experienced.

Rice didn't seem to be bothered. "Some places the dust is so bad you can't hardly see the team, and where the soil's white it'll about take your skin off."

There seemed to be wagons everywhere. It was as if with Daniel's arrival, the rest of the world had taken the opportunity to intrude, as well. She thought she had accepted the fact years ago that what they had was over. She would never have guessed it would be so upsetting to see him again. Her feelings were a mixture of fear that he could ruin her new life, anger that he refused to listen and sorrow for what was lost. How was she going to live so close to Daniel and never call him by name. *River,* she told herself again. *His name is River. I must think of Daniel as dead.*

"It won't always be this bad," Rice said, startling her. She turned toward him and saw the concern in his face. "You can wet your handkerchief and wipe the dust out of your eyes. It'll work better to breathe through when it's wet, anyhow."

"Thanks," Sarah said, ashamed to discover she was crying again. She found the canteen they kept under the seat and poured a small amount onto the cloth.

"We'll be stopping at the store soon," Rice went on. "You gonna buy anything?"

"I don't think so," she answered.

"I want to get something pretty for the von Schiller girls, but I don't know what. Besides, I don't think their mama likes me at all, only I can't understand what she says."

Sarah smiled at the boy's perplexed tone, glad for the distraction. "Maybe you should find something pretty for Mama, too," she suggested.

Rice wrinkled his nose but fell silent, and she guessed he was thinking over her suggestion.

Suddenly he called a friendly greeting, and River reined in beside their wagon. Sarah tried not to look at him but found him impossible to ignore.

"We'll make noon stop just past the Hollenberg Ranch so you and the others can go spend your money," he said with a grin.

"It's still there, then?"

"Looks like he's had a good year. He's added a stable that could hold a hundred horses, I reckon." Rice laughed in disbelief, and River went on. "It'll be a little later than the usual nooning, but it saves us stopping twice." His only acknowledgment of Sarah was "Ma'am," and a touch to his hat before riding away.

The sun was high enough for Rice to complain about hunger before they reached Cottonwood Creek. As they crossed, they could see the long low buildings of the Hollenberg Ranch a few hundred feet away. The stable was every bit as large as River had said, and Rice whistled in admiration. "Don't you want to come in, Miss Sarah?" He craned his neck to see, and Sarah worried he wasn't paying close enough attention to the team.

"I'll look forward to your description, Rice," she said.

When they stopped, Rice unhitched the oxen in record time. Eli was unpacking bread and last night's venison when he hurried by. "Rice!" Eli called, stopping him in his tracks. "Eat!"

"Miss Sarah can save me something," he said, backing away. "I'll eat it on the road." He turned and ran before Eli could argue.

"No-account fool boy," Eli muttered, and Sarah felt her pulse quicken when she heard River laugh.

"I suppose I better see he stays out of trouble," River said, reaching around Eli for a slice of bread.

"Well, who'll keep ya out of trouble?" Eli tried to pull the meat away before River could grab a chunk with his fingers.

River's arm was longer, and he soon balanced his prize on top of the bread. "You could come watch us both, Eli," he said, grinning.

Eli grunted and shooed him away. Sarah watched as his long easy strides moved him quickly toward the store. She turned to get her own lunch to find Eli eyeing her. She wasn't sure what he might have asked if Amy hadn't interrupted.

"We're gonna go to the store," the child called, running ahead of her mother and brothers.

"That sounds like fun, Amy," Sarah said, trying to pretend Eli wasn't still watching her.

Martha joined them in a minute, holding one small boy by the hand while balancing the other on her hip. "We need to look for a couple things," she said, a little breathlessly. "Would you like to come along?"

"How will you carry anything back with your arms full of boys?"

"Tom'll be along," Martha said, glancing over her shoulder.

"Let me watch the boys," Sarah offered. "I hadn't planned on going, anyway. You'll stay with me, won't you, Allen?" Sarah reached for the younger boy, who wailed and hid his face in his mother's shoulder.

Martha laughed. "You come with us. He'll go to you in a little bit. Or you can carry our things. Trust me, they won't weigh as much as he does."

Sarah ignored Eli's grunt as they started away. Amy's hand was soon in hers. "I think Lizabeth needs a new dress. You think they'll have one here?"

"Hush, Amy," Martha scolded. "The child doesn't understand money. The food seems to be lasting like we expected, but I'm almost out of thread. I think I'll try to find Tom a new shirt and use one of the old ones to patch everything else. Seems like all I do is mend. I tried mending as we traveled and almost ran the needle through my finger."

"I could help with some of it if you'd like. I plan to open a dress shop when I get settled."

"That sounds wonderful. I'll ask Tom if we could pay you a little."

"If you like to sew," Amy piped up, "you could mend my dolly."

"Amy," Martha scolded. "Your dolly's fine."

"Her leg's loose again, Mama."

Sarah looked down at the little girl. "I think I could mend your dolly, Amy. Bring it by the wagon as soon as we get back."

The little girl beamed up at Sarah as she skipped along beside her.

The store was crowded with emigrants, and Allen, who had stared at Sarah all the way up the hill, decided she was safer than the dark noisy building. His eyes never left her face as she carried him around the yard.

Young Allen wasn't the only one staring at Sarah. River had taken a look at the horses Hollenberg had for sale and had noticed Sarah with the baby as he turned toward the store. He froze, forgetting the horses and the people milling around him, aware only of Sarah and the small child in her arms. She was thinner than he remembered, and he remembered all too well.

She had left the sunbonnet at the wagons, and her hair shone with the sun's reflected fire. It reminded him suddenly of lamplight and red ribbons, ribbons he would loosen to allow her hair to cascade around her shoulders. He could almost feel the silken tresses between his fingers.

He watched her point out things to the baby, who refused to turn his head. After a few minutes he began to squirm, reaching toward the door where he had last seen his mother. River was surprised Sarah's thin arms could hold the determined child, but, after a brief struggle, she won the battle, pulling the little body against her chest. She rocked him slowly, and he gave in, resting his head on her shoulder. She began to turn in a circle, continuing the rocking motion, caressing the tiny head as she comforted him.

For a moment River was in a lamp-lit room, watching her dance with someone else. He felt the stab of jealousy and pushed it away. It was a remembered emotion and had nothing to do with how he felt now. He looked toward the waiting wagons to bring himself back to the present, but she was still in front of him, dancing with the baby in the dusty yard, and there was nothing he could do but watch.

When Rice joined her, she quit turning but continued the rocking motion. The baby looked up to see who had interrupted and, with a little shudder, settled against her again. Rice held something up for her to see. Ribbons. Sarah nodded as they discussed them. Finally Rice folded the ribbons inside a paper and carefully tucked them in a pocket. He looked around the yard, catching sight of River. He waved, and Sarah turned, as well. Their eyes met for only a second before she turned away. The family returned, and Rice came running toward him.

"I bought ribbons for the von Schiller girls," Rice told him eagerly. "I bought three like Sarah said. I'll give the light blue one to their mama."

"Ready to go, then?" River asked, looking over the boy's shoulder to find Sarah. She had started toward the wagons, having traded the baby for the purchases. She held the hand of a little girl who was crying harder than the baby had been.

Rice interrupted his thoughts. "Did you ever give a girl something like a ribbon?"

River looked at the worried face and laughed. "Once or twice."

"It don't seem like much."

"They'll like the ribbons if they like you."

"But I thought a present would help them like me."

"I'm not sure it works that way," River said. He glanced again at the retreating family. "Look, Rice, do me a favor. Tell Eli to pull out as soon as everyone is back. I'll catch up in a little bit."

"Sure thing," Rice said, and started away.

"And, Rice . . ." The boy turned back. "The girls would have to be crazy not to like you." Rice grinned and hurried toward the wagons and his previously forgotten lunch.

Chapter Four

"Now where's that fool boy gone off to?"

Sarah decided Eli was muttering, not asking, and therefore didn't require an answer. She could *guess* that Rice had gone to the von Schiller wagon, but she hadn't seen him go, and he hadn't told her. She saw no reason to share her guess with Eli.

"I was about to go for the wood," she told him. "Do you want me to look for Rice instead?"

"Well, I'll need more wood than ya'll find on the ground. Get River to go with ya and chop down one a them trees."

River had just entered the camp. He dropped his saddle and gear near the supply wagon. "I got better things to do," he said without sparing Sarah a glance.

"Don't see what. Ya already assigned guards, and ya ain't one a 'em. Don't see nobody askin' for yer help with nothin'." To illustrate this, Eli looked around the busy circle. "Go help Sarah bring in enough wood to fill the possum bellies in case we don't make it to the Little Blue tomorrow and have to stop in the hills somewheres.''

River glared at Eli before chuckling in defeat. ''I'll get the wood, but what do I need her for?'' He cast Sarah a dismissing glance, grabbed the ax and headed for the creek.

Eli called after him, ''To help ya find yer way back.'' He eyed Sarah curiously for a moment. She tried to pretend he hadn't embarrassed her. ''Fetch the water,'' he directed.

Sarah unfastened the buckets from the side of the wagon, glad River's long legs would keep him well ahead of her. She had barely left the camp when Rice caught up with her. He took one bucket from her and hurried on, making her walk faster. ''I'm sorry I'm late. Is Eli mad?'' He looked over his shoulder then walked faster still.

''I don't know, Rice. With him it's hard to tell. River's gone after the wood, and he sent me for water.'' To her dismay, Rice's pace was threatening to make them catch up with River.

''I'll get the water,'' Rice offered, taking the second bucket. ''See if you can keep Eli from being mad.''

Sarah stopped, too out of breath to argue, and watched the boy hurry away. At camp, Eli was muttering but no more than usual. She told him Rice would bring the water and went on to other duties.

She had no idea how to keep the grumpy old man from being angry at Rice.

Rice and River returned at the same time. Before Eli could do more than stand up, pointing his paring knife at Rice, River said, "Introduce me to the folks, Rice. I've barely met some of them. We can start with that German family." He threw an arm over the boy's shoulder, steering him away.

Sarah failed to hide her amusement from Eli. "Just a clever way to get outta work, if ya ask me, which ya won't. I suppose ya want to go, too. Well, go on. You ain't met all these people, neither. Ain't enough folks left for it to take long, anyhow."

He sat back down and resumed his potato peeling. Sarah looked at him in dismay. Eli's voice had been loud, and Rice and River had stopped, waiting for her to join them. Rice's eager face and River's glower left her torn for a second. But only for a second. She waved them away.

Supper was ready before they returned, and Sarah took advantage of the chance to look through her trunk. Somewhere there had to be something she could use to make Amy's doll a new dress. Her supply of fabric was small, and she had plans for all of it. Dreams more than plans, she decided. It was what she hoped would get her started as a seamstress, along with taking in mending and probably laundry, as well. Surely she could part with a corner of something. She went through it all again, trying to decide what she could spare.

"You missin' somethin'?"

Sarah jumped, almost knocking over the trunk. She steadied it as Eli climbed into the back of the wagon. His body blocked the light that came through the back flap. She turned up the wick on the lantern with an unsteady hand.

"No," she answered him. "I was just trying to decide on something."

"Didn't mean to spy, but ya looked like ya'd lost somethin'." Eli sat on a crate and showed no sign of going away.

Sarah considered a moment and decided the truth might bore him into leaving. "I was looking for something to use to make a doll dress."

Eli grunted, and Sarah waited for the muttering to start. "Won't need much to fit that shabby little doll ya was practicin' surg'ry on yesterday."

Sarah almost smiled. "That's the one," she said. She didn't look at him but carefully smoothed her pieces as she packed them back into the trunk.

"Pete had a couple extra shirts."

Sarah stared at him in surprise. He was scratching his whiskered chin. "One was kind of a bluelike gray color. Almost new, I think, when he tore it up some. Oughta work." He got up and moved some boxes, looking for Milburn's personal trunk.

There was barely enough room in the wagon for the two of them and all the things that were stored there. Sarah moved to the back and pulled the flap open further. She hoped Eli would think she was trying to give him more light. The last thing she wanted was him asking why the enclosed wagon made her so uncomfortable.

Eli found the trunk and opened it. "Got to go through all this stuff, anyhow. Guess it's Rice's now, but he won't miss the shirt." He found what he was looking for and closed the trunk, carrying the shirt to Sarah. As he handed it to her, he asked in a lowered voice, "Where'd you know River from?"

Sarah was so startled she was sure she jumped again. "I...I don't know what you're talking about," she stammered.

They heard Rice's voice and River's laugh. In a few seconds they would be at the fire. She clutched the shirt and wondered if its price was information.

After watching her a moment, Eli said, "Don't matter," and climbed out of the wagon.

Sarah stayed behind, closing her trunk and putting the shirt and her sewing box where she could get to them easily. Last, she blew out the lantern and, hoping she looked calmer than she felt, left the wagon.

The others had already filled their plates, and Sarah did the same, looking for a place to sit away from them. She needed time to think, to decide what to do about Eli.

"Sit here, Miss Sarah," Rice called, and she had no choice but to sit near him, near River.

"River said he didn't see no sign of Indians today, did you, River?"

Sarah tried to give the boy her full attention without looking at River. She heard River's negative response and looked quickly at her plate.

"But we might see some Pawnee anytime," Rice added, making sure Sarah knew he had his facts straight.

"Could." There was humor in the familiar voice, and Sarah couldn't resist looking up to see the face. He was trying not to smile as he continued to eat his meal, but there was merriment in his eyes as he gave the boy a sidelong glance. "You been scaring Miss Sarah with Indian stories?"

His eyes met Sarah's, and she held them for a moment before she turned to Rice, pretending her heart wasn't beating alarmingly fast. Were those blue eyes alone enough to cause it? Or was it fear that sent her pulse racing? Even now, she was sure Eli watched her.

"I told Miss Sarah there wouldn't likely be trouble but we are in Pawnee territory."

"It's Pawnee territory as long as they can keep it," Eli put in. "There's gonna be more folks who ain't satisfied to just pass through. Like that Hollenberg fella."

River chewed his food thoughtfully. "Now, some folks would say that anybody who can manage to take it from the Indians has a right to it. Maybe our Miss Sarah, here, would agree with that."

Sarah looked up to see the blue eyes on her, all humor in them gone. She heard Eli grunt; he didn't expect an answer. But River did. They both knew he wasn't talking about Indian land. Did he think she would offer some excuse in front of all these people? An admission of guilt? An apology? She felt her face turn red with anger. It took an effort to pull her eyes away from his piercing gaze.

"Excuse me," she murmured. She rose and carried her plate to the lead wagon. She didn't want to go back and sit with the others; she needed a little time alone. Slowly she stepped around the wagon, letting it block the firelight. The prairie was lit by the sunset's pale afterglow. The air away from the fire was crisp and clear. She let it cool her burning cheeks.

River watched Sarah leave the camp. He felt a twinge of guilt and fought against it. She had made herself so damn comfortable with Eli and Rice that he felt like an outsider. He couldn't resist the opportunity to remind her that he knew who she really was.

Still, it could be dangerous to wander away from the wagons. He took his plate to the back of the wagon and looked for Sarah without appearing to, he hoped. She was standing a short distance away, looking at the stars.

He grabbed his saddlebags and walked back to the firelight, choosing a different seat, one where he could see Sarah through the gap between the wagons. "Rice, let me see your hat," he said.

"What for, River?" Rice asked. The anticipation in the youth's eyes told River he could make a guess, however.

"Well," River began as he lifted an odd bundle from his bag, "you know the doctor's wife, Prudence? She was stomping around the camp one night when she let out this horrible scream."

"A snake," Rice whispered, watching as the cured skin appeared from River's bundle. River handed him the rattle and he rolled it in his fingers reverently.

River glanced at Sarah once more before he began folding the skin to hatband width. "I didn't know it was a snake at first. I was just glad she wasn't screaming at me. When she paused for a breath, we heard the rattle. I didn't think she was going to stand still for more than a second or two. In fact there was real danger that she'd faint away right on top of the snake. Hold this." He handed the hat to Rice while he searched his bag for his sewing kit. He glanced toward the wagons. Sarah had moved.

For a moment he was torn between finishing Rice's hat and going after Sarah. He told himself he was being ridiculous. There were things a person needed privacy to do; he couldn't go crashing after her.

"What happened?" Rice asked, drawing his attention.

River cut a length of heavy thread and threaded it on a needle before he spoke. "I decided speed was the most important thing under the circumstances, and I jumped right on the snake.''

''Wrestled with it for nigh on an hour, I suppose,'' Eli interjected. The other two ignored him.

''My boot heel came down just behind its head. I grabbed my knife and...'' He made a slicing motion with his hand.

''Did Mrs. Carroll faint?'' Rice asked.

''Nah,'' River said. They read each other's disappointment and laughed.

River looked up in time to see Sarah step over the wagon tongue. She hadn't made any sound that he could identify. It was as though he had felt her return. He was much more relieved to see her than he wanted to admit.

Rice drew his attention back to his project by rattling the tail. River took several lengths of the thread and fastened one end to the seam at the back of the hatband. As Rice handed him the rattle, he spoke again. ''I thought Ernest might faint when he saw me skinning the snake. He thought I planned to eat it, at first. Seems he'd seen my hatband but had never recognized it for what it was.''

''Did ya?'' Eli asked.

''Did I what?'' River winked at Rice as he handed him the hat.

''Did ya eat the snake?''

River glared at Eli for a moment, conscious that Sarah was watching him. ''I thought about smoking it overnight just for you, but I was afraid it'd turn up in my supper if I did.''

It was early afternoon the next day when River found the perfect campsite. This was beautiful country, and the place he had chosen was shaded by oak and cottonwood. Willows grew near the swift clear stream. He turned his mount and set an easy pace toward the train. They would reach this site in about two hours, maybe less. It would be early to make camp, but everyone could use the rest.

The day before, the train had made its way across the hills from the Big Sandy to the Little Blue River with no water between but what they had stored in their barrels. It had been a long day, and he had had to push them until nearly dark in order to get to the river.

It's what Milburn would have done. The thought came suddenly and made him smile. *And I would have been the first to argue with him.* He missed Milburn more than he would ever admit to Rice or Eli, but Eli had been right. The people of the train trusted him and followed his instructions.

Even Ernest and Prudence were causing him less trouble, now that they were with the larger train and River was officially in charge. Of course, they were easier to avoid with more people around.

Dr. Carroll had come to Eli's fire during supper the night before to report that his wife and brother were unhappy about traveling so late. The good doctor sat and drank two cups of coffee before he mentioned it.

"Well, you can go back and tell 'em you complained," Eli had told him cheerfully.

River grinned at the recollection. The grin didn't last. Also at the fire had been Sarah. Avoiding her wasn't as easy as he had thought. Because of the communal nature of trail life, they virtually lived together.

At camp she was always with Eli, and sometimes he simply had to talk to Eli. During the day, she was with Rice, and River found himself avoiding his friend because of Sarah.

What kind of lies is she telling the boy? he wondered. He had seen her charm work before, and Rice certainly was taken with her. He toyed with the idea of separating them by asking Eli to take her on his wagon, but how would he explain? He had promised to keep her secret, and he would, but that promise would last only as long as hers did. *If I get one hint that she's up to something,* he vowed, *Rice and Eli get the whole story.*

The train had come into view, and River put spurs to his horse to reach them. He pulled up at the lead wagon. "About three miles ahead is a clearing where the river turns left."

Eli squinted at him. "It'll be a little early to stop, won't it?"

"Yeah, maybe. We put in a hard day yesterday. I, for one, could use a rest."

"Won't never get nowhere restin'."

River knew to expect that kind of comment from Eli, but it irritated him, anyway. "It's a good camp, old man. Don't argue with me."

Eli cracked the whip over the backs of the oxen and muttered, "A body can't express himself without bein' accused of arguin'."

River refused to feel guilty. "I need to talk to Rice," he said, pulling on the reins.

"Wait!"

River rode beside Eli again.

"Been meaning to ask ya somethin'," Eli began. "Where do ya know Sarie from?"

River managed his most carefree shrug. "What makes you think I know her?"

"Ain't sure why I think so, just do." He thought on it and added, "She watches ya."

River laughed. "Eli, lots of women watch me." He pulled up on the reins and let the wagon move ahead. He could hear Eli, calling after him or talking to himself, River couldn't be sure. He wasn't going to bother to find out.

In a few minutes, he was riding beside Rice's wagon. The boy greeted him with a friendly hail. "We stopping early tonight?" Rice asked.

"You read my mind. Found a spot so pretty we can't pass it by."

"Miss Sarah's been asking me about Fort Kearny. I told her it's the second Fort Kearny. That right, River?"

"That's right. They moved it farther west to be more help to the emigrants."

This was at least the second time River had heard the boy ask to have his facts verified. Wondering if Sarah had been doubting him, he glanced at her, something he had been trying to avoid. She watched Rice fondly, which in itself worried him. He would have to talk to Rice alone, to warn him about Sarah.

He heard Rice thank him yet again for the hatband and realized he had watched Sarah too long. He told Rice to thank Prudence Carroll for finding the snake and excused himself, pulling up a short distance from the road to watch the wagons file by. Instead, he found himself looking after the second wagon, wondering what was going on in Miss Sarah Tanton's head.

That night he found his chance to talk to Rice alone. He joined the boy as he took the oxen to water and offered to help.

"I don't need help with the stock."

"I know you don't, Rice." River walked beside him. "I hardly see you anymore. How about practicing that running mount after supper?"

His face brightened then fell. "Miss Sarah asked me to read to her."

River eyed the boy suspiciously. "Can't Miss Sarah read?"

"'Course she can read!" Rice laughed. "She just likes me to read to her while she sews. She can't read and sew at the same time!"

They let the oxen wade into the stream. "It's early. Maybe you can read to her after we ride."

Rice shook his head. "Maybe, but I can't read after dark."

River felt a wave of frustration. "You can't ride after dark, either."

Rice looked at his friend, his eyes serious. "I don't want to disappoint her. She don't ask much."

River knew what he was about to say was in no one's best interest except his own, but he couldn't help himself. "Did it ever occur to you that she's just tricked you into doing some lessons?"

Rice grinned. "Yeah."

River wanted to swear and wasn't sure why. He had suggested the trick riding because he felt guilty about avoiding the boy. When Rice turned him down, he should have felt relieved. Instead, he was jealous. He told himself it was because he didn't—couldn't—trust Sarah Tanton. God alone knew what she wanted with Rice. A way to get to him, perhaps? He had to warn the boy.

"Look, Rice. Don't get too fond of Miss Sarah."

Rice looked startled. Suddenly he seemed to understand and laughed. "I don't like her *that* way. Not like I like the von Schiller girls. I know she's too old, but she's awful nice." He waded into the river and herded the stock back up the bank.

River sighed and fell into step beside him. "That's not what I meant. She's..." He struggled for a word to describe her without giving away their common past. "There's something funny about her. I don't trust her."

Rice looked at him sideways. "You just don't know her like I do. She's kinda shy. 'Specially around you." The boy gave his older friend a conspiratorial wink. "I think she likes you."

River stopped dead in his tracks. Rice led the oxen to the herd, and River looked after him. Finally he shook his head and stomped back to the wagons. *There's no talking to him,* he thought. *She's got him completely fooled!*

When he rounded the wagon, the first person he saw was the object of his wrath. He knew he should take a few minutes to cool down, but she was alone, and who knew when that would happen again. Sarah looked up from the fire she was building, and he saw apprehension in her eyes before she looked away. He watched her for a moment. "What do you want from Rice?"

It seemed she was going to ignore him. He fought the urge to take her by the shoulders and shake her. He stepped closer, ready to repeat the question. She stood slowly, and he thought there was the shadow of fear on her face. But there was something else, as well. Sorrow? Desperation?

"I don't want anything from him," she whispered. "Or you."

River wanted to laugh. She was good at this! For a moment, he had almost felt sorry for her. "I won't let you hurt that boy," he said softly. "Tell me what you want."

Anger flared in her eyes, and she turned away, intending to go back to her fire, to ignore him and his question.

"Answer me," he demanded, catching her arm and spinning her around.

She was lighter than he realized, and the quick jerk brought her up hard against his chest. Later, he would remember the gasp of alarm that escaped from her soft pink lips and the look of surprise in the deep brown eyes. Now, all he was aware of was the shock of contact and the voice behind them.

"Hey!" Rice strode quickly toward them as they stepped apart. "What's going on?"

"Sarah's skirts were too close to the fire," River said easily.

Sarah was too flustered to respond. She was sure her cheeks were flaming and her voice would shake if she tried to speak. Rice didn't give her time, anyway. He rushed to her side, concern evident on the young face. "You really gotta be careful, Miss Sarah. I seen a woman catch her skirts on fire once. It was awful scary. Are you sure you're all right?"

"I'm fine, Rice, really. I wasn't as close as I may have looked." She glanced at the dark scowl on River's face.

"Let me help you with the kettle frame," Rice went on. "Eli oughta be doing this. Where is he anyway?"

"You're doing a perfect impression of him yourself," River said, turning on his heel and walking
away.

"What's got under his saddle?" Eli joined them
from the opposite direction. "He's been in a prickly
mood all day."

Rice shuffled his feet. "I think he's mad at me. He
asked me to do some trick riding with him, but I said
I couldn't 'cause I was gonna read to Miss Sarah."

"Well, that sounds about right. Wouldn't want
nothin' to interfere with his play." Eli's grumblings
turned unintelligible as he went to the back of the
wagon and removed ingredients for supper.

"Rice," Sarah said softly. "We can read anytime.
How often do you get to do something with River?"

She watched several emotions play across his face
as he looked in the direction River had taken. "I do
like reading about knights and such, Miss Sarah," he
said finally. "But, well . . ."

"Besides," she interjected, "if you're going to do
some trick riding, I'd like to watch."

The young face brightened. He started away at
once but turned back to thrust the kettle into Sarah's hands. Sarah couldn't hold back a small chuckle
as she watched him run to find his friend.

Eli's loud grumbling cut it short, and she hurried
to hang the kettle on the frame, which had already
started to warm. Eli was glaring at her with his hands
on his hips when she turned around. "Well, go on

with ya!'' he said. ''I heard what ya told the boy. I don't need none of your help, anyhow.''

She didn't wait for him to change his mind.

River held the pinto's halter and looked at the boy above him. Rice sat high in the tree, poised to jump from the branch. ''I can do it with the horse moving,'' he yelled to his friend.

''I know you can,'' River said with a smile. ''First do it this way.''

Rice pushed away from the branch and landed smoothly on the horse's bare back. The horse side-stepped a little but settled down quickly, and Rice slid off. ''Walk him under me this time,'' he said, barely short of breath.

''All right.'' River led the horse away as the boy climbed the tree again. The landing was nearly as smooth as before. ''Let's try it once more,'' River said as Rice slid from the horse's back. ''Be ready for anything.'' Rice grinned and scrambled up the tree.

This time River led the horse at a fast walk toward the tree. At the last possible moment he turned and went around the trunk, bringing the horse under Rice from the opposite direction. Rice saw it coming, grabbed the branch where he sat and turned around as he lowered himself onto the horse's back.

River nodded his approval.

''Let me show you what I've been practicing,'' said Rice, breathless more from anticipation than exertion.

River raised his eyebrows. "Practicing on what?"

"Mr. Milburn's black."

River shook his head. Milburn's horse wasn't as reliable as the pinto, and he was surprised Milburn had given the boy permission. Of course, the black was Rice's now.

River relinquished the pinto's reins and leaned against the tree as he watched the boy ride a few yards away. He couldn't help but be pleased with the evening. Rice was showing considerable skill at riding and was quick to figure out any trick River could show him. The boy was obviously having fun, as well.

Part of his pleasure came from knowing he had won a small victory over Sarah. She had made plans for Rice, but the boy had chosen to be with him instead. He would make the most of it.

Rice rode by at a good gallop, dropping out of sight on the horse's far side as he passed the tree. He pulled himself upright again and reined around. River applauded the feat and caught the reins as Rice dismounted.

"How many times did you fall, trying to learn that one?"

"Too many to count," admitted the boy, laughing. "Show me the running mount again. I can't never get that."

"It'll get easier as you get taller." River clapped the boy's back as he led the horse a few steps farther from the tree.

* * *

Sarah watched from the shadow of Martha's wagon. She had been afraid to follow Rice any farther. If she was too near, her presence might be a distraction and cause him to get hurt. She tried to tell herself it had nothing to do with not wanting River to see her.

Occasionally Martha had come to stand beside her, and the two women had exchanged exclamations at the daring tricks they saw performed across the meadow. But Martha had dinner to prepare, and only Amy remained with her now.

River leaped onto the back of the moving horse and set him running toward the trees. The spectacle gave Sarah several moments of alarm as the rider risked life and limb, first one way then another.

"I can't do that," said Amy.

"Me, either," Sarah agreed, smiling down at the wide-eyed girl. "I don't think I even want to try."

"I do," said the child, still staring at the running horse.

"Don't try it until you're a lot bigger."

"Or find a little bitsy horse." Martha, coming up behind her, laid her hands on Amy's shoulders. "Dinner's ready." The four-year-old ran toward the fire. "Want to join us?" Martha asked Sarah.

Sarah shook her head. "I should be back helping Eli." She wanted one last look. River had dismounted, and Rice held the reins as River explained something that required more than a little gesturing.

"Just don't let him catch you watching him like that," Martha whispered. "He'll read everything that's in your heart."

"I was watching Rice," Sarah said quickly.

"Uh-huh." Martha laughed as she turned to join her family.

With Martha gone, Sarah allowed herself the pleasure of really studying the man she once loved. He stood, his back to the tree, calling instructions to Rice. The strong, warm voice reached her ears. She watched him lean his shoulders against the tree and allow one long leg to cross the other at the ankles. He waved to Rice, then folded his arms as he relaxed to watch. The fringe on the buckskin jacket danced with the movement. The jacket and boots fit River as well as the fashionable suits had fit Daniel. It made Sarah curious about the changes she couldn't see.

He had discarded his hat and the wind ruffled his golden hair, and Sarah remembered the texture as if she had just run her fingers through it. His beard was barely visible from this far away. Had it grown enough to be soft? She could imagine the sparkle in his blue eyes, though she couldn't see it.

The boy and horse flashed between them. Sarah barely noticed. River applauded and shouted to Rice. Sarah didn't even know what Rice had done.

River's head turned then, and he looked toward the wagons. Sarah had the feeling he looked straight at her. She had been sure she was in enough shadow that that wasn't possible. But then he was in the shade of the tree, and she could see him quite clearly. Martha's warning came back to her, and she found it difficult to handle his gaze, even at this distance. She waved goodbye to Martha and the family and walked to Eli's fire.

River watched Sarah walk away and wondered how long she had been watching. He smiled at Rice. "You'll have that one down in no time. You hungry?" At the boy's nod he added, "It'll be getting dark soon. Take care of the horse?"

"Sure thing. Can we work on shooting next time?"

"Depends on where we are. Now go, before Eli burns up all the food." The boy led the horse away, and River glanced toward the wagons. He would check to see that all the guards were in place and knew who their replacements were. After that he could eat and turn in.

He felt reluctant to return to camp. A few minutes ago he had been planning to gloat over a victory that now seemed hollow. He just wasn't sure about Sarah Tanton. When he thought of what she had done, he knew he couldn't trust her, but sometimes she seemed changed. It was almost as if she were someone else. It left him wondering if it was an act.

He had to get her alone, get her talking, watch her face, maybe figure her out. He chuckled at himself. He was standing in the gloom of evening, staring at the wagons where he had last seen Sarah, telling himself he was going to figure her out. "That," he muttered, starting toward the first guard, "is not very likely."

Chapter Five

Friday morning the train pulled away from the river and followed the army road once again. It ran roughly parallel to the stream, far enough away to be unhampered by the trees. Sarah thought the army had cared too much for efficiency and not enough for beauty. She would rather have kept to the shade of the trees and meandered with the river.

She and Rice walked beside the wagon. Rice, whip in hand, kept the team moving. "Awful pretty here, ain't it, Miss Sarah?" he offered.

It was his third attempt at conversation, and Sarah scolded herself for not being better company. She murmured her agreement, wishing she could be as easily contented as young Rice. He sprang back from disaster while merely the possibility of a threat had her jumping at shadows. Who was she kidding? She had jumped at shadows before Daniel reappeared, and she probably would all her life.

"I'm sorry about last night," Rice said.

Sarah looked at him sharply and saw the sadness in his face. "What are you talking about?"

"I figured I hurt your feelings last night, going off with River . . . or somethin'."

Sarah sighed and squeezed his arm. "My mood has nothing to do with you. Folks are just like that sometimes. Don't think that you're to blame."

Rice nodded. "You really don't mind that I didn't read to you last night, Miss Sarah? I do like King Arthur and all, but . . ."

"Of course not, Rice. We'll have a lot more evenings to read. Mr. Milburn would be pleased to know you're enjoying his gift."

Rice clearly liked the idea. "He got it for me in St. Louis more'n a year ago. I 'spect he thought I never would get it read."

It was a good sign, she thought, that he could talk about Milburn with a smile on his face. "Well, last night I enjoyed watching you and River ride. You're both very good."

Rice's grin broadened. "You think so, Miss Sarah? Did we scare you?"

Sarah laughed at the mischief in the boy's eyes. "Is that why you were doing it? To scare me?"

"Nah. But it's no fun if it looks easy."

Sarah laughed.

Abruptly Rice hollered and waved. She knew River must be coming, but she didn't turn to look. She didn't like the way her heart either plummeted to her stomach or leaped to her throat every time she saw him. She was scared of him, attracted to him and resentful all at once. She could hear the pounding of his horse's hooves and finally looked up. The handsome face wore a broad grin. *Throat this time,* she thought ruefully. Now she couldn't look away.

River reined the pinto and dismounted, falling into step beside them. "Want to ride for a while, Rice?" he asked.

Rice looked at the wagon seat, starting to shake his head. River laughed and held the reins toward him.

"Sure do!" The boy handed Sarah the whip, taking the reins eagerly.

"No funny stuff," River warned. "Just ride with the wagons."

Rice nodded and swung into the saddle. He waved as he sent River's pinto trotting toward the end of the train.

Sarah was smiling after him. It took a second to realize she was now alone with River. She turned and found him watching her intently. Her shock must have been easy for River to read on her face. She couldn't help it; throat to stomach was a long drop.

She hurried to catch up with the wagon that had moved on while they had not. The oxen were slowing, and if they stopped she wasn't sure she knew how to make them start again, though she had watched Rice often enough.

Before she had gone a dozen steps, River caught her around the waist, slipping the whip from her hand. "Whoa there!" he called. "Let's ride." He lifted her to the step as the slowly moving wagon came to a stop. There was no room to argue; she had to either grab hold or fall.

River climbed up the side of the wagon after her and cracked the whip over the backs of the team. She settled herself on the seat, automatically going still to hide her nervousness.

"We didn't finish our conversation last night. I'll ask again. What do you want with Rice?"

Sarah took a deep breath and let it out slowly. How could she explain what Rice had come to mean to her? She hadn't fully understood herself until she had thought of losing his friendship.

When she didn't answer, he spoke again. "I've never known you at a loss for words."

That brought a humorless laugh to her lips. "Do you know what prison was like, Daniel?"

He shook his head. "All I know is you weren't there long enough."

Sarah felt tears come to her eyes and was grateful for the bonnet that hid her face. "It wouldn't have taken much longer," she managed to say softly.

"What's that supposed to mean?" He shifted his weight a little on the wagon seat, and Sarah wondered if it wasn't the conversation that made him uncomfortable.

She didn't care. She would tell him this much at least. "We couldn't talk, Daniel. Unless it was necessary for our work, we weren't allowed to talk. It's called the Silent System and is supposed to give us time to think. I watched it drive more than one inmate crazy." Her voice cracked at the end, and she swallowed hard.

Much as she wanted to make him understand, she realized she wasn't able to talk about the past six years, not yet. But now, while he was here alone with her, was her chance to explain the night that had changed everything. She took a deep breath and began. "Daniel, six years ago—"

He cut her off. "Was six years ago. I'm more interested in now."

His refusal to listen made her angry. It was a welcome change from the tears she had felt a few seconds before. "All right," she said softly, "let's talk about now, Mr. River Whatever-you-call-yourself. Why change your name?" She pushed the bonnet off her head and turned to watch him. "You weren't accused of anything six years ago. Why the new identity if even I have the courage to use my own name?"

River had the grace to look embarrassed. "It's not really a new identity," he said.

She looked him over and asked incredulously, "It's not?"

River returned her gaze, feeling suddenly on the defensive. "No, it's not. Look, a lot has happened in six years . . ."

"Not for me."

He let that hang in the air and fought a surprising urge to tell her he was sorry. She had been through a hell he couldn't even imagine. He found himself wondering how long it would take her stiff body to relax if he drew her into his arms, and decided conversation was the best defense against such fantasies. "I saved a little Indian girl from drowning," he said. "A chief in her family's tribe named me Saves Child from River."

A slow smile played on Sarah's lips, surprising them both. "And you liked it."

He grinned a little sheepishly. "Well, I was working for the army, leading the Indian scouts. It didn't hurt to have an Indian name."

Sarah tried to reconcile this with the Daniel she remembered. Finally she shook her head. "Why did you come west, Daniel? Your father must have been against it."

River chuckled. "I would imagine you're right. I didn't bother to ask. I just left. The old man's probably disowned me by now."

Because of me? she wanted to ask, but didn't dare. She looked for traces of hurt on his face. If he felt any, he hid it well.

"What you did added just a little too much strain to our relationship," he continued. "But some time ago I realized it was for the best. I'm not sure when I would have broken away from him, otherwise." He pushed his hat to the back of his head and looked across at the horizon for a moment, taking in the rolling hills and vivid blue sky, before he smiled down at her. "I like what I'm doing."

Sarah returned the smile and nodded. She wanted to tell him she was happy for him, but somehow it was harder to put into words than it should have been.

River found himself staring at the sad eyes and sweet lips and had to turn away. But God, it was difficult! Memories of Sarah Tanton came back to him unbidden, memories of dancing and parties, laughter and love, of the sweet feel of her in his arms. *I was such a fool,* he thought, trying to shake away the feelings. He had been certain that the pain had wiped all that from his mind.

"That's not what I wanted to talk to you about," he said gruffly. "I want to talk about Rice."

"He's very fond of you," she said quietly. "I understand he thought of Milburn as his father. Do you realize he's expecting you to take over that position?"

River was astonished. He had been prepared to ask her intentions, not have her question his.

She misunderstood the look and continued quickly, "For all his size, he's still a boy and too young to be completely on his own. What will you do when this train reaches its destination? Does the boy figure in any of your plans?"

River tried to look serious in the face of Sarah's growing anger but failed and laughed.

Sarah couldn't understand why. He couldn't have become so heartless that he didn't care about the boy. No, she had seen how much Rice meant to him.

Maybe he thought she was treating him like a baby. How dare he make light of her greatest concern! She was so angry she could hardly speak. "I won't see that boy abandoned!"

River raised a hand to ward off the daggers her eyes were throwing. "He won't be. I promise." He got control of his laughter and watched her. If this wasn't genuine anger, she was an accomplished actress, indeed. Finally he spoke, "Don't be mad. I didn't mean to laugh at you. I just didn't expect a lecture."

Sarah hadn't forgotten his question of the night before with its unspoken accusation. Anger gave her a resolve she hadn't felt much lately. She looked unseeing at the scene around her and spoke with as steady a voice as she could manage. "You asked last night what I wanted from Rice. There is something, and I'm willing to lie to get and keep it." She turned her face in his direction, and he watched the anger slowly fade to sadness. "Friendship," she whispered.

He hadn't known what she would say, but somehow he wasn't surprised. "God knows why, but I believe you. You won't lose it because of me."

Sarah sighed deeply and relaxed for the first time. River watched her a second before pulling his hat down firmly over his brow and mumbling, "Now where's that boy ridden off to?"

Not all of Sarah's anger had been spent. She was still disgusted with herself for being attracted to this man who so obviously disliked her. "Get down and look for him." The words were out before she thought.

River was secretly pleased. This was closer to the Sarah he remembered. "All right, I'll do that." Before she had time to protest, he put the reins in her hands and climbed over the side, jumping away to avoid the wheels.

Sarah wanted to call after him, but she was afraid to look back, afraid, in fact, to move at all. What was she supposed to do? Her arms began to ache almost immediately, she was holding the reins so stiffly.

The oxen plodded on as if they hadn't noticed any change, and she began to relax. As long as nothing unusual happened, she would be all right. As long as she didn't need to turn, stop, slow, hurry...

Before she had quite panicked, Rice rode up. She watched in horror as he went from the back of the horse onto the wagon seat. The horse turned quickly and trotted off, answering River's whistle.

Rice grinned as he took the reins from her wooden fingers. "River teaching you to drive the team?" he asked cheerfully.

"I almost forgot." Eli emerged from the supply wagon with a small brown bottle. "Rice, take this to that German fella. He's got a toothache, and I want him to try it. Ya remember how we used it?"

"Yes, sir," answered Rice, closing the book and setting it beside Sarah's sewing basket. "But it didn't do my tooth no good."

Eli put the bottle in the boy's hand as he came to his feet. "Well, it might help his. Just go, and don't argue. Ya got some way of making him understand what to do?" At Rice's nod he continued, "Stay till yer certain he understands."

The boy grinned at Sarah's wink and started away. Eli called after him, "On second thought, ya best stay and watch him do it so yer shore."

Eli sat down where Rice had been and watched Sarah intently. She went back to her sewing, trying to ignore him. He wouldn't let her. "Wanna tell me how ya know Daniel?"

Sarah stabbed her finger with the needle and gasped, bringing the wounded digit to her mouth. Had he said *Daniel?*

Eli came to his feet. "I didn't mean to scare ya!" He sounded disgusted. He went to the fire and lifted the coffeepot, mumbling to himself, "Never seen a gal so jumpy."

"Everything's quiet," River announced, coming out of the shadows. At the fire, he held his cup under the pot so Eli would fill it.

Eli grumbled harder.

"What's wrong with her?" River asked, indicating Sarah, who still clutched the bleeding finger.

"Nervous as a treed 'coon."

Sarah glared at them both.

After one sip, Eli set his cup aside. "Now, where is that fool boy?"

Sarah looked at him in surprise. "You just—"

"Yer right. I'll just have ta go look for him."

Before Sarah could speak he stomped away. "He..." she began, pointing after him.

"What?" River sat down beside her and picked up Rice's book. He absently turned the pages, stopping at an illustration of a castle with a knight in the foreground.

"He—oh shoot!" A drop of blood formed on her fingertip. Concerned she would stain her sewing if it didn't stop, she pressed her thumb against the wound. River gently pulled her hand toward the light. "It's just a scratch," she said, trying half-heartedly to pull away.

"Must have gone pretty deep." He wrapped a handkerchief around the finger and closed his hand over it.

"It's nothing," she protested. "I just didn't want to ruin the dress."

River eyed the small pile of gray cloth on her lap. "That's a dress?"

Sarah laughed, and River found himself captivated by the sound. "A doll's dress," she clarified.

Their eyes met, and River found he didn't want her to turn away. "You don't laugh much, do you?"

His voice had dropped to a softer tone, a seductive tone that she well remembered. His nearness, his blue eyes, the warm touch of his hands produced a nearly forgotten quiver in her stomach. She basked in it a moment before she remembered what had caused her to poke her finger. "Daniel, does Eli know your real name?"

River shrugged. "Maybe. Probably. Why?"

Sarah tried again to pull her hand out of his grasp, but he held it fast. "I thought he might have heard me call you Daniel."

River grinned. "You do it all the time."

Sarah's voice dropped to a whisper. "He's asked me where we knew each other. Just now, he set us up to be alone. He's probably listening."

River seemed unconcerned. "He's asked me, too. It gives him something to think about."

"But, Daniel, what do I tell him?"

River turned her hand loose and came to his feet. "I don't care, Sarah. You said you could explain. Try it out on him."

"But he won't care about an explanation." Her voice dropped to a whisper again. "I've been in prison. That's enough to..."

River saw her perplexed look as she searched for words. "Enough to what? It won't make any difference to Eli."

"Then why does he keep asking? What will he do with the information?" Sarah watched him intently, unaware that she unwrapped and rewrapped her finger.

River shrugged. "He's a nosy old man. He likes to know everything, but he's not a gossip. He'll keep it quiet if you ask."

Sarah took a deep breath. "He didn't want me working for him in the first place. He'll want to leave me in Fort Kearny when he finds out I've been in prison and I'm a . . . a . . ."

River saw her cheeks turn pink as her quiet voice trailed off. A slight smile touched his lips. He didn't stop to wonder why his voice was suddenly soft. "What? A fallen woman?"

Sarah turned her face away, and he knelt beside her. "Leave out that part," he teased.

"Daniel, be serious." She looked into the handsome face and longed to reach out and touch it. This was the Daniel she remembered, the Daniel she missed.

"All right," he said. He took her hand and unwrapped his handkerchief from the finger. He told himself this was getting dangerous; he should move away from her and quickly. He also wanted an excuse to stay. He used the handkerchief to wipe away the blood and gently tested the wound. "I'll be serious," he promised. "But you have to relax. If you don't want to tell him anything, don't. But don't expect him to quit asking questions while you're so jumpy. You've let him spook you."

He took his handkerchief and stood. She wanted to tell him that everything spooked her. Even him— maybe especially him. Instead, she tried to sew, but her hands shook. Her stitches would be crooked, or she would poke herself again.

He retrieved his coffee cup and found a place to sit that put the fire between himself and Sarah. He didn't want to watch her but there was little else to watch. She looked frightened and lost, and he began to feel sorry for her. Perhaps she had already been punished enough; perhaps she truly wanted to start a new life.

He cursed himself for a fool, being taken in again by those big brown eyes! Why did she insist she had an explanation? Was she forgetting that he had been there? In a way, he would like to hear this crazy tale. He wondered if he could get Eli to repeat it after she told him. He didn't question that she would tell Eli, he only wondered why she hadn't already. Maybe she hadn't figured out anything plausible yet.

He watched her carefully fold the tiny pieces of cloth and place them in the sewing basket. Damned if he didn't find himself liking this woman who sewed doll dresses for little neighbor girls and worried about the well-being of young boys.

Sarah was glad to see Eli and Rice return. They strolled leisurely into camp together. Eli, looking from Sarah at one side of the fire to River at the other, seemed disappointed. She was more convinced than ever that he had intentionally left them alone.

Rice took his place beside Sarah, pleased with his visit to the von Schiller wagon. He related it to her

eagerly, managing to leave out any mention of Mr.
von Schiller's toothache.

The next day, the train left the Little Blue and followed the divide toward the head of Elm Creek. As
the wagon rocked along, Sarah listened to Rice. "All
of a sudden it just don't seem right," he concluded.

"Do you think the girls are unhappy? Are they
fighting?"

Rice shook his head. "I don't think so."

"Well, unless you've started liking one more than
the other, I don't see anything wrong with the way
things are."

"But I thought you was just supposed to have one
girl."

Sarah tried hard not to grin at him, he looked so
puzzled. "When one girl becomes special, she should
be your only girl, but for now, you and the von
Schiller girls can all be friends."

"I don't want to be just friends, not like I am with
you and River."

Sarah nodded her understanding. "I'd just give it
time, then. Maybe one of the girls will suddenly seem
special."

"Or one of them will decide I'm special."

"Exactly," Sarah said. "Until then, enjoy their
company."

Rice was grinning at Sarah and almost missed the
fact that Eli's wagon was slowing to a stop. He pulled

back on the reins and stopped the team a little too close to the lead wagon.

Rice leaned over the side of the wagon to see what was ahead of Eli. Sarah leaned over her side, as well, then drew back with a gasp. She grabbed Rice's sleeve, pulling him upright, and pointed.

"What?" Rice asked, straightening. A half-naked Indian rode past their wagon. His head, held high in pride and defiance, had been shaved except for a strip down the center from forehead to neck. A long lock of hair hung down his back. Two other Indians followed, and they positioned themselves at intervals along the side of the wagons.

"Pawnee," Rice said. "We got to pay them tribute." Even as he said it, Sarah saw River ride toward one of the Indians. They talked, using mostly gestures, then River wheeled his horse and rode toward Eli's wagon. In a moment he returned carrying a sack, which he handed to the Indian.

"Does this mean we're safe from them now?" Sarah asked.

"We weren't never in much danger," Rice said. "If we decided not to give them nothin', they'd probably just let us move on. But maybe they would follow and steal what they want in the night."

Sarah shuddered at the thought of the savages sneaking into camp in the dark. "I'm glad River paid them," she said.

"'Course, they might try it anyhow. You can't never tell," Rice went on. "I heard once about a

Pawnee sneaking into camp and stealing a blanket right off a fella without never waking him up.''

While Sarah was trying to decide if Rice was teasing her, River rode up beside their wagon. After a brief greeting, he looked back toward the receding band of Pawnee. ''I guess I can understand why some folks call them beggars, but to them, sharing food is a sign of friendship. Most whites would say they think so, too, though they forget it when they're asked to share with Indians.''

''I was just explaining it to Sarah,'' Rice said.

''Don't be scarin' her with Indian stories,'' Rice warned his young friend.

''No, sir,'' said Rice seriously. Sarah wondered if he was afraid he had already said more than he should have. She wanted to reassure him that she wasn't close to panic yet, but she would wait until River had left.

''We'll camp outside the circle tonight,'' River said before he put spurs to the pinto and rode toward the next wagon.

''Outside the circle?'' Sarah asked.

''That means the stock will be corralled inside the circle of wagons. Indians like to stampede the cattle, but it's the horses they want. They won't likely try nothing if the horses are all inside.''

Sarah thought this arrangement would make the travelers themselves more vulnerable.

''Hey!'' the boy shouted. ''There won't be no dancing if we're outside the circle!''

Rice was right. They made a late camp, corralled the stock and posted extra guards. The next morning, River announced the train would travel at noon, giving them the morning to check their wagons. A small party went out to hunt but didn't venture far from the camp.

Sarah took the opportunity to call on the Williams family and deliver the doll dress she had finished. Amy skipped to the wagon to find her doll. "I'm grateful for all you've done for Amy," Martha said.

Sarah smiled. "I haven't seen her around as much lately. You know she's always welcome, in spite of what Eli says."

Martha brushed a strand of hair out of her eyes. "She's finally decided to play with the Hess boy. He's five. She didn't like him at first because she's used to being the oldest. He won't let her boss him like she does her brothers."

They didn't visit long; both women had work to do. Sarah left, reminding Martha to send Amy over to visit anytime. After the noon meal, Rice and Sarah sat on the wagon seat for nearly an hour, waiting for River to give the word to pull out.

"They sure don't like traveling on Sunday," Rice commented.

A voice behind them seemed to rise an octave. Rice leaned over the side of the wagon to watch the argument. "It's the doctor's wife. She just joined her brother. River's starting to get real mad." He sat up and grinned at Sarah. The arguing made Sarah uncomfortable, but Rice seemed to think it was fun. She was afraid these new malcontents would lead another revolt. In a moment the voices were ominously silent, and Rice looked behind them again. "It's over," he announced.

Sarah wished she could see, too, but she didn't want to climb out of the wagon and be caught watching River again. "He didn't hit anyone, did he?"

"Nobody hit anybody." River's voice made her jump. He appeared on Rice's side of the wagon, and she turned away to hide her reddening face.

River walked past without further comment and untied his pinto from the side of the lead wagon. Once in the saddle, he waved to Eli, and the wagon started forward almost immediately. Rice cracked the whip above the backs of the oxen, and they were on their way.

Sarah had tried not to watch River as he rode in front of them, but the white patches on the horse's painted coat caught the sun and drew her eye in his direction. Rice was right, he was angry; it showed in every line of his body as he sat on the restless horse, rifle across his lap, watching the wagons pass.

Rice's grinning face came into her line of vision. She hadn't realized how intently she had been watching River. She turned away, embarrassed.

"Bet he give them what for, huh, Miss Sarah?"

Sarah nodded her assent.

The boy went on, "I can't see how come they're so upset. River gave them the morning and promised them a day at Fort Kearny."

"I'm sure it's the principle of working on Sunday that bothers them," she said. Rice shrugged, and Sarah smiled to herself. At least she didn't have to worry about a theological debate with Rice.

Chapter Six

Chapter Six

Wednesday morning found the train camped two miles above Fort Kearny. They had passed the fort in late afternoon, and Rice had observed that the last two miles had been about the longest all day. Whether he was referring to his desire to get to camp or the way the sand dunes slowed the wagons, Sarah had agreed. Now, as she helped Eli fix the breakfast, she knew Rice was hurrying through his morning chores, eager to go into the fort.

"Well, here's the list and some money." Sarah turned as Eli stuck his head out of the lead wagon and began to climb down. She looked around before she realized he was talking to her. "You and Rice better take the supply wagon. Got a brake beam worrying me on this one."

Sarah tried to cover her surprise as the old man put the paper and coins into her hand. She hadn't expected to be going into the fort, but the prospect of seeing it with Rice made her feel as eager as the boy.

When River and Rice came to the fire to eat, River made himself comfortable, as if he had been looking forward to a leisurely breakfast. Rice, on the other hand, grabbed up his food even more quickly than usual, and Sarah was afraid he would choke.

"Slow down, Rice," River admonished. "You'll give us all nervous stomachs just watching you."

"Sorry." Rice made an effort to eat more slowly. "You coming with me, River?" Sarah thought the question was probably meant to get his friend to hurry.

"Nope. I'll let you do the shopping. I'll go in a little later and see what news I can pick up."

Rice looked across at Eli, who answered his unspoken question. "I'm sending Sarie with ya."

Rice and Sarah exchanged smiles, and Rice went back to eating as hurriedly as ever. It took every ounce of concentration for Sarah to avoid looking at River. The prickling on the back of her neck convinced her he wasn't returning the favor.

Rice finished his breakfast and ran to get the team. Sarah finished soon after. River watched her with narrowed eyes as she checked the list, asking Eli a question about one of the items. The old man made fun of her for not understanding, but if it bothered her, she didn't let it show.

River couldn't help but notice that she never looked in his direction. He thought it was curious but decided she was giving him the cold shoulder for suggesting she tell Eli her so-called explanation. That had been days ago, he realized, and they had barely spoken since. It made him wonder what, if anything, she had told Eli.

When Rice returned, River was surprised to see Sarah move to help with the team. He glanced at Eli, but the old man didn't seem to notice.

Finally the wagon pulled out of the circle, and River waved goodbye to his young friend. He turned to refill his coffee cup and found Eli staring at him. "I reckon you got my morning planned," he said, returning to his seat with the steaming cup. "Where do we start?"

"With this here wagon. It's fixin' to fall apart, in case yer interested."

River gave a noncommittal grunt. "Are you grouchier than usual, or have I just not noticed till now."

"Ya just ain't noticed."

River laughed, but Eli ignored him.

"Like ya ain't noticed how unhappy Sarie is."

River looked across the camp, giving himself time to bury the resentment the comment caused. Several emigrants were leaving for a trip into Fort Kearny, a few in wagons but most on horseback or on foot. He took another slow sip of his coffee before he answered Eli. "I don't think she seems particularly unhappy."

"Aha! I said ya don't notice nothin'."

River cast Eli a withering look, but the old man wasn't discouraged.

"I know all 'bout ya and her and how mean ya was to her," he said.

"What!" River sprang to his feet, nearly spilling his coffee. "I was mean to her?"

"Well, I'm glad to hear ya admit it." Eli dumped his coffee cup and put it with the other dishes. He moved to unfasten the grease bucket from the side of the wagon.

"I don't know what she told you, but—"

Eli cut him off. "Don't wanna hear no more 'bout it." He took River's cup from his hand and thrust the grease bucket into it. "Ya should be ashamed."

River stood fuming for a full minute while Eli turned to the dishes, ignoring him. *What kind of crazy story did she tell?* he wondered. He moved to grease the wagon wheels, mentally cursing both Sarah and a foolish old man who would believe what she said.

At the last wheel, Eli came to look over his shoulder. "Gotta use a little more 'an that."

River straightened suddenly, causing Eli to fall back a step. "Do you want to do this?"

"Mean, that's just what ya are," he grumbled.

River sighed in exasperation. He finished the wheel and returned the bucket to its place.

Eli spoke the moment he was done. "Now, ya gotta check the brake beam. I think it's coming loose."

River eyed him a moment. "What did she tell you?"

"Who?" asked Eli, moving to the other side of the wagon to inspect the brake shoe in front of the rear wheel.

River gritted his teeth and followed. "What did Sarah tell you?"

"Enough. Now crawl under there and make sure the beam is still in one piece."

River slid under the wagon and tried to concentrate on checking the brake beam. Did Sarah expect him to suffer Eli's temper in silence? He had promised to keep quiet, but if she was going to lie, he was going to defend himself.

He found a bolt that was working loose and tightened it; otherwise the brake beam seemed fine. When he slid out from under the wagon, Eli was crouched nearby watching him. River sat with his back against the wagon wheel and glared at the older man.

"She's been in prison," Eli stated.

A suspicion began to form in River's mind. "She told you that?"

"I'm right, ain't I?"

River grinned. "She didn't tell you anything. You're guessing."

"I can guess more 'an that. Ya meant somethin' to each other, didn't ya? I bet ya promised to marry her."

The two men watched each other, trying to read the other's mind. Finally River spoke. "You can guess all you want, Eli, but keep it to yourself. I promised her I'd keep quiet about her past, and you're not tricking me into telling you."

"I was right, though, weren't I? Sarie don't hardly talk, don't like bein' inside the wagon, and she jumps worse'n a grasshopper. 'Sides, she knows ya, and ya scare her. That much I know for sure. My guess is she's been in prison, and ya know all 'bout it."

River's expression didn't change.

"Am I right?" He tried to stare River down. Failing, he nodded slowly. "I'm right. And ya were again' her, somehow. Are ya the reason she went to prison? Was it yer word that sent her? I know ya done somethin' to hurt that girl."

River came to his feet.

Eli looked up at him. "Was it murder? Did she kill yer wife? Er maybe her own husband?"

River gave Eli a withering look as he considered just how much he should say. Eli was intentionally making crazy guesses in an effort to get information. River realized that at least part of Eli's plan was working. He didn't want the old man to think Sarah was a murderer. "She went to prison for robbery. But keep it to yourself, Eli. For her sake."

Ernest Ortman nearly stumbled in his haste to get back to his wagon. Prudence would want to hear about this!

He had been on his way to talk to River. Prudence had sent him to complain about the late travel of the night before. He tried to get himself worked up again, remembering how tired and haggard his poor sister had been, trying to fix their supper in the dark. He couldn't quite do it; he was too excited.

He had heard the old man talking to River. Waiting, not wanting to interrupt, he had heard the old man mention Sarah. He couldn't help but listen after that. Then he had hurried away. Even now he took a quick look behind him. When he was almost to his wagon, he called out to his sister. His voice came out a croaking whisper. "Prudence. Prudence."

She answered weakly from the wagon. "In here."

His poor sister was lying on her bed, such as it was, trying to rest. She didn't remove the damp cloth that was draped across her eyes but spoke as Ernest climbed into the wagon. "What did you tell him?"

"I didn't get a chance to tell him nothin' a'tall," Ernest began, still breathless from hurry and excitement.

Prudence took the cloth from her eyes and glared at him.

"That River fella was talking to the old man, Eli, and—"

"And you can just go back and wait till they're done," Prudence interrupted.

Ernest was undaunted by his sister's stern face. "But let me tell you what I heard them sayin'."

Prudence was suddenly interested. She even rose up on her elbow to listen.

Ernest announced, "Sarah's been in prison."

Prudence glared at her brother a moment, watching his face fall in light of her reaction. After she had let him squirm a moment, she asked, "Who's Sarah?"

Ernest was plainly disappointed. Such a juicy bit of news should have earned him more respect than this. But his poor sister had been too busy to get acquainted around the train, he reminded himself. "She's the young woman that travels with Eli, River and the boy, Rice."

Prudence's eyes narrowed. "A young woman traveling on this train has been in prison?" She settled back onto her bed and replaced the damp cloth. "You're imagining things."

"No," Ernest whispered fiercely, leaning toward her. "I know what I heard. Eli was saying he knew Sarah had been in prison, and that River fella told him to keep it to himself. And Sarah is the name of the woman with that bunch."

Prudence pulled the cloth from her eyes and gazed at the canvas overhead. "I don't remember a Sarah. What do you know about her?"

"Well, she's young, like twenties, I'd say. Rides the wagon with Rice. Sometimes she's with the Williams family, you know, the one with all the babies. She's real small and has pretty brownish red hair and big brown eyes."

"Does she—" Prudence tried to interrupt, but Ernest had warmed to the subject.

"She's real quiet and don't hardly ever smile, but when she does it's like . . . like . . ."

"Ernest!"

His attention quickly flew to his sister's plump face. She glared at him, and when she was sure he felt properly chastened, she asked, "Does she act strange—you know—like she's different?"

Ernest had to think about that a moment. He had certainly watched her as much as possible. She hadn't ever seemed to notice him. In fact, she hadn't seemed very sociable, though he hadn't found fault with that until now. "Well . . ." He hesitated. "Now that you mention it, I guess she does act a little odd."

Prudence sat up, glad to see her brother coming back to his senses. "Well, we can't have a crazy person on the train with decent folks. Did he say why she went to prison?"

Ernest's eyes grew large. "Robbery."

"Go get my husband. We need to decide just how we're going to handle this matter."

River stepped out of the post commander's office and surveyed the activity around him. Fort Kearny was little more than a circle of frame buildings with a parade ground in the middle, but, as always in the spring, it was filled with emigrants, trappers, Indians, oxen, mules and wagons. The sights and sounds were so much a part of the place for River that it was hard now to think of it without them, though he had certainly been here in the off-season often enough.

He walked across the porch to lean against a post, trying to think about the fort and his short stint as an army scout and to forget about Sarah, Eli and the promise he had broken. His attention went to the sutler's store, where most of the activity was centered. His gaze was drawn to Sarah. How could a woman in such a plain dress stand out in a crowd?

He looked away. She was with Rice, he didn't have to worry about her. He should check around, see if any of his old friends were still around, gather as much news as he could. He found himself turning to watch Sarah again. His eyes could settle on her without even searching.

The bonnet had been pushed off her head, and the sunlight danced like fire in her hair. She was standing by the wagon, supervising Rice as he loaded the supplies. The boy was talking and would stop to finish what he was saying before going for another load. The job was taking twice as long as it should have, but Sarah didn't seem to mind. Even at this distance, River could see her smile and nod to the boy.

Before he knew it, he was walking across the parade ground toward them. He wasn't even sure when he had made the decision to step off the porch. Rice waved as he approached, and Sarah turned cautiously toward him.

"Me and Miss Sarah's almost done," the boy said. "You want to ride back to the camp with us?"

River found it impossible not to smile at his young friend. "You better work more and talk less, or you'll never get done."

"Yes, sir," Rice responded, but he was still smiling as he turned toward the store for another load of their purchases.

With the boy gone, River realized he was standing very close to Sarah. She had barely looked at him since he had joined them. *I make her nervous,* he realized, and wondered why. *Has she got some reason to feel guilty?*

Sarah was all too conscious of River's nearness. Rice had been talking about his friend, and she had been soaking it all in. Now he stood beside her, and she was afraid her feelings would show. She wanted to say something that would break the tension, some casual comment about Rice's conversation, but she found herself tongue-tied, as she so often did. Around River it was always worse. She kept her eyes toward the store, hoping River wasn't looking at her, afraid to turn and see.

River watched the still profile with a certain amount of discomfort. He was the one feeling guilty. His conscience told him he had to warn her before she got back to Eli. "I need to talk to you," he said, and Sarah jumped.

She turned toward him, trying to govern her expression, hoping he wouldn't know she was shaking inside.

He stepped back to lean against the wagon, focusing his attention on something over her left shoulder. How could she look so sweet and vulnerable? He didn't dare look in her eyes.

Rice stepped between them and tossed a sack of flour off his shoulder onto the wagon bed then scooted it more snugly into place. "That's everything," he announced.

"Do me a favor," River said, smiling at the boy's eager nod. "The pinto's tied across the parade ground. Ride him back to camp for me."

"Yes, sir! You gonna give Sarah another driving lesson?"

The ghost of a smile played on Sarah's lips at River's surprise and vanished quickly when his eyes met hers.

"Something like that," he said, feeling himself slide into the deep brown pools he had tried to avoid.

"You want I should go back now?"

With an effort, River pulled his gaze back to his young friend. "Whenever you're ready."

"Yes, sir!" Rice repeated, obviously pleased at River's show of confidence. "I'm ready now."

He cast Sarah a proud grin before he hurried away. Her feelings were mixed. She was happy for the boy, but now she was alone with River. Her feelings about that were confused in themselves.

She watched River's back as he secured the tailboard. Rice could have performed the same task just as expertly, but Sarah was conscious of River's greater strength. It was a physical reminder of how much power he had over her. His knowledge of her past could ruin her future. She didn't even want to think of what he could do to her if he knew she still loved him.

"Shall we?" River motioned toward the front of the wagon. His easy grin made Sarah want to turn and run. Instead, she took a moment to remind her legs how to work, then walked, calmly she hoped, toward the front of the wagon.

River's warm hand took her elbow to help her aboard, and she settled onto the seat. River climbed up beside her, released the brake and called to the oxen. Sarah watched his hands as he negotiated the wagon through the crowd. In a way she wished he did have a driving lesson in mind. That seemed less frightening than some of the things he might want to talk about. He always made her too nervous to say what she meant.

When they had left the fort behind them, River glanced at his companion. She sat very still and straight beside him, almost at attention. He felt another pang of guilt, and it made him angry. This was her fault after all; she was the one with the prison record. *But I'm the one who let Eli trick me into telling.* Blaming the old man wasn't going to make things easier for Sarah.

He studied the small hands that rested on the dull brown fabric of her lap. They were showing signs of hard work, yet he had never heard her complain. He had to admit she had changed a lot in six years. River turned away from her, surprised at the direction his thoughts were taking. Staring resolutely at the backs of the oxen, he got it over with. "Eli knows you've been in prison."

Sarah didn't move. She wanted to pretend she hadn't heard him right, pretend he was talking about something else.

"Did you hear me? Eli knows. He guessed it." He braced himself for a tirade. He had broken a promise. He would let her get it all out, then he would try to explain.

Sarah watched a wagon pull out of a circle a short distance away without really seeing it. She had known this would happen from the moment she recognized River. She took a deep breath and let it out slowly. "What did he say?"

River stared at her in disbelief. Where were the angry tears? The accusations? Had she known he would tell and planned for it? God, had she expected Eli to take her side? What kind of plotting went on in that pretty little head?

When River didn't answer, Sarah concluded the worst. Eli wanted her off the train. That's why River had needed to talk to her. He was taking her back to camp to get her things from the other wagon, and she would be on her own. She would never see Rice again! River had sent him on ahead, and Eli would make sure he was busy. She wouldn't even have a chance to say goodbye.

It was more than she could handle, and she panicked. Without a word she jumped to her feet and climbed from the moving wagon.

"What the—" River pulled the lines, and the oxen began to slow. He reached a hand toward Sarah, but she had already gone over the side. He knew she had landed safely when he saw her running across the prairie, her skirts held in her hands and her bonnet swinging against her back.

He swore under his breath as he directed the oxen off the track and pulled them to a stop, setting the brake. In a moment, he was on the ground running after her. His long legs ate up the distance between them, and he caught her arm, bringing her to a breathless stop.

Other wagons were passing near them. Three camps were spread out on the plains around them, and the fort was still in sight, but to them they were alone on the prairie.

Sarah struggled to free her arm, and River caught her by her shoulders, fighting the urge to shake her. Travelers were run over by wagon wheels too often for him not to know what she had risked to get away from him. The fact that he had climbed out of the moving wagon a few days before didn't enter his mind. "Are you crazy?" he yelled when he had caught his breath.

Sarah was about to collapse. Her breath came in lung-burning sobs, but still she tried to pull away from him. She wanted to run and run and never stop.

Finally, she realized how fruitless her struggles were and let him pull her against his chest.

"Damn, Sarah!" He took a deep breath and made a conscious effort to lower his voice. "You scared me." He smoothed her hair away from her face, soothed the racing pulse at her temple. "There's no reason to run."

Sarah felt the strength begin to return to her legs, only to have them turn to jelly as he continued to caress her. She wanted to surrender to the solace of his arms, to forget there was a damning past and an uncertain future, to pretend there was only here and now. *For a moment,* she told herself. *Only for a moment.*

River felt her relax against him and wondered at her reaction. She never did what he expected. He often scolded himself for thinking he could ever understand her, but it was difficult not to wonder when she constantly surprised him. And equally impossible not to be affected by her body in his arms.

"You've got nothing to worry about," he said finally. "I just wanted to warn you that Eli knows. He won't cause you any trouble."

She reluctantly pulled away but refused to meet his gaze. "How do you know?" she whispered.

River took a step backward, telling himself he was glad the contact was broken. The fact that he wanted to pull her against him again made him angry. He didn't want her to feel so good in his arms. He tried to hide the unwelcome feeling in resentment toward

Eli. His voice was rough when he answered. "The crazy old fool has decided it's my fault."

Sarah looked at him in disbelief. Eli had disliked her from the moment Milburn had hired her. Surely River had misunderstood.

River watched the brown eyes widen. She *looked* absolutely innocent. He tried to search her face for any sign of duplicity but recognized the danger in gazing at her for too long. He took her arm and propelled her across the prairie. "Let's get back to the wagon before somebody steals it."

Sarah hurried along beside him, trying to figure out what had happened. One moment she was in his arms, hiding from an uncertain future, the next moment he was telling her nothing had changed and dragging her back to the wagon. The old Sarah in her wanted to remind him *he* had no reason to be angry with *her*. *She* had no influence over Eli. One look at his stony profile convinced her to keep her thoughts to herself.

The ride back to the camp was passed in silence, each of them remembering the brief embrace and neither daring more than a glance at the other. As they neared the circle of wagons, River noticed the Reverend Fleenor watching them. He looked at Sarah, but her attention was on Rice, walking with the von Schiller girls.

When he had brought the wagon into line behind Eli's, he looked again for Fleenor, but he was no longer in sight. He tried to brush away the odd sense of foreboding that had started when he saw the reverend watching them.

Sarah touched his arm, making him jump. "I should have known Eli would guess," she said softly.

River looked at her and was caught in the deep brown eyes. "I guess I should have tried to deny it."

"No. I don't want you to lie to your friend for me. I'm sorry he blames you," she went on. "I'll try to explain."

It struck River that he could easily fall under her spell again. The thought was both infuriating and frighteningly appealing. He pulled his eyes away. "Don't bother," he said, and climbed quickly from the wagon. He turned to help Sarah, dreading the electricity the slight contact was bound to cause. As soon as her feet were safely on the ground, he stepped away from her. *I don't know why I let Fleenor trouble me,* he thought as he unhitched the team. *Sarah's the one I need to worry about.*

A voice behind Sarah made her jump. "I was hoping I would find you alone."

She had walked to the river intending to do the laundry, but the dust kicked up by so many wagons and stock made her wonder what she hoped to gain. She had tried to concentrate on the task, blocking out all thoughts of the future or of River, and had even less success with her mind than she had with the clothes.

She turned now to discover the Reverend Fleenor standing behind her. "I didn't mean to startle you," he offered, removing his broad-brimmed hat. "I would like a word with you but Mr..." He waved his hat toward the wagons. "Mr., uh, Eli... well..."

Sarah nodded her understanding as she came to her feet. She told herself to relax. The reverend had always seemed friendly, but she couldn't stop her heart from pounding.

"Have you repented, Miss Tanton?" He didn't wait for an answer but plunged on. "Whatever sin you committed, God is ready to forgive you."

Sarah swallowed hard before she found her voice. "What sin are you talking about, Reverend?"

"That's between you and God."

"Then isn't repentance, as well?"

Fleenor's fingers began to work their way around the hat brim. "Of course, Miss Tanton. But sometimes we need someone to help us along the road to salvation."

"Why, specifically, do you think I need help?" She held her breath. *Say you've noticed I don't attend your services. Say you're calling on all the members of the train.*

"Miss Tanton, I don't want to betray a confidence, but I've been told you served time in prison."

Sarah felt the world spin for a second but steeled herself. She was determined not to let his words destroy her; she had already panicked once today.

"You haven't asked me if it's true. You haven't asked if I was guilty."

The reverend's voice was soft. "Is it true, Miss Tanton?"

Sarah straightened her back and tried for a confidence she didn't feel. "Yes, it's true. But I was not guilty."

"But you were being punished for something. Otherwise, the Lord would have prevented it." At Sarah's startled look, he tried to explain. "The Lord does nothing without a reason. At the very least He wants you to learn something."

Sarah tried not to let this opinion bother her. But she couldn't stop herself from wondering if he was right. Had God meant for her to go to prison? And who on the train had told the reverend? It was more than she could sort through while her mind was screaming, *Everyone knows! Everyone knows!*

As she tried to retreat to her laundry, he caught her arm. "Please understand, Miss Tanton, decent people on this train will want you to leave. If I can assure them that you have repented and been forgiven..."

"I suggest you leave her alone."

Sarah jumped again, this time with instant recognition. "Daniel," she whispered.

The reverend nodded. "Of course, sir. I was only..."

"Nice day for a stroll, huh, Reverend? But Sarah has work to do."

"Of course. Mind what I've said, Miss Tanton."
He placed his hat on his head and nodded to River,
then turned to walk toward the train.

Sarah whirled away and resumed her washing.
River watched her kneel on the bank for a full minute before he asked, "What did he say?"

"That someone told him I've been in prison." She
scrubbed at a shirtsleeve more vigorously than it deserved.

"Not Eli."

Sarah gave a humorless laugh. "No, I don't think
Eli would run to the reverend."

River studied the tense shoulders as he tried to
think. "Someone must have overheard," he suggested.

"I wouldn't be surprised. We don't exactly have
thick walls around here."

River was getting tired of talking to her back. He
let himself ignore what she was suggesting, that he
should have known there was a chance of being
overheard. "Now look," River said, kneeling beside her. "This isn't my fault. I didn't tell Eli anything."

Sarah's hands stilled on the garment. She turned
slowly to look at him. "I know," she whispered.

River watched her profile as she went back to
work. She was becoming quite good at keeping
emotions from showing on her face. If he didn't
know better, it would be easy to believe her only interest was the small stain on the sleeve of that shirt.

After a moment he rose to his feet and walked away. He had work to do, and he ought to dismiss her as easily as she dismissed him. Only he couldn't. As he made the rounds, he found himself thinking about Sarah, her flight across the prairie and her strange reaction at the stream. The Sarah he remembered would have laughed in their faces, and his.

He decided it was not a good idea to think about that Sarah. It brought back too many memories, not all of them pleasant.

Chapter Seven

A couple of hours after leaving Sarah, River approached the Carroll and Ortman camp. With a glance around the circle, he realized he had left it until last. *Natural desire to forget it entirely,* he thought.

Prudence Carroll was viciously attacking a potato when she noticed him. She put down the potato and rolled the knife handle in her hand as she scowled at him. He tipped his hat and tried to give her a cheerful greeting, but she interrupted. "I sent my husband to talk to you," she informed him.

"Is that right? I must have missed him. I've been around seeing if folks have any problems."

"We most certainly *do* have a problem." She came to her feet, wiping her hands and the knife blade on her soiled apron. "You must do something about that Tanton woman."

River let a smile spread across his face, but his eyes remained cold. "What did you have in mind, ma'am?"

Prudence glared at him. "I want her off the train," she stated. "I let the good reverend persuade me to wait until he talked to her before I informed the rest of the train of her abominable reputation."

"Abominable?" River quirked an eyebrow at her, trying not to let his rising anger show.

She shook the knife at him. "The woman's a convict! Don't pretend you don't know what I'm talking about, either. Ernest got it from your own lips!"

"From behind my back. Ernest eavèsdropped, Mrs. Carroll." So it was Ernest. He should have guessed.

"No matter. Doesn't change the facts." She tipped her chin a good inch higher.

River's eyes narrowed. "Sarah's past is her own business."

Prudence inhaled sharply. "There are decent folks on this train!"

"I'm sure there are, and if any of them hear about it, they'll most likely ignore it."

Prudence opened her mouth to speak, but River, completely fed up with the woman, turned on his heel and strode away.

Sarah felt numb. If only she could convince herself it didn't matter; what other people knew or didn't know had nothing to do with who she was.

But it did matter. Some of these people were her
friends, and they might not remain so. Rice, Martha, even Eli. It hurt to think how they would look
at her now.

She finished the laundry and gathered the wet
clothes into a bundle, barely aware of what she was
doing. The reverend had her so confused even the
comfort she had taken in her own innocence deserted her. She hadn't committed the crime she had
paid for, but she wasn't totally innocent, either. She
and Daniel had shared a rather wild youth. She could
well imagine herself being punished for other things.

Color rose to her cheeks as she thought about it.
She had been Daniel's lover without benefit of marriage; by most everyone's standards, that made her
as bad as the reverend said. In fact, some would see
it as worse than robbery.

Her feet carried her toward the wagons without
any help from her brain. She was aware of a sense of
alienation, made more painful because she had begun to think of that circle of nine wagons as home.

She hung the clothes over the line between Eli's
wagons and tried to pretend she would never have to
speak to anyone again. *Silence, just like prison,* she
thought with a shudder. She immediately withdrew
the wish.

Soon the laundry was hung up to dry, and she
ducked beneath it to enter the circle. Eli and Dr.
Carroll were sitting near the fire, sharing a pot of

coffee. "Fetch a cup, and come join us, Sarie," Eli called.

Sarah considered facing whatever the men had to say to her without the stimulant, but her hands were cold from the washing, and the warm cup would give her a little comfort. She went to the back of the lead wagon and, with cup in hand, stepped to the fire. Dr. Carroll rose to pour her coffee, and they indicated a seat between them.

"Doc here's got a theory," Eli said. "Sounds a bit peculiar, but it might be worth a try."

Dr. Carroll leaned toward Sarah. "I don't want to alarm you, Miss Tanton, but I'm sure you've already heard of cholera."

Sarah straightened in surprise. This was not the subject she had expected them to be discussing.

Eli misunderstood her reaction. "We ain't got no case of it, Sarie. We was just talkin' on it."

"Back home we'd heard how cholera takes so many travelers, and Eli has seen cases himself," the doctor continued. "I've been reading all I can find on the subject, and several sources, including army surgeons, have advocated boiling all drinking water."

Sarah looked from one man to the other, and Dr. Carroll explained quickly, "I can see you're skeptical, but, as I understand it, it works like this. When the water is boiled, the toxic substances rise to the top and can be skimmed off or strained away through a cloth." He waited for Sarah's reaction, clearly hoping for an encouraging one.

"Kills the bug, too," Eli added cheerfully.

Sarah looked from one to the other and didn't know what to say. Disease on the trail had been something she had tried not to think about. She didn't see how her opinion would matter to either of these men, anyway. Finally she echoed Eli's words. "It's worth a try."

The doctor smiled at her acceptance. Thanking Eli for the coffee, he rose to his feet. He murmured a goodbye to Sarah before walking away.

"Nice sort," Eli said.

Sarah turned cautiously to look at him, wondering if he had been waiting for the doctor to leave before bringing up the subject uppermost in her mind. Instead he stretched and said, "I reckon it's time to start supper."

River was still fuming from his encounter with Prudence Carroll when he saw her husband leave Eli's fire. He couldn't help but worry what the man might have said to Sarah. The doctor hurried toward him and, signaling for quiet, motioned for River to follow him out of the circle.

River didn't bother to hide his irritation. "Your wife said you wanted to talk to me."

"Yes," Carroll began. "I wanted to warn you for the young lady's sake. The wife's got a bee in her bonnet, you might say."

"So I understand."

Carroll looked at the younger man and sighed. "I can see you know all about it. It will be hard for the lady, but eventually Prudence will find something else to interest her."

River gaped at the doctor. "Your wife wants Sarah thrown off the train!"

"But if you and Eli support Miss Tanton, there's not much Prudence can do even if she gets some others behind her."

"Wouldn't it be easier to just curb your wife?"

The doctor looked taken aback by River's temper. "Well—no," he said finally. "You can't really blame Prudence. It was the way she was brought up, you understand. She and all her family are pretty secure in the knowledge that they are right."

"Then tell her she's wrong!" River strode back to the wagons. He knew that venting his anger on the doctor was an effort to deny his own responsibility for the situation.

Just before he reached his camp, he stopped to watch Sarah. It was hard to tell what she was feeling. She worked the same as she always did, quietly and efficiently. His conscience urged him to go to her, but he wouldn't know what to say. He clenched his fists in frustration then shoved them into the pockets of his jacket.

One pocket wasn't empty. He pulled out a small paper-wrapped parcel and stared at it a moment before recognition dawned. He had bought this on a whim at the Hollenberg Ranch and had forgotten it.

He unwrapped it now to reveal a length of bright red ribbon. He fingered the satin surface, remembering how foolish he had felt after he bought it. But then, as now, he had pictured the ribbon in Sarah's chestnut hair and remembered how her eyes used to sparkle at every gift he gave her.

The memory of a special gift intruded. Sarah sat in the middle of the bed, laughing with delight. She was dressed only in her chemise, petticoats and corset. A very charming outfit, he recalled. Her hair tumbled freely around her shoulders, catching the lamplight. He stood and watched as she opened the box, flinging the paper aside impatiently. He could still hear her soft gasp of surprise before she turned her smile on him. "Red, Daniel?" she teased.

"Of course."

She scrambled off the bed and threw her arms around his neck, kissing him on the cheek. "You're so sweet to me, Daniel," she whispered, before returning to the gift and lifting it out of the box. A bright red dancing dress.

The red dress.

He quickly rewrapped the ribbon and tucked it into his pocket. He had far too many memories of Sarah. Why he even thought of giving her gifts was more than he could understand. She wouldn't want them anyway, not from him.

* * *

To Sarah, it felt like the calm before the storm. Eli moved about the fire with less conversation than usual, failing to criticize even her most awkward cooking techniques. River joined them, took a bridle from his gear and began to mend it without speaking to either of them.

The fish on the spit were nearly ready, and Sarah had begun to relax, when Rice hurried into camp.

"Is it true, Miss Sarah?"

Sarah looked up from the potatoes she was testing. She didn't need to ask what he was talking about.

"The old bat didn't waste any time," River said, laying the bridle aside and coming to his feet. He had some thought of moving close to Sarah to offer his support before he stopped himself.

Rice had only come to the edge of the camp as if he couldn't bare to come any closer. "Folks are saying you was in prison. It's not so, is it, Miss Sarah?"

Though the confusion and hurt she saw on the boy's face made her want to lie, she felt she had no course now but the truth. "Yes, Rice. It's true."

"But why didn't you tell me?"

The boy was nearly shouting, and River moved toward him. "Take it easy, Rice."

"I thought I was your friend." He glared at Sarah. "You don't keep secrets from friends."

River laid his hand on Rice's shoulder, but the boy turned away. He left the camp at a run, and Sarah started after him.

River stopped her. "Let him go," he said gently. "Give him time to cool off and think about it."

Eli spoke from behind them. "He's just bein' a fool boy. He'll be back when he gets hungry."

Sarah wasn't convinced. Rice had left the circle of wagons, and it seemed like a big prairie out there, full of dangers for a boy alone. She hoped he would head for the von Schiller wagon. River's hand was on her arm. He urged her back toward the fire.

"Let's dig in," Eli said cheerfully.

River forced a chuckle at the old man. "Rice isn't the only one who lives by his stomach." He hoped his smile reassured Sarah.

"'Course not," said Eli, carefully removing the tender fish from the spit. "Everybody does, whether they know it or not. Now Sarie here, she worked hard to make this supper. I don't aim to miss it just 'cause Rice does. Do him some good to see what hungry's like."

Sarah and River exchanged a brief glance before taking their plates from Eli. River related his visits with several of the emigrants, and Eli explained Dr. Carroll's plan for purifying water. Sarah knew they were both trying to make her feel as if nothing had changed. Eli even tried to draw her into the conversation, but she could bring herself to do little more than nod. River had enough sense to leave her alone.

She had lost Rice. The truth made no apparent difference to the grumpy old man who hated her anyway, but the friendship she had with the young boy would never be the same. Sarah felt the spark of anger ignite inside her and quickly smothered it. Blaming Eli or River would do no good. She had to find her way from this point forward.

In spite of Eli's words about Rice going hungry, she noticed he wrapped a portion of fish and two potatoes in a damp cloth and left it on a rock by the fire. "'Course, I may just be feedin' a coon," he said with a chuckle.

As she helped Eli clean up from the meal, she stole glances toward the food as if its being there would somehow tempt Rice into returning.

When she finally climbed into the wagon to sleep, it was still where Eli had left it. By morning it was gone.

Sarah became occupied with the usual activity of preparing to leave. She saw little of Rice except when he ate, and then he refused to look at her. River, Eli and Sarah barely spoke. When it was time, Eli directed her to the lead wagon and helped her into the seat before climbing up beside her.

It was Thursday morning, May 26, Sarah reminded herself, and grimaced. Rice was the one who always kept track of the days to make sure they didn't miss a Saturday night. She glanced at Eli, but he seemed to have already forgotten she was there. It promised to be a long day.

Sarah saw River ride ahead of the lead wagon and wave his hat as signal to begin. He reined the pinto up a short distance off the track to watch the train. She couldn't pull her eyes away from him as Eli started the wagon moving. He seemed completely relaxed, watching the circle of wagons uncoil, and Sarah was reminded of Milburn. She would never have imagined Daniel taking on something like this.

Presently they passed him, and there was nothing to see but the wide, flat prairie. A few cottonwoods grew along the river, but otherwise the view was undistinguished all the way to the low hills that lined the north and south horizons.

Eli was not inclined to converse, and they rode silently for hours. Sarah's mind skipped from one uncomfortable thought to another, and she missed Rice, with his distracting banter, all the more. When she could stand it no longer, she asked to walk until the noon stop. Up close the prairie was no more interesting than it had seemed from the wagon, and Sarah knew the fault lay more with the beholder than the gently waving grass.

That night they camped on Plum Creek, and Eli sent Sarah out with a large sack to gather buffalo chips. The possum bellies were both full of wood, but Eli was eager to have a buffalo chip fire. She was the only one on the prairie gathering fuel, the others choosing to cut what little wood was available or use up their stored supply.

She tried to ignore the isolation. She had been more lonely in prison, certainly. Here she was free. Taking orders from Eli wasn't the same as taking them from the guards, and she could argue with him if she wanted to. The thought made her hands shake; she *had* thought of Eli as the warden since she joined the train. Perhaps she had been unfair.

The evening meal passed much as the morning's had. Sarah considered trying to get Rice alone, but he avoided her. She decided he had as much right to his anger as anyone.

She cleaned up the last of the dishes and was turning to the fire when River was suddenly beside her. He took her arm and led her outside the circle. When the wagon was between them and Eli's fire, he stopped her. His hand lingered on her arm before he dropped it self-consciously. Just above a whisper, he asked, "Are you all right, Sarah?"

"How do you mean?" There was an edge to her voice, though she had meant it to sound as soft as River's.

She saw his face harden and knew he had heard it, too. "Is Eli giving you trouble?" he asked.

She shook her head. Part of her wanted to blame River, but she couldn't. The rest of her wanted to run into his arms.

He was watching her closely, and she wondered what he could read on her face. Finally he spoke again. "Rice'll come around."

She closed her eyes, slowly releasing a breath. An instant later her eyes flew open as she felt his hands on her shoulders. He had stepped closer, and she was nearly in his arms!

"Sarah," he whispered.

She stepped away from him. Her lips formed a soundless "no" as she backed out of reach.

"I didn't mean to do that," he said, holding a hand toward her as if she were a wild creature he was trying to coax toward him. "I'm sorry, Sarah. I just want to..."

River dropped his hand and sighed as she fled for the wagon. Exactly what had he wanted? Somehow with Sarah it was easy to forget. For a moment, he considered following her. Deciding that would be the height of foolishness, he headed for the herd. He had a full three hours of watch to consider how his physical desire had gotten the better of him for a moment. *God, what if she hadn't run?*

Late in the morning, the third day out of Fort Kearny, Eli elbowed Sarah. "Looky what we got here," he said, pointing. A caravan was coming toward them. Sarah had been watching the distant hills move almost unperceptively past and hadn't noticed the other train. "Buffalo skinners," Eli explained. "Can you smell 'em?"

Sarah glanced at her companion to see if he was teasing. The wagons were so far away she could scarcely make out any details. Eli cracked the whip above the team's backs and fought the lines as the oxen tried to turn aside. By the time he had them headed in the right direction, they were well off the track.

Sarah could smell the hides now, a strong wild scent of fur mixed with putrid meat. The hunters themselves seemed as dirty and shaggy as the hides piled in the wagons. Eli's oxen tried to turn again as the wagons came alongside. He let them pull farther away to give the hunters a wide berth. Sarah was glad when they were past and the wind had blown their smell after them.

"Can't hardly blame the ox for wantin' to avoid 'em," Eli commented.

Sarah pretended the comment had no hidden meaning for her. Rice was the only one actually avoiding her. There was little time for socializing anyway, and other than a few haughty glances, things weren't so very different from what they had been before. Except for Rice. Sarah's mind echoed Eli's words. *Can't hardly blame the boy for wanting to avoid me.*

At the noon stop, Sarah threw together a cold lunch while Eli helped Rice and River water the teams. As the men were returning to eat, Prudence Carroll marched toward the lead wagons. River saw her coming and hurried to meet her, hoping to spare Sarah whatever the woman had come to say.

"If you hurry there's still time," Prudence called.

"Time for what?" River had to turn and follow as Prudence bustled past him, not pausing until she stood face-to-face with Sarah.

She glared at the younger woman as she caught her breath. "Time to catch those hunters," she said.

"I'd as soon catch a fever," Eli said, but Prudence didn't hear.

She pointed a stubby finger at Sarah. "She can go back with them."

River saw the shock at this suggestion on Sarah's face.

Eli grunted and, taking his lunch, walked away. River watched him go with a little envy. He was in charge and had to set her straight, preferably without making her too angry. "Mrs. Carroll," he began.

Prudence turned to face him. "We should have left her at that fort, but the reverend made me wait."

"Mrs. Carroll," he tried again.

"I'm sure they will take her if you don't tell them much about her."

River took the woman's arm. "Allow me to escort you back to your wagon," he said, propelling her away from Sarah.

"Thank you, but I'm sure you should go as soon as possible. It's been at least an hour, and they seemed to be moving rather fast."

River congratulated himself for holding his temper. The woman obviously didn't realize he wanted to strangle her. Keeping his voice at a reasonable volume, he said, "Sarah will leave the train when, and if, she wants to."

"You can't mean to let her—"

River silenced her protests by making her walk faster. He could see both Ernest and the doctor waiting for them and said quickly under his breath, "Stay away from Sarah," then let her go.

"I intend to do just that," she responded, and huffed toward her family.

River stomped back to the front of the train, thinking of several things he wished he had said. She was the one he should have left behind. She was the one that ought to be riding back with the buffalo skinners. He pictured her fat body sitting primly on the pile of hides, a lace handkerchief held over her nose. He smiled at the thought.

Sarah was alone at the wagons when he arrived. Eli and Rice had gone to bring in the teams. Sarah handed him his lunch and turned away, busying herself with nothing in particular. River watched her, certain she was fuming. He didn't think she would stand quietly and be insulted again. As he walked toward the grazing pinto, he wished he hadn't hurried Prudence away quite so quickly. It would have been good to see Sarah put the woman in her place.

During the afternoon's march, Sarah tried not to think about what had happened. She tried not to wonder what Rice thought of the woman's suggestion or why River had returned with the smile on his face. She tried but failed. At camp, Rice's haste to unhitch the teams reminded her it was Saturday. There would be a dance tonight, the first since the train had divided, the first since River had joined them.

While she and Eli fixed the evening meal, River warmed a small pan of water at the fire and hung a mirror to the side of the wagon. When Sarah realized his intention, she tried not to watch. It was impossible. There was something very intimate about seeing him slowly scrape the razor across his cheek and jaw. In normal conditions it would be something only his family, his wife, would see. She tried to remember what Eli had just asked her to do.

In her continuing effort to ignore River, she kept her attention on Rice through supper. She thought she saw his youthful exuberance threaten his resolve to ignore her. He seemed more embarrassed than angry now. For the first time, she let herself hope River had been right when he said the boy would come around.

As soon as Rice left for the dance, Sarah became conscious of River's gaze. He made her even more nervous than usual. She ate hurriedly so she could take her plate to the back of the wagon and move farther away from River.

She and Eli had begun to clean the dishes when River brought his plate to them and leaned a shoulder against the wagon. He tipped his head toward the small band that had begun to play. "You coming, Sarah?"

She looked at him in surprise and shook her head, then had trouble looking away. His freshly shaved jaw seemed to invite her touch. His blue eyes sparkled with mischief, and she wondered if he read her thoughts.

Eli answered for her. "I can do this without ya. Get on out there and have yer fun."

"No, thank you," she said, quickly returning her eyes to her work.

River wasn't dissuaded. "I know you like to dance, and we've got so few dancers."

Sarah was aware of Eli standing beside her. She wished River had made his offer in private, then remembered what had happened the last time they were alone. There was no better way to discourage him than with the truth. Looking him in the eye, she said, "I'm not wanted there."

"I remember a time when that wouldn't have mattered," he countered.

"Six years in prison has a subduing effect," she said.

Eli grunted, whether in disgust or appreciation it was impossible to tell. He continued his work as if he weren't standing in the middle of a personal conversation. Sarah saw River cast the old man an annoyed glance and had to smile.

The smile faded as his gaze fell on her again. She tried to return it unflinchingly but was relieved when he finally shrugged and turned toward the dancers. "When you change your mind, come on over." In a moment he was dancing with one of the von Schiller girls while Rice danced with the other.

Turning back to her work, she found Eli watching her. "Get yerself over there, and show 'em they ain't got ya cowed."

Sarah shook her head. "I don't want to spoil their fun."

Eli grunted. "Some fun! Pickin' on one scrawny gal. Go make Rice dance with ya!"

"No," Sarah said firmly.

A broad grin split the old man's face. "I knew it," he stated before returning to his work.

Sarah eyed him curiously, but he didn't seem inclined to tell her what he knew. Deciding to leave the rest of the dishes for him, she took her sewing to the fire.

Eli wouldn't let her work in peace. "Ya waitin' for someone else? That'll make 'em both jealous, River and Rice. Serve 'em right, too."

Sarah moved closer to the firelight. Eli continued to mumble over the dishes. After several minutes of relative quiet with the music and laughter in the background, Eli moved to the fire. He sat where he could watch her and the dancers. She didn't look up but wasn't surprised when he spoke.

"Ortman," he said. "That's who ya oughta dance with." He laughed in anticipation. "About makes his sister come apart at the seams!"

Sarah sneaked a peek at the gleeful old man and tried not to smile. It was just the thing she would have enjoyed a long time ago. And River was right, she wouldn't have cared what the others thought. Now she wanted to call as little attention to herself as possible.

When she didn't respond to Eli's suggestion, his humor returned to normal, and he sat grumbling for several minutes. Suddenly he spoke to her again. "How come you let people think you robbed somebody?"

Sarah let her sewing drop to her lap. "What makes you think I didn't?"

Eli shrugged. "You got more fight than you let on, too."

Sarah shook her head. "Not anymore."

Eli grunted. He seemed to watch her with some anticipation. She imagined telling him the whole story. It would be a relief to set the record straight with someone, but she wasn't sure Eli would believe her. Somehow, the thought of dredging up a past she was trying to forget brought a lump to her throat.

Eli was still waiting, and she finally spoke. "I don't think they know about the money. Prison is enough, and I can't deny that." She picked up her sewing, hoping Eli would see it as a sign the conversation was over.

He swore under his breath. "Ya just gonna let 'em win!" He stomped away, leaving Sarah alone at the fire.

Chapter Eight

The next morning, Sarah looked up from the dough she was kneading to see Amy holding up her doll for Sarah's inspection. "See what happened to Lizabeth's old dress?"

The stitching had come out of the tattered sleeve seam, leaving the tiny piece of fabric dangling. Sarah had to smile at the child's solemn look. "That's easy to fix," she assured her. "If you want to leave the dress, I'll mend it tonight." She wiped her hands on her apron and reached for her sewing basket. "You can put it in here," she said.

"But if I take her dress off, she'll be naked."

"What about the dress I made for her?" Sarah asked, kneeling to the child's level.

"Mama threw it away."

Sarah gave an involuntary gasp, and the little girl began to whimper. "I . . . I'm sorry."

Sarah pulled her into her arms. "Don't be sorry. It's all right." Suddenly the little body was pulled from her arms, and Amy cried out in alarm.

Sarah rose to her feet to find Martha in front of her. The frightened child clung to her mother's leg and sobbed softly as Martha patted her back. "I— I'm sorry," Martha stammered. "It startled me, seeing Amy... I mean." Her eyes seemed to skip around the camp looking at everything except Sarah. "She needs to learn to stay closer to the wagon." The mother turned away, dragging the child with her.

"But, Mama," Amy protested.

"What have I told you about coming here?" Martha scolded.

The last words weren't intended for Sarah's ears, but Martha's behavior had made her feelings plain, anyway. As Sarah watched the mother and child arrive at their own fire, a short distance away, she became aware of an audience. River and Rice stood together across the fire. She didn't wait for their reactions but turned to her bread, pretending she had never been interrupted. She fought the impulse to see if they were still there. She didn't really want to know if they felt pity or pleasure at her embarrassment. Most of all, she didn't want them to know how she felt. She didn't look up until Eli berated her for kneading the bread too long.

River had stood helplessly as the mother dragged her child away. The pain he read in Sarah's face held him in shocked silence as the full implications of what she was confronting cut into his heart. Prudence with all her bluster was easier to dismiss. Who cared what that old bat thought, anyway?

A short time ago he had tried to warn Rice away from her the way the young mother had warned her daughter. He thought he knew Sarah to be a thief and a deceiver, but for some odd reason he couldn't convince himself she deserved this. He was more than a little tempted to go to her, to offer her comfort.

His attention was drawn away from Sarah as the boy beside him turned and ran. River wanted to call out to him, but the silence seemed too heavy to break. He took one last look at Sarah's stiff profile before following Rice. He caught up with him where the horses were picketed. Rice had gone straight to Milburn's black. River noticed the boy's slumped shoulders. "You hiding from something?"

River was surprised to see him jump. Rice had been so engrossed in his own misery, he hadn't realized his friend had followed. "Naw," he said, trying to sound casual.

River stepped forward and caught the halter, rubbing the black's nose. "I know how it is. Sometimes you just need to come see your horse."

He watched Rice out of the corner of his eye and thought he saw the ghost of a smile. Finally Rice spoke. "You heard what that woman said. She tried to pretend, but she wasn't a bit nice. And that fat old

Prudence wanted to send Miss Sarah away with the buffalo hunters."

"I feel bad for Sarah, too," River admitted.

"But I don't want to feel bad for her. I want to be mad at her."

"Maybe you've been mad long enough." The horse tossed his head, and River let the halter go. In the distance he could see the small hunting party returning. He clapped Rice on the back and pointed. "Want to go meet them?"

Rice shook his head. River watched the boy turn his full attention to the black. After a moment he said, "I have work to do. Don't wait too long before you see if Eli needs you."

A slight nod was the only indication that Rice had heard. River smiled as he left him. Sarah would be riding with Rice again. He wondered momentarily why that thought should make him happy. He tried to put her out of his mind and concentrate on the business at hand. He had to meet the hunters and see that the game was equitably divided among the families.

At the wagon, Sarah had seen the hunters come in. She tried to distract Eli by pointing them out, but he wasn't interested. "Ya ask me, yer better off. Didn't never need that mouthy little gal hanging around, anyhow," he was saying. "'Go home!' I'd say. Didn't I have to say it all the time?"

Sarah took a deep breath. Eli, she had learned, had been within earshot when Martha had come for her daughter. He had wanted her to have some time to herself, he told her, and had left her alone until he had to rescue the bread.

While Eli put the loaves into pans and set them in the sun and Sarah cleaned up from mixing, he told her the opinions of the other travelers shouldn't bother her. In the process, he pointed out several slights Sarah hadn't noticed. She knew he was trying to reassure her, but it was making her more depressed. As he talked, it occurred to her that Eli always acted as if the rest of the train disliked him.

"And old Mrs. Prude," he continued. "Ya didn't want her as a friend, nohow."

Eli's name for Mrs. Carroll startled Sarah into glancing at him. From the corner of her eye she could see Rice approaching and turned quickly back to her work. She didn't want to embarrass the boy by staring at him.

Eli caught the reaction, looked around to find the cause and grunted. "Ya shouldn't make it so easy for him to ignore ya," he grumbled, not quite under his breath.

Sarah cast him a reproving look, afraid Rice might have heard.

Rice went straight to the supply wagon and in a moment came to stand beside Sarah. She didn't look up, certain he was only after something in the wagon. Finally he set the volume of *King Arthur* on the tailboard in front of her. "Could I read to you this evening, Miss Sarah?"

Sarah laid a hand gently on the book, resisting the urge to rest it on the boy's arm instead. "Of course, Rice," she said, barely daring to look at him, afraid tears would come to her eyes. He smiled and hurried away.

"That weren't no apology," Eli grumbled loudly.

"Hush!" Sarah glared at him. Her reaction seemed to tickle him, and he chuckled and muttered as he got the fire ready for the bread.

A short time later, River brought over their camp's share of the meat. Eli set about carving off a large chunk to roast for supper. "Show Sarie how ta jerk the rest," he said.

Sarah had no idea what he meant, but she joined River obediently. He set two cutting boards on the tailboard and pulled the bone-handled knife from its sheath on his thigh.

"Wash up," Eli said. Sarah bit her lip to keep from laughing at River's expression, but they both complied.

"Cut a chunk you can handle," River said, demonstrating. "Then slice it in thin strips about an inch wide." He cut a chunk for her and handed her the knife. Sarah did as he instructed, amazed at how sharp the knife was.

Once he had seen that she knew what to do, she expected him to go on to some other job. Instead he pulled a thin knife from the top of his left boot and stayed beside her, skillfully slicing the meat. She worked more slowly, uncertain about both the task and her companion.

As he finished with one large chunk, he looked at her. "Did Rice come by?" His tone was low enough to exclude Eli.

She nodded, giving him a slight smile. He flashed his broad grin in return.

The grin confused her. He already made her nervous, standing so close; now she was afraid she would cut herself. He had gone back to work, but she could only watch her hands shake.

After a moment he spoke again. "I'm sorry about what's happened."

Sarah held the knife firmly against the cutting board. If it didn't shake, her voice wouldn't. Or so she hoped. She met his eyes. "I don't blame you," she said.

"I know. But I'm sorry just the same."

She tried to pull her eyes away from his, but he stared at her with an intensity that held her. Finally a nervous laugh allowed her to break free. "You're forgiven," she said, and went back to work.

She knew River was still looking at her. She tried to watch what she was doing and not his hands, which were suspiciously idle. When he grabbed another chunk of meat, she sighed with relief. In a moment she was cutting the last piece; they were almost done. She would be able to wash her sticky hands and ease the tension building in her shoulders.

River hollered at Eli to get the line to hang the meat on.

"Get it yerself," Eli returned.

"Go get it, old man, unless you want blood all over the insides of your wagon. I don't want to wash my hands twice."

Eli grumbled, but he went to the supply wagon, and River cast Sarah his easy grin. In a moment Eli returned with the line and moved a crate for River to stand on while he hung the string high on the side of the wagon. When he was ready, Sarah handed the strips of meat to him, and he draped them over the line.

"How long will these take to dry?" Sarah asked.

"Three or four days," River replied, laughing when she wrinkled her nose in distaste. "What's the matter? Don't you like a little fringe on your wagon?"

Sarah smiled, and River found himself staring at her again. He forced his eyes away. If he wasn't careful, he would be gaping at her and fall off the crate.

Sarah was surprised to discover she was enjoying herself. Her hands were sticky with blood, Eli was grumbling in the background, but River was teasing her like the old days. Her mind was too slow to tease back the way she used to. Or maybe it was fear that stopped her, the same fear that made her think twice before she spoke and dread being inside the wagon.

River must have read something of her thoughts on her face because he watched her intently. She forced a quick smile. "What do we do if it rains?"

River wasn't fooled into thinking that was what worried her, but he played along. "Then we yell at Eli for not letting us dry it over the fire tonight."

Eli's grumblings increased in volume. When River hung the last strip of meat, he said, "I'll help you clean up."

Sarah grabbed the bucket and soap and followed him. He didn't head straight for the river but led her at an angle toward a plum thicket on the bank. Sarah's mind was so filled with conflicting emotions she didn't think to question why he chose this particular spot. Yellowing petals on the ground gave evidence that the bushes had recently been in full bloom. Sarah wished she might have seen the blossoms when they were snowy white. It seemed a shame to step on the petals, which had once been so pure.

River led her to the bank on the far side of the thicket. He filled the bucket for her but was content to wash his own hands in the slowly flowing stream. When she handed him the soap, he caught her hand, as well. Sarah couldn't free it for fear of dropping the slippery soap. River used both hands, and she drew away, hoping he hadn't seen what so simple a contact did to her.

"I'm finished," she said, emptying the bucket into the thicket. She meant to go back without him, but he was on his feet in an instant.

"Wait," he said. "You've got some on your face."
His cool hand rubbed gently at her cheek.
"There." He smiled down at her but didn't draw
away. In a moment his lips were warming the spot his
damp fingers had cooled.

Sarah felt her knees tremble and dropped the
bucket to steady herself against his strong chest. His
lips trailed across her cheek to claim her lips. The feel
of his cool, damp hands on her back brought Sarah
to her senses. The purpose of the plum thicket suddenly became clear.

She tried to break away, but he caught her arm.
"Sarah, please. I need to talk to you."

"Talk?" She eyed him accusingly.

"I know. I'm sorry." She tried again to break free,
and he talked faster. "Sarah, meet me here tonight.
Please. Do you think you can find it in the dark?"

"No."

He released her arm and watched her hurry away.
The bucket lay on its side at his feet. He bent to retrieve it and turned to find the soap. "What gets into
me?" he muttered. "I'm letting that woman drive me
crazy. Again."

He was thinking much the same thing when the
stars came out, and he paced beside the plum thicket.
I must be crazy. She isn't coming. She had told him
she wouldn't come; there was no reason to be here
losing sleep. Yet if there was any chance she might
change her mind, he wanted to be waiting.

What was it he hoped to tell her, anyway? How much he still wanted her? No doubt she could guess. That the past didn't matter? He would be lying if he told her that.

Maybe he just needed to tell her he knew she had changed, that he wanted to start over. He took off his hat and raked his hand through his hair. Most of the changes he could see he didn't like. He had been delighted the few times her behavior reminded him of the past. In the past, he reminded himself, she had robbed his father's store.

He shoved his hat back on his head and paced. He had lied to her. He didn't want to talk. He wanted to get her alone, as far from the others as he could, and make love to her. If he told her that, it ought to earn him a good slap in the face.

It doesn't matter what I wanted to tell her. She isn't coming. Resigned, he started around the plum thicket and froze midstride. She *was* coming. He could barely see her, picking her way in the dark. He moved to meet her and led her to the far side of the little thicket.

"I was afraid you wouldn't be here," she said.

"You said you weren't coming." He still held her arm; he didn't want to let go any sooner than he had to. Her hair was loose, and the breeze blew a lock across the back of his hand.

"I reconsidered," she admitted.

River grinned and started to pull her toward him and felt her stiffen. He dropped her arm and watched her back away a step.

"Daniel," she warned.

Coax her back, he thought. "I love it when you call me that."

Sarah couldn't see his face but heard a hint of humor in his voice.

"It brings back memories," he added softly. He began to close the distance between them.

"You said you wanted to talk. I thought it might be my chance to explain."

River took a deep breath. "Sarah, you've already told me you weren't there, but I know what I saw."

"But you've never listened to me."

"Shh." He reached out and gently touched her cheek. "I don't want to hear your lies. I have other memories of your lips."

He moved toward her so slowly Sarah felt hypnotized. His lips had claimed hers in a slow, gentle kiss, and his arms had drawn her body against his before she could pull herself out of the spell. And it was a powerful spell. It made her lips go soft under his. The gentle intrusion of his tongue brought Sarah to her senses.

As soon as he felt her stiffen, he let her go. The disappointment and frustration didn't surprise him. The longing and regret did.

Sarah struggled to catch her breath. "How can you want to kiss me when you still think the worst of me?" she gasped.

River shoved his hands in his pockets. "I don't know," he whispered.

Sarah felt a moment of desperation. She couldn't make him listen, but maybe she had time to plant one idea in his head. "Do you remember Linda Neff?"

It was too dark to tell if the question surprised him. He took his time answering. "Yeah, I remember her."

Sarah bit her lip. Why was it so hard to talk about it? He said he didn't want to listen, but he was here with her; why couldn't she blurt out the truth? She even had proof! She ought to wave it under his nose!

Suddenly she knew why she didn't. She wanted him to believe her, trust her, without the proof. Foolish as it seemed, she wanted him to believe in her without having to hear her tell it. If he couldn't, he didn't love her. Not the way she loved him.

River was curious about her mention of Linda. She had been one of their group of friends, but neither of them had particularly liked her, as he recalled. It irritated him more than it should have. He was having difficulty carrying on a conversation with her while the moonlight and breeze played in her hair. How was he supposed to stand here so close to her and not touch her? Her long silence made him want to fidget.

Finally Sarah spoke. "She's dead." It wasn't what she had intended to say, but none of that mattered now. She turned and started away.

River caught her arm. He felt a surge of anger at her for being so unmoved by the setting, the moonlight, the nearness of their bodies. And anger at himself for being nearly overpowered by it. "I'm sorry to hear that," he said. "She was more than willing to offer me comfort after your betrayal."

Sarah's steps faltered, but only for a moment. She hurried toward the wagons. It had been a mistake to come. She should have followed her instincts and stayed as far away from him as possible. Now she would have to try to sleep with the memory of his kiss and the knowledge that he held her in such low regard.

He admitted to going to Linda when she was arrested, or Linda had gone to him. She shouldn't have been surprised; it explained a few things. But for him to brag about it now and to suggest he wanted her even as he called her a liar was too much to bear.

She pressed her hands to her burning cheeks. After six years, after all he had said and done, when he had moved to kiss her, she had wanted him, as well.

From the riverbank River had watched her go, reaching a hand out toward her then letting it fall helplessly at his side. Why couldn't he hold his tongue?

He paced the little area beside the plum thicket again, cursing himself. She was the one who always brought up the past. Why mention Linda Neff now? She had been easy to forget until Sarah reminded him. Sarah, he would never forget.

He took a deep breath and started back. He knew where he had gone wrong. He had lost his temper. He and Sarah would get along fine, he decided, if they just didn't talk.

Monday morning Sarah was in the wagon seat, enjoying Rice's chatter. It was barely midmorning, and she had already heard how the von Schiller girls were improving their English, their father still had a toothache, and maybe their mother liked him after all.

When they decided to walk for a while, Rice helped Sarah down and started the team moving again. "I saw you walking by Eli's wagon," he said.

Sarah nodded; she had thought of that at the time. Wanting to put Rice at ease, she said in a loud whisper, "It's a little boring riding with Eli."

Rice remained serious. "I kept wishin' you'd fall behind and have to ride with me."

"But, Rice, I thought you didn't want me around."

The boy shrugged, keeping his eyes on the team. "I did, and I didn't."

Sarah laughed. "Don't feel bad about it now. I'm just glad we can be friends again in spite of my past."

"Your past don't bother me none," he said. "I just thought you would have told me something that important."

Sarah watched the young profile for a moment. "There are lots of reasons people keep secrets. I wanted to pretend that part of my life never happened. I'll bet there are some things you don't want to talk about." At his skeptical look she added, "Or there will be. What if one of the von Schiller girls kisses you? Will you come tell me first thing?"

Rice grinned at her and turned away.

The rest of the day was spent in relaxed conversation, but River was always on Sarah's mind. She tried to nurse the resentment and deny the attraction but it wasn't possible.

In the evening, they made a camp near the Platte and traveled the next day through the same featureless prairie they had been crossing for several days. Sarah thought there might be fewer trees, and the valley seemed to have narrowed.

On Wednesday Eli pronounced the meat dry enough to take off the line, and Sarah helped him put it into sacks. The jerky didn't look good to Sarah, and she was happy to learn it was to be saved rather than eaten right away. For once there was plenty of wood, and Sarah helped Rice refill the possum bellies.

Thursday morning River roused the travelers early. It had been a starless night, and before first light they could feel the threat of rain. "The road up here can get awful muddy," Rice explained. "Worse than some other places. It's so level the water can't go nowhere."

Sarah had trouble seeing how this stretch of road could be much worse than others they had traveled, but River seemed to think so. He started them off early and pushed them until nearly dark. Even though the skies continued to be heavy and gray, there were only a few light showers. When they reached a camp that was past the worst of the lowlands, River called a halt.

In spite of Eli's protests, River rigged an awning against the side of the supply wagon, then went to check the stock and the guards with barely a word to any of them. He knew it wasn't the rain that had put him in this mood. He had been angry enough at Sarah to never want to see her again. Well, that wasn't a new feeling. But avoiding her made it worse, not better. *Damned if I don't feel guilty about the way things have gone!* he thought. What business did she have making him feel guilty?

It was raining steadily by the time the evening meal was prepared. Sarah thought the little tent seemed cozy when she and Eli brought the food and joined Rice. However, in a few minutes River, dripping rain from his hat and slicker, joined them, and the little space became close and tense.

River had avoided Sarah all week much as Rice had the week before. It had made life easier for Sarah. She had begun to believe that what she had mistaken for love was only memories. She couldn't possibly be attracted to someone so heartless. Now, with him so close, she had no idea what she felt.

If Eli noticed the tension, he chose to ignore it. He sat with his back to the wind, barely under the canvas cover. "Well, River," he said conversationally. "I hear yer name was Dan'el back in the states."

River glanced at Eli. The old man was still curious about his and Sarah's common past. He braced himself for more questions and answered calmly, "That's right."

"Had a rich daddy?"

Rice spoke up. "Sarah's family was poor, and her folks died when she was young like mine did. That right, Sarah?"

She nodded. She could sense River's foul humor and wondered why Eli didn't. Still, she was curious where Eli would take the conversation. He was after something.

"How'd a rich boy end up out here in these humble surroundin's?" He waved his spoon in a circle to indicate their little camp and winked at Sarah.

River guessed the rich daddy had been a shot in the dark. "Punishment for something, I reckon," he said, showing more interest in his dinner than Eli's conversation.

Eli chuckled. "Yer old man run ya off, didn't he?"

River glared at him over his cup for a long moment then determined that was all the information the old man was going to get. He was in no mood for this.

Rice glanced from one man to the other and looked questioningly at Sarah. She shrugged, and he kept silent.

After a moment, River added, "You're free to follow his example and run me off anytime."

Eli chuckled. "'Fraid not. Milburn made ya the boss."

"Then maybe I should fire you."

This struck Eli as particularly funny.

The rest of the meal was spent listening to the rain on the canvas and Eli's occasional chortle.

As they were finishing, a gust of wind blew a heavy shower of rain into their shelter. "Told ya this here tent weren't no use," Eli said. He gathered the dishes into the empty cooking pot as the wind increased. In less than a minute, it was threatening to tear the awning away from the wagon and poles that supported it.

Eli set the pot inside the supply wagon and hollered at Sarah to head to the lead wagon for shelter. She could hear Rice and River fighting the wind as they removed the awning before it was lost.

Inside the wagon, Sarah shook water from her skirts and, after lighting the lantern, went to the front to draw the pucker string closed. In the soft golden light, the wagon seemed warm and familiar, and she experienced less of the panic she expected to feel with both ends shut. She decided not to tie the back closed, however, unless the rain began to blow in.

She took off her muddy shoes and her outer garments, spreading them across some crates to dry. Her hair was wet, also, and she went to her trunk for a blanket and a towel. Taking a seat beside her trunk, she threw the blanket around her shoulders and found the walnut jewel box to catch the pins as she removed them from her hair.

The last pin fell into the box just as the back flap of the wagon swept open. She closed the box and dropped it into her trunk. She would have to tie the canvas closed after all. She started to rise and gasped. River was standing just inside the wagon. She sat in startled silence as he removed his hat and slicker, showering the surrounding crates with rain.

Chapter Nine

Finally, Sarah found her voice. "What are you doing here?"

"Getting out of the rain." He smiled at her as he took in the simple white undergarments not entirely hidden by the coarse dark blanket.

Sarah pulled the blanket tighter around her shoulders, conscious of his gaze. "Use the other wagon," she said, alarmed that her voice shook.

"Too crowded." He sat down and began removing his muddy boots.

"But you can't stay here."

"My gear's in here. I'm not getting my blanket wet running from here to the other wagon. Besides, like I said, it's too crowded over there." He set his boots near her shoes and stood to look around the small enclosure. "Where do you sleep?"

Sarah swallowed hard. Pointing toward the spot where he stood, she said, "There in the back."

"Curled up here?" he asked, indicating the small area uncluttered with crates. At her nod, he shook his head. "I need more room than that."

As she huddled under her blanket, he began rearranging the contents of the wagon, placing crates that were the same height along one side, turning others on their sides or stacking them. He made her get up so he could move the box she was using as a seat, and she found herself retreating to the front corner of the wagon. After a while he seemed satisfied with his arrangement and motioned her toward a barrel he had placed beside her trunk.

She sat down and retrieved her towel, trying to decide how she would dry her hair without letting the blanket slip from her shoulders. She watched him toss his knapsack and bedroll onto the bunk he had made. He unrolled his blankets, and she knew she ought to run. If he wouldn't leave, she should.

The rain, falling gently now with only an occasional gust of wind, made a soothing sound on the canvas. Perhaps that was what lulled her into accepting his presence.

River sat on his bunk and studied Sarah. She was trying to dry her chestnut hair with one hand while the other clutched the blanket to her breast. He ought to leave her alone, for his own sake as well as hers. This woman had gotten a hold on his heart once before. He had tried to convince himself he was immune to her, but he knew it wasn't true.

There was something sweet about her gentle face, something innocent. The pink tinge that rose in her cheeks made him doubt what he thought he knew about her. Those soft, moist lips weren't the lips of a liar. Those weren't the eyes of a thief.

She looked up, her cheeks darkening further under his gaze. "Shouldn't you be watching the stock?" she asked, trying to sound disdainful but failing.

River grinned. "I'd rather be watching you."

Sarah turned away. With her old hairbrush, she worked on the tangles in her hair, conscious always of River a few feet away.

River saw the blanket slip down one almost bare shoulder as Sarah slowly brushed her hair. "Do you remember . . . ?" His voice trailed off as he realized what he was remembering: Sarah, a younger Sarah, carefree and unpredictable, brushing her hair. They were in a hotel room he had rented. His father's money had made it possible for him to get away with nearly anything, and Sarah's grandmother had never seemed to care where she was. He remembered lying on the bed, gazing at her as she sat in front of the mirror and brushed her hair.

His body began to ache as his mind filled in more details: Sarah walking gracefully toward him, Sarah's hair spread across the pillow, Sarah's soft, sweet body in his arms.

He wasn't sure when he had come to his feet and moved toward her, but he found himself standing over her, reaching out to touch the soft, damp hair.

Sarah felt his nearness and turned, unable to ignore him. One look, and she couldn't turn away. His eyes seemed to capture her, the desire in them speaking to the longings in her heart. His question still hung in the air, and she whispered, "Yes. I remember."

A smile touched his lips for a moment, and he buried his hand in the mass of hair that glistened in the soft lantern light. "God help me, Sarah, I don't think I ever got over you."

Sarah came slowly to her feet, unaware of the brush as it slipped to the floor. It seemed as if River's eyes compelled her to rise up to meet them. She may have had one brief realization that what would surely happen was wrong, but it passed quickly.

Slowly she rose on the tips of her toes, her lips drawn to his by a force as old as time. River's hand slipped to the back of her neck, and he lowered his head to meet her.

His lips were gentle against hers as if he held back, afraid she would turn and run as she had before. Sarah knew she wouldn't run, couldn't run. Not this time. She had known this was inevitable when he came into the wagon. Six years slipped away, and she was his woman again.

River drew her carefully into an embrace; her warm body beneath the thin garments was tantalizing to his arms. He wanted desperately to feel her skin against his skin, to take her quickly and end this sweet torture. At the same time, he felt a need to move slowly, to make her feel what he was feeling. Sarah's lips, parting sweetly beneath his own, told him it was possible.

Sarah's hands strayed across his shoulders to wrap around his neck, pulling his mouth more firmly against hers. She marveled at the feel of the hard muscles in shoulders much wider than she remembered. And she knew she remembered exactly.

Slowly, River drew his lips away, pulling her arms from around his neck. Sarah's eyes flew open in shock. Had he kissed her only to entice a reaction from her, to prove to her and himself that she wanted him?

One look at his face, and she knew she was wrong. Passion smoldered there along with what she had once been certain was love. She wouldn't trust that guess so easily again.

"It's warm in here," he whispered, quickly shrugging out of his jacket. "Don't you think?"

His teasing voice brought back memories so clearly she felt like the old Sarah again. She shook her head, but her eyes sparkled. "I think it's cold." She reached for the blanket lying in a heap at her feet, but he took it from her hands, tossing it carelessly onto his bunk.

"I'll keep you warm," he murmured. One hand at the small of her back brought her against him while the other found the ribbons on her chemise. The look in his eyes alone could heat her flesh. Her hands moved to the front of his shirt as her eyes returned the favor.

River had the impression that this was too easy, then realized why. "No corset?" he whispered.

"It seemed an unnecessary expense." She kissed his ear since it was so close to her lips.

In moments their garments were puddled at their feet and they stood entwined again, River's need to feel her body without restrictions, satisfied only to make him more aware of stronger needs. He trailed kisses across her shoulder and groaned as she moved against him. Her soft body, more slender than it had been the last time he loved her, seemed fragile in his arms.

He hungered for her, but he could not imagine pressing her down on the hard, uneven bunk. He scooped her up into his arms, enjoying the way she wrapped her arms around his neck. He sat on his bunk with her on his lap and buried a kiss in her hair before lying back, pulling her down on top of him.

Sarah kissed the stubble on his jaw and the soft skin below his ear. Warm desire filled her and washed away all other thought. She let him guide her body above his, bringing the two of them together. Their hearts beat with the same rhythm; her movements complemented his. Though so many things had changed, this hadn't.

With an effort, River held his passion in check, slowing his pace to match hers. Her soft hair swept against his face, and he turned to inhale its sweetness. The curve of her hips beneath his hands inflamed him almost unbearably, yet he couldn't stop himself from caressing the soft, smooth skin. When he thought he would surely lose control or go mad, he felt her body tense against him and, with a muffled cry, her breath quicken. Her movements became an even more exquisite torture, and he abandoned any hope of patience.

Sarah surrendered to River, to Daniel, to the love she still felt for him. Now her love found expression in every fiber of her body, every nerve crying out to him, every muscle shuddering from the effort of loving him.

Slowly, very slowly, Sarah felt her body return to her possession. It tingled, warm and damp, as if newly reborn. Reason was trying to return, as well, but she pushed it away.

River eased her off him until she lay snuggled against his side, her head pillowed on his shoulder. He found the blanket he had earlier discarded and spread it over her. They heard the low rumble of distant thunder, and River groaned. "You were right earlier," he whispered, brushing a strand of hair away from her face.

"Hmm," she sighed, not remembering having said anything and not wanting to be reminded now.

His breath tickled her ear as he whispered softly, "I really should be watching the stock."

Sarah fought a nearly irresistible urge to giggle. She knew she was still in a sort of dreamland and reality was only a moment away, but she wanted to cling to the dream as long as possible.

"I'm sorry to leave you, sweetheart," he said, pulling his arm from under her and replacing it with his knapsack. "But I want you to promise me two things."

Sarah tried to move closer to him as he moved away. He tucked the blanket around her and rose from their bed. Her eyes were closed, and he bent to kiss her forehead before turning to find his clothes. He dressed quickly then sat beside her, listening to her even breathing. With one hand caressing her cheek, he spoke to her again. "Sarah, you have to promise me two things."

Her eyes fluttered open, and she sighed.

"First," he said, "don't hate me in the morning." He kissed the corner of her mouth as if that might entice her to agree.

Sarah's brain wasn't ready to consider what had happened between them. She smiled at the gentle kiss and closed her eyes again.

"Second," River whispered, "don't hate yourself."

The lips Sarah remembered tasting so hungrily touched her again, on her cheek this time. She barely heard him murmur, "Go to sleep," before she obeyed.

River rose quickly and donned his slicker and hat. He extinguished the lantern and felt the chill of the damp night air as he parted the flap and left the wagon. Another rumble of thunder seemed ominous to his ears.

Sarah awoke slowly. Early-morning sounds drifted in to her, but the closed flap of the wagon kept out the first light of dawn. She stretched on her hard bed, rubbing a sore shoulder, and came suddenly awake. She was stark naked! Memory of last night returned, and she sat up quickly, reaching for her clothes.

Eli could open the back flap any second! Most of the cooking supplies were stored in this wagon. With the flap closed, she couldn't tell how late it was. Oh God! What if he had looked in already? Or worse, what if River had told him not to—and why?

Sarah dressed as quickly as she could and pinned up her hair. After hastily folding the blankets, she even moved one of the crates, feeling certain the arrangement looked like a bed for lovers even with the blankets gone.

Throwing her shawl around her shoulders, Sarah took a steadying breath and stepped to the back of the wagon. She knew putting off her appearance would only make matters worse. Eli was sitting by the fire, and she approached him, prepared, she thought, for anything.

"'Morning, Sarie," he greeted her cheerfully. "Rough night, huh?"

Sarah was sure her mouth dropped open. He knew everything and wasn't going to be polite about it! She was mortified.

"What with all the ruckus, I figured you could use a little extra sleep." Eli filled a cup with coffee and handed it to Sarah, who took it automatically. "Coffee and the pot ended up in t'other wagon, anyhow."

Sarah sipped the coffee, wishing it was the steam that made her face burn. Should she offer an explanation? What possible explanation was there?

Eli was still talking. "We ain't in no hurry to move out, I reckon, on account a the mud. Good thing, too. I don't think I got a nickel's worth a sleep. Between the storm and River coming after Rice to corral the stock in the circle, and them horses millin' around, I got to sleepin' good about the time I shoulda got up. Well, I reckon it weren't much different for ya so I let ya sleep."

Sarah discovered her knees were shaking and sat down on a barrel near the fire. Had she really slept through all that? She wanted to ask where River was but didn't dare. She asked about Rice instead.

"He's off with River. I got me a hankerin' for some flapjacks." He winked at Sarah. "Got a little maple syrup hidden away."

When he went to the lead wagon to start their breakfast, Sarah tried to relax. She couldn't shake the feeling he would look into the wagon and know what had happened there.

And what of River? How would he treat her this morning? Would his behavior give them away? Would he even try to keep last night a secret?

Oh, how could I let it happen? she asked herself. *I deserve to be shunned by all the good people of this train.* The coffee tasted bitter, and she set the cup on the ground. She was no better now than she had been all those years ago. She gave in to her lowest desires even when she knew they were wrong.

She watched Eli stir the batter and knew she should offer to help. She needed to pretend nothing had happened, but she couldn't hide the awful truth from herself.

She shivered and leaned closer to the fire, wondering about River. What must he be thinking of her now? Was he laughing at how easily she had given in to him? Now that it had happened once, was he planning to take her again whenever he wanted? To her shame, the thought made her tingle with anticipation.

"'Mornin', Miss Sarah." Rice was all youthful energy as he trotted into camp. "How come breakfast ain't ready?"

"Now, ya don't got no call to be complainin'," Eli scolded, bringing his long-handled skillet to the fire. "I ain't let ya starve yet, have I?"

Rice hardly seemed to hear Eli. He sat down near Sarah. "Wasn't that something when the horses got excited last night? I thought they was gonna run off in the storm, but River got 'em settled down."

Sarah looked up to see River walking toward them. His slicker had been discarded, but his hat was still wet. The shoulders of his buckskin jacket were dark, indicating a last, unexpected shower. Sarah looked at the shoulders and remembered how the hard muscles had felt under her hands, how the strong arms had held her. She should look away before Rice and Eli read the thoughts her eyes must surely reveal. Instead, her eyes moved to River's face as if she hoped to discover what he was feeling. When his eyes met hers they seemed to hold her, and it was too late to turn away.

River watched the deep brown eyes telegraph uncertainty. She looked more beautiful than ever this morning, with her hair hastily pinned up and the campfire warming her cheeks. As he watched, the color in her cheeks deepened, bringing a slow smile to his lips.

In the past Sarah would have come to meet him and wouldn't have cared who was watching. He knew better than to expect that now. Now she was shy.

Or pretended to be. The thought caught River by surprise, and he turned away to greet Rice and Eli. Did part of him still suspect her of putting on an act?

Would he ever be sure of her again? And why did it suddenly seem desperately important?

Sarah was glad to see River's attention turn from her. She got up to set out the plates and cups, worrying Eli would wonder why she had waited so long. He was kneeling at the fire, flipping the first flapjack.

"That one's mine," Rice said, taking a plate from Sarah and holding it toward Eli.

"Now, how ya figure that?"

Rice grinned. "I got my plate ready first."

Eli grumbled, and River laughed.

Sarah found herself watching River again. Dark circles around his eyes and one deep crease between his brows suggested he had gotten very little sleep, if any at all.

In a minute, Rice took his flapjack to the tailboard of the wagon to cover it with butter and syrup. Eli poured more batter into his hot skillet and asked, "We gonna be pullin' out later or sit around here all day?"

"Oh, we'll pull out," River answered, smiling up at Sarah as she handed him a cup of coffee. "I'm just not in any hurry."

Sarah turned away, praying Eli hadn't seen the look in his eyes. Or hers.

"It'll be slow goin' in this mud."

"I know." River stretched tired muscles to their limit and relaxed with a sigh. It was a wonder he didn't feel worse, after a night of hard work in a cold rain. He glanced at Sarah, who knelt beside Eli with another plate, and knew the reason he didn't.

She held the hot flapjack toward him, trying not to meet his eyes. He pointed toward the tailboard. "Fix it up for me, would you?"

Sarah took the plate to the wagon, pausing with the knife over the butter crock. She had to swallow hard before she could speak. "How much butter and syrup do you like?"

River smiled at her, shrugging. "I'm easy to please."

Sarah felt her face warming again.

River had to admit he was enjoying Sarah's discomfort. It proved she wasn't taking last night lightly. Whatever she was thinking, he had to talk to her. It wasn't going to be easy getting her alone again. He accepted the plate she handed to him and flashed her another bright smile. He would find a way.

Later that day, as River rode ahead of the train, he thought more about Sarah than the area he was supposed to be scouting. The rain had come hard the night before, packing the ground rather than leaving it muddy the way a long, slow rain would have. There were places near the river, however, that had washed, and he was trying to find the best route around them. His sharp eyes could save a broken axle, but all he wanted to think about was Sarah.

He had not really intended to seduce her when he had gone into the wagon last night. He had meant to get his blanket and go. One look at her sitting in her petticoats with the lantern light dancing in her hair and he had been lost. She had simply brought back too many memories.

More and more when he was with Sarah, the good memories would come back with startling clarity. At first, the anger and the pain of betrayal had been all he could recall when he saw or thought of Sarah Tanton. Now, the turn of her head or the sound of her voice would bring back vivid images of dances or quiet walks or making love with Sarah Tanton.

Six years ago he had managed to convince himself that he had never really loved her. How could he have loved someone so false? Everything his parents had warned him about her had turned out to be true, and he decided he must have known it all along.

But he had been lying to himself. As more of the good times were reenacted in his mind, he was forced to admit that he had loved her. He wasn't sure if he still did, or if he was simply responding to the memories. The only way to find out was to get better acquainted with Sarah Tanton. He grinned to himself. Last night had been a very pleasant step in the right direction.

A movement at the edge of his vision made him pull the pinto to a sudden stop and curse himself for his inattention. Lapses like that out here could get a man killed. Ahead, nearly on the riverbank, was a wrecked wagon and two, no, three men. He sat and studied them. He counted three oxen and one horse.

The men were wandering aimlessly around the wagon. *Or hopelessly,* he thought. Part of the wagon was bogged down in the mud, but even at this distance he could tell there was more wrong than that. He guessed something had broken while they were trying to pull it out.

"Easy pickin's for the Indians when they find 'em," he mused. The pinto pricked its ears toward the voice. River watched the camp for a moment more, then kneed the horse. "Let's go introduce ourselves," he said.

He studied the three travelers as he rode toward them. One was shorter than the others with a heavy build. He moved around the camp, stopping at a corner of the wagon for a moment, in front of first one man and then the other, gesturing and yelling. River was close enough to hear the man's voice before anyone in the camp saw him coming.

One of the men pointed, and the short one hurried to the back of the wagon, sinking in mud to his boot tops. He cursed loud enough for River to hear as he pulled a pistol from the wagon.

"Ho, the camp!" River yelled.

The short man took up a combative stance in front of his companions and watched River ride in. River tried not to be put off by his behavior. The man was prepared to defend his property against a stranger, and River shouldn't fault him for that. Still, something about the man's hard face kept River on guard.

"Looks like you've had some trouble," he said, dismounting a few yards away. He dropped the pinto's reins on the ground and stepped forward.

"What's it to you?" came the response.

"Nothing, I reckon. I just thought you might be needing some help."

One of the others spoke. "We're waitin' for another train. Ours went off and left us."

"Shut up, Herman," snapped the one with the pistol. "Don't need to tell everyone our business."

"There's a train a couple hours behind me," River offered. "You can pack what you can on the backs of your oxen and travel along with it."

"They got an extra wagon?"

River studied the man for a moment. He was beginning to wish he had ridden on past. "No," he answered. "You might get one at Fort Laramie, though."

"How far's that?"

"About a hundred miles. We'll be there in a couple of weeks."

"Hell," the man muttered. He turned to his companions, and Herman took an involuntary step backward. "That's too damn far to be comin' back for things."

"Whatever you leave behind won't likely be here tomorrow," River said.

The man swore again. He paced around the camp, apparently undecided, and River studied his companions. One seemed to be only a little older than

Rice and watched the stocky man warily. The other, the one called Herman, caught River watching him and grinned, nodding in greeting.

Finally the leader came back to face River. "I guess we ain't got much choice."

"Doesn't look like it. My name's River," he said, offering his hand.

"The hell, you say! That damned old Eli talked about a River. The train comin' ain't Milburn's train, is it?"

"The same," River answered, trying to remember everything Eli had told him about the folks who had pulled out and their leader in particular.

The man swore again, then laughed. "The old coot musta kicked off right away if the train's that close behind. Bull Gaines's my name. That there's Herman Kirby, and that's my nephew Nathan. I can't believe we're about to join that same damn train."

River hesitated a second before taking the hand. He added the reference to Milburn to everything else he disliked about the man. "We better start packing," he said.

Two hours later, when the train was visible in the distance, Bull and the others were nearly ready. They had argued some over what would be left behind, but Bull had won each time.

"It's going to be inconvenient as all hell unloading all these things every night," Bull said. "Maybe someone'll let us put some of it in their wagon."

"Might," River said, noncommittally. "In exchange for your oxen helping to pull the load."

"I ain't wearin' out my stock pullin' somebody else's wagon!" Bull responded, puffing out his chest like a rooster ready to fight.

"Suit yourself," River said mildly. He whistled once, and the pinto trotted toward him. "I'll ride back to the train and let Eli know you're coming. You can fall in as the train goes by."

River gathered up the reins and swung into the saddle. In a moment he was galloping toward the train. It felt good to put some distance between himself and the Gaines party. He wished he had told Bull to sit tight and wait for an empty wagon to come along.

He pulled up next to the lead wagon and wheeled the pinto around to walk beside it. "Remember a hard case named Bull Gaines?" he asked.

Eli swore under his breath, started to speak and swore again.

"That's what I thought," River said.

"Is that who's waitin' yonder?"

River nodded. "Their wagon broke down, and the rest of the train went off and left them."

Eli snorted. "No more 'an what he woulda done. I suppose ya told 'em to come right on back in with us."

River looked in the direction of the broken wagon. "Didn't have much choice." Eli grumbled his understanding, and River reined the pinto around and let the wagon pass.

Sarah was on the next wagon beside Rice. He watched it come toward him and returned the boy's hail. He tried to catch Sarah's eye, but she ignored him. With a chuckle he wheeled his mount again, ready to walk it alongside the supply wagon. He would suggest Rice ride the horse, so he could give Sarah another lesson on handling the team.

The wagon had nearly caught up with him when he heard his name called. He groaned. Ernest Ortman was hurrying toward him, waving his arms as he tried to get his attention.

River took one more look at Sarah and caught her watching him. She turned away, but not before he could flash her his biggest grin. He urged the pinto toward Ortman with considerably more good humor than he would have imagined possible.

Ernest was winded when he reached him, so River dismounted, intending to walk beside him. "What's the problem?" River asked, trying to sound cheerful.

"How long...we gonna...keep goin'...in this mud?" Ernest demanded, bracing his hands on his knees as he bent over trying to catch his breath.

River pretended to think it over. "Oh, I'd say till about dark."

"Well, it's such slow goin'... it ain't hardly worth it, is it? I mean, shouldn't we just... wait while it dries up?"

"Are you stuck again, Ortman?"

Ernest had finally caught his breath and shook his head indignantly. "No, I ain't stuck again, but Prudence is awful upset at having to walk. Telling her she had to get out to lighten the load was downright mean of you. I let her back up in the wagon a while ago, but now she's saying her shoes are ruined!"

Ernest's voice had risen with each word. River set his hat back farther on his head, and Ernest heard the dry clatter of the snake's rattle. His voice turned humble. "I was just thinking maybe we could stop till the ground dries up a little."

River tried not to lose his temper. "How long do you suppose that would be, Ortman?"

"Well, you should know that better'n me."

River looked away from Ernest as he tried to come up with an appropriate response, one that wouldn't get him into trouble. His eyes fell on the wagon that was about to catch up with them. Prudence Carroll was in the seat, her large hands handling the reins as if she were a boxer waiting for her opponent. She glared defiantly at River.

He glared back. "If I stopped this train every time your sister is unhappy," he said slowly, "it'd take longer than you'll live to get to California." He turned and swung into the saddle, congratulating himself for biting back the curse he had wanted to include.

As River cantered away, Prudence pulled the team to a stop beside her brother. Ernest stared after River for a moment, his knees shaking, then he climbed into the wagon. He took the reins from her and called to the team in a weak voice.

Prudence looked at him and looked at the oxen standing placidly where she had stopped them. With an exasperated groan she took the reins back and bellowed at the team. As they started forward she elbowed her brother. "What is the matter with you? Did you tell him we wanted to stop?"

Ernest stared at the spot ahead that was River and the pinto. "I told him, Prudence," he said. "But I think he threatened me."

Chapter Ten

River sat on the pinto's back, watching the herd of oxen graze. It had been two days, and he hadn't found a way to get Sarah alone. It wasn't that she avoided him, it was just that his duties on the train had kept him busy. Between wagons bogged down and complaints from short-tempered travelers, it would have been a rough two days even without the addition of the Gaines party.

He glanced toward the sunset and judged that the stock had been grazing for about an hour. He waved at Williams and Hess, who were on foot near the river, and the three of them began herding the stock toward the wagons. After nearly losing the horses in the storm, he had realized how undermanned the train was and had decided to corral the stock inside the circle at night. It saved on guards and was a good precaution under any circumstances.

Ernest Ortman had complained, as River had expected. River had explained that the area was roamed by the unpredictable Sioux, and a train this small had to be careful. The animals, Ernest had replied, rubbed against his wagon at night, frightening poor Prudence. River had suggested that if their stock was lost his sister would be more than frightened, but he wondered now if it had come out the way he had intended. Ernest had taken offense. In fact, upon reflection, Ernest had seemed unusually nervous approaching him with his complaint in the first place and extremely upset when he left.

River shrugged it off. Ernest wasn't the only one who had been unhappy with the situation. Rice had been looking forward to a dance and was sure he couldn't talk the folks into having one outside the circle. However, another train had overtaken them late in the afternoon and camped nearby. Even before the oxen were unhitched, plans were being made to pool their musicians and have a dance in the area between the two trains. As he dismounted to help Williams and Hess tie ropes between the two wagons to close the corral, River could see Rice heading for the other train, holding hands with both von Schiller girls.

At the fire, Eli and Sarah had supper ready but he told them to go ahead, wanting to shave before he ate. He could see Sarah's reflection in the mirror and caught her glance in his direction more than once. It amused him but he didn't think she would like knowing it. Years ago they had been able to tease each other about everything. She would have teased him for going a week or more between shaves. He would have teased her about watching.

As he finished, Eli was trying to urge Sarah to eat more of his rabbit stew. "I've known mice to eat more'n ya do."

River wiped the last of the soap from his face. "Knew these mice well, did you?" He gave Sarah a wink when she turned in his direction.

"Well, I've had worse company, and that's a fact. But it weren't mice I was talkin' about, it was Sarie here. Don't you think she needs more meat on her bones?"

River let his eyes rove slowly over her, grinning when her face began to color. "I don't know, Eli. I'll have to study on it some."

Sarah came quickly to her feet and busied herself gathering a cup and bowl for River. She dipped up his stew and tried to hand it to him without looking at him. Eli's chuckle told her he was enjoying her embarrassment. No doubt River was, too. He took the bowl she offered with a murmured thanks and sat down, but she had a feeling he still watched her.

"Sounds like they got themselves quite an orkeestra," Eli commented as the first discordant strains could be heard. "What is that awful squawk? Lordy! If any Sioux are listenin' they'll think we're on the warpath fer sure."

River shrugged. "Maybe somebody's singing."

Eli grunted. "Bein' tortured by those selfsame Indians, more likely."

"Could it be bagpipes?" Sarah offered.

The preliminary noise died for a moment, before beginning again, this time with all the instruments in full swing. Eli listened for a moment, shaking his head. "This I gotta see."

As he disappeared around the curve of the wagon circle, River set his bowl on the ground. "Let's dance," he said, coming to his feet.

"I told you last week, they don't want me there."

"More than half of those folks don't know anything about you. Let old Prudence stick her nose in the air if she wants to. Come dance. With me. Please."

She shook her head. River was already standing over her, pulling her to her feet. "Daniel, no."

River grinned down at her. "Then dance with me here." He led her a little farther from the fire and pulled her into his arms. Her feeble attempts to draw away were met with the barest tightening of his arm around her. "This is about as close to that music as I want to get, anyway," he said, swinging her around.

She laughed, raising her head to look up into his face, and quickly turned her attention to the fringe on his jacket. This dance, as he called it, could turn into an embrace if she didn't keep her head.

"Do you remember what you promised me?" he asked.

"Promised?"

"Two nights ago."

His voice was just above a whisper. She could feel his breath stirring the hair at her temple and knew he had leaned closer. This was crazy. She should be running, not following as he led her around in slow, seductive circles. She barely managed to say, "I don't remember promising anything."

"That's what I was afraid of." He stopped dancing and, with his hands on her shoulders, held her away from him, compelling her face to turn up to his. "I asked you to promise not to hate me."

She swallowed, remembering vaguely. "I don't hate you."

He smiled gently. "And I asked you to promise not to hate yourself."

Sarah struggled to escape, but his hands were too strong. "Don't run away from me," he pleaded. "I don't want you thinking what happened between us was wicked."

"Of course *you* don't," she protested, angry at him for trying to manipulate her and herself for being so susceptible.

"Sarah." His voice was coaxing. "You're too hard on yourself nowadays. You used to be—"

Her temper flared. "Don't tell me what I used to be. I used to be in prison, and you were the first to say I belonged there."

River drew away, but his grip on her shoulders didn't loosen. He stared into the angry face, reading hurt and shame, wishing he could take it away. Finally, he whispered, "Maybe I was wrong."

Sarah's face registered shock at his words. After a moment, her eyes narrowed, and River knew she wasn't sure she had heard the truth. Anything more he wanted to say would have to wait for another time.

"Dance with me, Sarah," he murmured. He wanted to coax her back into his arms, but she still eyed him suspiciously. "That's all I want from you tonight." He gave her a little shake, breaking the rigidity in her body. "I just want you to dance with me."

His voice was seductive, and she knew she shouldn't listen. But she did so love to dance. In spite of everything, she wanted very much to be in his arms. He sensed when her resolve weakened and pulled her close again.

The music had changed to a slow, mournful tune, or at least that's how the lovers heard it. Their bodies swayed against each other, more in time with the crickets and bullfrogs than with the band, which seemed to drift farther and farther away.

Near the wagon, just outside the light of the fire, Eli watched and congratulated himself.

Sarah let the night breeze play gently across her face. She had barely slept. Instead, she had sat at the back of the wagon and stared into the darkness, trying to sort out her feelings for River. An evening of dancing in his arms had been at least as confusing as the night of love a few days before.

She reminded herself he hadn't stood by her six years ago, and she would be a fool to put too much trust in him now. When the train reached its destination, he would abandon her again. She had no place in his plans, whatever they were.

Well, her plans didn't have to include him, either. She would earn her living sewing and mending for people, taking in laundry. She might even go to one of the mining towns, where she had heard a woman could earn good money washing miners' clothes if she could stand the primitive conditions. She wouldn't need River.

It had all made sense when she left Albany. Now it seemed like a very lonely life. In her heart, she knew she had never stopped loving Daniel, and though he had changed some, she couldn't help but love him now as River.

She had shied away from her feelings the way she shied from everything else. She didn't want to hide any longer. Last night, when they had danced in the firelight, she had realized how much she wanted to be near him, even if it would last only a few months.

She was grateful when the sky began to turn gray and she could give up all pretense of trying to sleep. She had decided last evening what she would do and had spent the night trying to convince herself it was right. Whatever River was willing to offer, and for however long, she would accept. It could be the last time in her life she would love anyone.

As she came to her feet and folded her blanket, she couldn't help thinking of her decision as a fall into sin. It brought a rueful smile to her lips. In truth, she had fallen long ago; she wouldn't blame herself now for trying to enjoy what life was left for her. Only in theory could she think of her time with River as wrong; when she was in his arms it seemed more right than anything else in the world.

It was still dark inside the wagon, and she found her trunk by feel, trading the blanket for the better of her two dresses. She slipped into what she had begun to think of as her Sunday dress and wondered what Reverend Fleenor would think of the description. It was her Sunday dress because she wore it on Sundays while she washed the other one.

She moved to the back and put on her shoes. She didn't need any light to know how worn they were, and she didn't have a second pair. There was little chance these would hold together all the way to California. With a sigh, she wondered what the price of shoes would be at Fort Laramie, if there were any available, and wished she had thought to buy extra before she left the states.

Sarah knew the moment Eli was awake; he always muttered under his breath as he rolled from his blankets. She stepped out of the wagon, and when she saw which direction he went, she went the opposite. Since trees had become scarce on their journey, Sarah had seen other women go out in small groups, standing in a circle of spread skirts to provide privacy for one another. She hadn't asked to join them. Instead, she had sought the cover of darkness each morning and evening to relieve herself. Since she and Eli were normally the first ones up, she simply headed away from him.

The first ones up except for River, she thought as she walked away from the train. Sometimes he slept near the banked fire until Eli woke him with a booted toe. Other times he would come into camp carrying his bedroll, making her curious where he had slept.

When she was far enough away from the wagon she knew no one could see her, she stopped and listened a moment. This procedure always made her nervous; she imagined the complete humiliation of being discovered. As soon as possible, she made her way back to the wagon.

Eli was there to meet her. "We oughta tell the reverend to start prayin' for bushes," he said in a low tone.

Sarah hoped the darkness covered the color rising to her cheeks. She found it mortifying when Eli spoke so openly about such things. He had even provided her with an empty lard can to use as a chamber pot inside the wagon if all other possibilities failed. She was embarrassed carrying it away to empty it, but appreciated his surprising thoughtfulness.

She made no reply to his remark but added buffalo chips to the fire. The fuel caught and a small circle around her was bathed in pale light.

At the edge of that circle River raised himself on one elbow. He spoke softly, his eyes on the woman by the fire. "What are you two doing up so early? It's Sunday."

Sarah's eyes met his and held. He could hear Eli at the back of the lead wagon. "Well, we got work to do, even if ya don't. There's bakin' and washin' and..."

River found Sarah's shy smile completely captivating. The fire warmed her cheeks and made the fine hairs that escaped the tight knot rise with its heat.

"If that t'other train's agonna pull out or..."

River didn't listen to Eli's tirade until Sarah suddenly glanced in the old man's direction. He was annoyed at Eli for distracting her even before he realized what had caught her attention. Eli had mentioned Bull Gaines.

He managed to recall what he had only half heard. Eli had suggested that Bull Gaines could leave with the other train. Why had Sarah reacted the way she had? His eyes narrowed as he watched her. She didn't look at him again but rose, moving to the tailboard of the lead wagon to busy herself with breakfast preparations.

River shoved his hat on his head and came to a sitting position just as Rice crawled out from under the wagon, clutching his boots. "Did Eli say Gaines was leavin' with that train?" the boy asked.

"I was hopin' it, not sayin' it," the old man corrected. "Weren't nobody rightly listenin' to me."

River grinned at Rice, who was trying to step into his boots without falling down. He pulled his own boots on and came to his feet. "Well, you can't blame us, Eli," he said. "Your prattle gets to be like a cricket's chirp, so constant we don't hear it anymore. Till it gets damn annoying."

Eli grunted.

Sarah bit her lip, afraid she would make his temper worse if she laughed. She looked at Rice, expecting him to be in the same predicament, and was surprised to find him watching her seriously.

"Miss Sarah, Gaines was askin' after you last night," Rice said, coming closer.

Sarah shuddered, remembering Gaines's crude comments and his rough fingers on her cheek. She turned back to the tailboard to set out the dishes, hearing them clatter in her shaking hands.

Eli had sliced bacon and spread the pieces in his long-handled skillet. He carried it to the fire, glaring at Rice. "He can ask all he wants as long as he stays away from my wagons."

River looked from Eli's scowling face to Sarah's rigid back and wondered what he had missed besides the division of the train. He was annoyed with Gaines for whatever had caused this reaction but annoyed at Rice and Eli, as well. This wasn't the first time his friends' conversation had included Sarah and left him out.

The boy continued. "He said he was watchin' for you, and then he danced with Gretchen."

"Gretchen?" Eli and River spoke at once.

"Von Schiller," Sarah informed them.

River and Eli exchanged a look, but Rice spoke to Sarah. "I didn't want him to dance with her, but she said not to try to fight him. I didn't know what to do. He didn't dance with her very long, and afterward she told me he couldn't understand what she said so she pretended not to understand him, either."

Sarah felt for the boy, wanting to protect a young lady but powerless against a man the size of Gaines. She walked to him and laid a hand on his arm. "You both did the right thing. I don't think he'll bother her again."

Rice's eyes were downcast. "He called her a dumb immigrant."

Sarah suppressed a smile. "That's probably a good sign, Rice." He looked into her eyes, saw the smile there and returned it with a slight nod.

River watched the exchange with surprise and growing anger. Rice was his friend, but he took his problems to Sarah! When had she learned to comfort someone? She and Rice had obviously become very close friends. And when would one of them tell him what there was between Sarah and Bull Gaines? Feeling completely excluded, he took two water buckets from the side of the wagon and left the camp without a word.

Rice followed River with two more buckets, and Sarah watched them go, wondering what River was thinking. She couldn't understand how he could change from frankly appraising her across the fire to coolly ignoring her.

"Ya got yer man jealous," Eli said, and snickered.

Sarah looked at the grinning, leathery face and answered as calmly as she could, "I don't have a man, let alone a jealous one."

"Shows what ya don't know." He didn't seem to care that she had turned her back and was busily doing nothing at the tailboard. "Ya done it twice. First by mentioning Gaines, then by smilin' away at young Rice there."

Sarah whirled around. "I didn't mention Gaines, you did!"

Eli turned to study her, and she had a feeling he was reading more on her face than she wanted him to. She was relieved when he turned back to the skillet and stirred the bacon around with a long wooden spoon. After a moment he chuckled.

"Oh, shut up," she muttered, and he chuckled harder.

"If we're in such a big hurry, why don't we go with *them?*" Herman pointed at the neighboring circle, where the men were hitching teams and the women were packing away equipment.

Bull glared at the man until he looked away. "I'll decide what's best," he said. He squatted by the fire and poured himself another cup of coffee. "This train'll do fine." Herman sat near the fire, nodding in agreement. Nathan was washing the dishes from their breakfast.

When Bull was sure he had their undivided attention he went on. "See, boys, I had one regret when we left their company a ways back. Leavin' behind that little Tanton gal. You know who I mean?" At their nods, he sat down on the one camp stool he had found room to pack and stretched his legs in front of him. "Yes, that little gal could make travel right pleasant, don't you think?"

"I like those German girls, myself," said Nathan.

"Dumb as mud." Bull sneered at Nathan, who shrugged and resumed his work. "But that Sarah, I think I'll pay a call on her this afternoon." He grinned at Herman's nod of approval. "Say, Nothin', ain't that boy at Eli's camp about your age?"

Nathan eyed his uncle a moment before answering. "Yes, sir."

"Well, maybe you two could think up somethin' to do for a while. Go look for snakes or somethin'." He laughed at the boy's scowl. "And Herman here's been wantin' to talk to that old man, Eli. Ain't ya, Herman?" He laughed even harder at Herman's confused nod.

"Where did Eli go?"

Rice joined Sarah at the back of the lead wagon.

He and River had made the rounds to see that all the travelers had checked their wagons and made the necessary repairs. River had sent him back to see if Eli needed any help.

Sarah was rolling out a crust to go with the dried apples Eli had inexplicably decided should be baked into a pie. She winked at Rice when he stole a piece of the soaking fruit. "He went off with that simple fellow who travels with Gaines. He said something about his oxen, I don't know. He wasn't making much sense, but he seemed worried so Eli went to check."

Rice reached for another apple slice, but Sarah caught his hand. "Save some for the rest of us," she teased.

"Aw, you sound just like Eli."

Sarah gave him a pained look. She started to respond but saw Rice's attention had turned elsewhere. A young man was standing near their fire.

"Hi," he said hesitantly.

Sarah took in the dirty clothes and shaggy hair. She searched her mind for the boy's name, but all she remembered was his uncle. "Aren't you the Gaines boy?"

"Yes, ma'am. Nathan's my name."

Sarah knew she was letting her dislike of Bull influence her reaction to him. She watched his gaze go from her to his toes for a moment before settling on Rice. "You wanna go do somethin'?"

Rice eyed him suspiciously. "Like what?"

Nathan shoved his hands in his pockets and shrugged. Sarah could see the uncertainty and shyness in his eyes and a touch of defiance, as well.

He glanced over his shoulder before he asked, "You got a horse? Maybe I could borrow Uncle's, and we could ride up to those hills."

Rice shook his head. "It's not a good idea to go riding away from the train."

Nathan shrugged again. Sarah could see he was trying to pretend he didn't care if Rice sent him away. His feet, however, seemed rooted to the spot.

Sarah looked from one young man to the other. "Maybe the von Schiller girls could help you think of something."

She had expected to see Rice's face brighten, but he remained serious. "Which one do you like?" he asked. It sounded like a dare.

Nathan laughed. "I don't even know 'em apart."

Sarah felt Rice relax. "I'll introduce you," he said.

As the two boys walked away, Sarah saw Nathan turn to glance at her. There was something strange about the boy, something that made him seem older than he looked. She couldn't put her finger on it. She shrugged, mimicking the boy, and returned to her piecrust, which had gotten dry and crumbly while she had been distracted.

"Well now, if you ain't a sight for sore eyes."

Sarah almost dropped the crust she had been trying to turn into the pie plate. She spun around to face the man who had sneaked up behind her. With sudden certainty, she knew Nathan had been sent to lure Rice away.

Bull was leering at her. "And cooks, too! Now ain't that fine? What you makin' there, honey?"

Sarah wanted to demand that he leave, but she was too terrified to speak. She had been uncomfortable around him before, but this time they were alone.

"Aren't you glad to see me?" He took a step closer.

Sarah told herself he wouldn't dare touch her, but the look on his face made her uncertain. She had laid out a knife to trim the crust, and she glanced toward it involuntarily.

She saw Bull's eyes dart to it, as well. His smile was repulsive. "You don't need to worry, honey. I'm not going to hurt you. I just thought we could get to know each other."

Sarah watched him, afraid to look away. She knew she was acting like a fool; he hadn't said or done anything threatening. She tried to force herself to relax.

"You're shore quiet." He eased toward her again, and she drew away. "I like the quiet ones."

"So do I." Sarah jumped and looked past Bull as he spun around to confront the new arrival. The glare on River's face was more threatening than Bull's had been.

River watched Gaines look him over and knew he was being measured for a fight. He did some measuring of his own. Bull Gaines was a bully. Though he was shorter than River, he was probably stronger. However, just glaring at him was enough to make him back down. River was sure Gaines would want to pick the time and place that would work best to his advantage. He wouldn't want to depend on a fair fight.

"I was just havin' a talk with the lady. Didn't know you'd already staked a claim."

"Now you know," River said with a thin smile.

"No hard feelin's, then?"

River did not respond.

Bull glanced back at Sarah once, tipping his hat. "Ma'am," he said, and walked away.

He had disappeared around a wagon before River turned his attention back to Sarah. She was trembling. All he had to do was open his arms, and she ran into them.

Sarah pressed her forehead against the soft leather of River's jacket and closed her eyes. "I don't like that man," she murmured.

"I'm glad." River wrapped his arms more tightly around her.

Sarah was afraid she would start to cry and knew she was overreacting. She thought she ought to explain. "He scares me," she whispered.

River pressed a kiss against the top of her head. "I know."

Sarah felt herself beginning to relax within the warm embrace. She knew it was time to pull away, but she wanted to linger. She spoke again, prolonging the rare feeling of finding comfort in his arms. "I'm sorry he came back to our train."

"Right this minute, I'm kinda glad."

"What?" Sarah lifted her head, but River's arms kept her from even trying to pull away.

He smiled down at her. "I couldn't have planned this better myself." He lowered his head to claim a slow and gentle kiss.

Sarah was sure River's arms were all that kept her from dissolving into a puddle at his feet. Something in the pit of her stomach seemed to flutter to life as he molded her body more snugly against his. His lips moved over hers, enticing them open, and she tried to lift herself upward to meet the kiss.

A small sound behind her startled her. She and River were locked in a very intimate embrace in broad daylight where anyone could see them! She tried to pull free of River's arms, but he released her reluctantly, keeping one arm around her waist.

Eli was working diligently with the neglected pie-crust. River and Sarah watched him ignore them. Sarah felt she should explain herself, but her head was whirling in crazy circles, and she had no idea what she should say. After a moment, the old man started to whistle.

"Could you keep that down?" River said. "We're busy here."

Eli laughed without looking up from his work.

River started to draw Sarah back into his arms. "Daniel!" she scolded in surprise. She knew her face was burning, and she didn't dare look either Eli or River in the eye.

River chuckled softly and whispered, "Later," next to her ear. With a soft kiss on her temple, he walked away.

Sarah watched him go with a mixture of longing and embarrassment, and a remnant of the earlier fear. She gave herself a moment before she took a step toward Eli. "Bull Gaines used his friend and nephew to get me alone."

Eli glanced at Sarah. "Well, that Herman fella's silly yammerin' is finally makin' some sense. Gaines didn't count on River, though, did he?" Sarah blushed, and Eli laughed, then he went on. "Rice's off with the nephew, then?"

Sarah nodded. "They went to the von Schiller wagon."

"Rice'll be all right." Eli peered at Sarah. "You all right?" At her nod he went back to his work. "Wish I could say the same for this pie."

Chapter Eleven

Sarah stood beside the left rear ox as she had seen Rice do and tried not to worry. She didn't like being responsible for the team even when they were standing still with the wagon brake set. Rice had assured her all she had to do was stand back and watch.

In reality, it wasn't the wagon that had her worried or even the tall cattle beside her. It was River. He was wading across the South Platte with an armload of willow branches.

Earlier, River had directed Rice to pull his wagon out of line, explaining it would be the last to cross. Rice had left her in charge of it and had gone to help River cut branches from the willow trees near the river. Sarah wondered idly how many travelers would do the same before all the willows finally died.

Now, River was sticking the branches into the sandy bottom to mark the crossing. Rice had told her the river wasn't more than two feet deep even if it was nearly a half mile across. Rice and Eli were collecting chains and ropes to fasten the wagons together, and Sarah stood out of the way and watched River.

She expected him to disappear at any moment, sucked into the quicksand Rice had talked about. She knew both men would have laughed at her fears. The moving sand on the bottom of the river didn't really work that way. Rice had explained that a drop from a firm surface to a soft one would jar the wagon and perhaps break an axle or wheel or even tip a wagon on its side. River's willow flags were meant to help them avoid the worst of these places.

The wagons would be fastened together to keep them moving. It wasn't safe to stop on the unstable sand. The horses would be ridden across ahead of the wagons to pack the bottom. All the stock were to be watered so they wouldn't be tempted to stop and drink halfway across.

"Mules are the worst," Rice had said. "They won't even try to get themselves out of quicksand. They'll just sink right in till they drown."

Sarah had laughed at the time, having been reminded of Eli's scorn for mules, but now the picture made her worry more about River. Every time she saw him pause for a moment, she imagined he was sinking into the sand.

"Ya gonna keep him from drownin' by starin' at him?"

Eli's voice made Sarah jump. She had to blink twice before her eyes could focus on him, having stared too long at the sun-reflecting water. Eli continued, "He'll be fine without ya levitatin' him up till he walks on the water." He fluttered his hands toward the water like a conjurer and chuckled even though she didn't. "I come to get the team to take 'em to water."

Eli began unhitching the oxen, and Sarah tried to help him while she continued to watch River. The water came barely up to his knees, and he was approaching the middle of the river. "Rice told me the women will walk across instead of ride in the wagons," she said.

"I reckon. It helps pack the sand for the wagon wheels." Eli came out from between the oxen and grinned. "Especially someone like Prudence."

The joke helped Sarah keep her voice steady in spite of her growing fears. "Is that what River wants me to do?"

Eli was quiet, and Sarah wasn't sure he was going to answer. Finally he asked, "You scared of water, too?"

Sarah had to smile. "No. I guess that's one thing I'm not scared of. I was just thinking about..."

Her voice trailed off, and Eli grunted. "About them other women and how they like to treat ya? Well, I don't think that's what River's got in mind, anyhow."

Sarah glanced at him curiously then paled. "I'm not ready to drive the team across something like this!"

Eli let out a hearty laugh. "Not likely."

Sarah sighed with relief and laughed, too. Eli led the team away from the wagon, chuckling occasionally as he went. As Sarah listened to him, her relief turned into annoyance. She wasn't that bad with the team, was she? He still hadn't told her what River did have in mind. Probably just to ride in the wagon beside Rice.

Rice had talked with a certain amount of excitement about how a wagon would tip over once in a while, spoiling possessions and sometimes causing a family to lose everything. He hadn't mentioned drownings. "I'll probably be the first," she mumbled, and scolded herself. She would talk herself into being afraid of water if she wasn't careful.

After a few minutes, Rice brought the team of oxen and rehitched them. He helped Sarah onto the seat and moved the wagon into line with the rest.

When he jumped down to chain the wagon to the one ahead, Sarah realized the wagons blocked her view and she couldn't watch River anymore. She started to climb down from the wagon, needing to know he was all right.

"River says you're supposed to wait here," Rice said.

"I won't go far," she assured him. She walked away from the train until she could see River again. He was nearly at the opposite shore, and it was a minute before she realized he was now moving toward their side of the river.

Rice was jogging toward the bank. She saw him mount River's pinto and ride into the shallow water. Sarah divided her attention between Rice, as the pinto splashed along the trail of willow branches, and River, as he made his way more slowly toward him. She sighed with relief when they met and River swung himself up behind Rice, only to gasp audibly a moment later when the pinto stumbled.

But the pinto recovered quickly and, in a short time, was plunging up the muddy bank onto dry land. They stopped for a moment at the group assembled on the shore. She could imagine River giving them last-minute instructions and knew it was time for her to get back onto the wagon seat. It was hard to pull herself away, however. She had been so worried about River that she wanted to assure herself he was all right.

Rice turned the horse and put him at a canter toward the end of the train. She walked slowly to the wagon as she watched them, smiling at the look of excitement on Rice's young face.

He pulled the pinto to a stop next to her and slid to the ground. "I'll see you later," he said as he walked past her to the wagon.

It took Sarah a second to realize he had been talking to her. River had moved into the saddle and was grinning down at her. He leaned toward her, offering her his arm. "Put your foot in the stirrup," he instructed.

Sarah hesitated a moment, then hiked up her skirt and did as he said. She grabbed his arm, and he pulled her up behind him. She tried to arrange her skirts into a semblance of modesty but failed.

"Hang on," he said, turning the pinto toward the river. Sarah wrapped her arms securely around his waist, expecting him to kick the horse into the pace he and Rice had set.

By the time they had walked slowly past two wagons, Sarah realized this was as fast as River intended to go. "What are you doing?" she asked.

"I'm taking you across the river. Any objections?"

"No, I mean, why are we going so slow?"

River laughed. "I can show you off to these folks better this way."

The driver of each wagon was watching her ride past with her skirts hiked up almost to her knees. She tried again to pull them down, but that seemed to make matters worse.

"Will you hold on?" River scolded. "I could go faster if you held on."

Sarah nearly sputtered in exasperation. "I was holding on, and we were just . . . Never mind. Is this better?" She slid her arms around his waist again until they nearly met.

"This is." He pulled her tighter against him until she could clasp her own wrists. Her body was pressed against his broad back. His right hand caressed the back of hers.

"Daniel, this isn't..." She tried to pull away, but he kicked the pinto, and they sprang forward. All she could do was cling to him or fall. The wagons seemed to fly past, and in no time they were pulling up beside the group that waited at the bank. Sarah had to struggle to catch her breath.

"Horses first," River said. "You ladies on foot follow, then the Gaines team before the first wagon. Water's not deep. Just follow the flags and keep moving."

Before River reined the pinto into the water, Sarah caught a glimpse of Prudence Carroll gaping at her. She wanted to tell the woman to close her mouth before she caught a fly. She muffled a giggle against River's back.

"What's funny?" River let the horse pick its way along the line of willow branches.

"Mrs. Carroll," she said softly. "I think we've shocked her."

"Good for us."

Sarah rested her cheek against River's buckskin-covered back and enjoyed the ride. Mostly the pinto walked sedately through the water, but occasionally, when he stepped onto the softer sand, he plunged forward in order to get a more solid footing. As a result, Sarah had to cling tightly to River, not that she wanted to loosen her hold. She couldn't think of a more pleasant way to cross the South Platte.

River pressed his palm against Sarah's hand at his waist. He traced the fine bones and slender fingers with his thumb. He hadn't really intended this to be an announcement to the train, but he didn't regret that interpretation. It had seemed like the safest way to get her across. He didn't think he could have watched her cross in Rice's wagon or even Eli's. He would have spent the entire crossing worrying about her. This way, she would be safe on solid ground, and he could keep his mind on the rest of the train.

The north shore came too soon for Sarah. It seemed they had barely begun before the pinto was struggling up the slippery bank. River reined to a stop well away from the river and helped her slide to the ground.

"I have to see to the others," he said.

"I'll be fine."

"Just wait here for Rice. Eli won't be able to stop until all the wagons are across." River looked back. The first of the horsemen were just coming up the bank; the few women on foot were well behind. There were no signs of trouble.

He turned to Sarah, still smiling up at him, and bent to touch her face. She moved closer, and he kissed her quickly before putting spurs to the pinto.

Sarah touched her fingers to her lips as she watched him go. The five horses were all out of the water by the time River reached them. She could see that most of the children were on horseback. One of the von Schiller girls rode her father's horse while the other was on Rice's black. Each had a Williams boy in front of her. The reverend's wife rode her husband's horse with their little girl while Mrs. Hess led the horse her five-year-old son rode.

Sarah searched quickly for Amy, discovering her still in the water with her mother and the other three women. She seemed very small with the water coming nearly to her waist. Martha was too far along in her pregnancy to carry her, and the other three women were old. Sarah wondered if the child wouldn't have been safer in a wagon.

The women on horseback had ridden where River had directed and were dismounting. One lone rider headed toward her. Bull Gaines. He had left it to his partner and nephew to lead his oxen and had ridden across in comfort.

She felt a pang of guilt; she had done the same. She should have walked across and let Amy ride with River. She watched the little girl struggle through the water while Gaines's oxen slowly narrowed the space between them.

"Pretty day, ain't it?"

Bull had dismounted nearby, but she kept her eyes on Amy. "Yes, it is," she answered politely.

"The ladies was all abuzz back there, seein' you with that River fella. Seems I wasn't the only one didn't know he was your man."

Sarah chose neither to look at Bull nor to answer him. She caught her breath as Amy slipped and went under for a moment. Martha helped her to her feet and urged her on.

"Well now," Bull said. "Maybe you're not so happy to have them sayin' it, after all. You and me could make them forget that gossip and start some of our own."

Sarah was barely listening to Bull. She watched River reach the group of women and bend over the side of the pinto. In a moment, little Amy was in front of him, and he was headed back to shore.

Sarah let out a sigh of relief.

"That's what I thought."

The triumphant ring in Bull's voice brought Sarah around. Too late, she understood what he was saying. She shook her head, backing away, but his strong fingers closed around her arm. She tried to wrench herself free, but he pulled her against him. She struck out blindly, pushing and scratching at his face, while the blood pounding in her ears nearly drowned out the terrible sound of his laughter.

For a moment Sarah thought she had screamed. The voice had been a child's, and Bull pushed her away. River, one arm around a frightened Amy, glared down at Bull from the pinto's back. "I thought you understood. Sarah's mine."

Amy was crying and reached out to Sarah. She stepped forward, and River released the little girl into Sarah's hands without looking away from Bull. Sarah crumpled to her knees as she set the child on the ground. Amy's clothes were soaked and Sarah wrapped her arms around the shivering child.

Bull glared up at River. "I haven't heard nothing like that from the little gal here."

"I think you have."

"This?" Bull touched a cheek and shrugged at the blood that came away on his fingers. "She don't want me thinkin' she's easy, that's all. Ain't that right, missy?"

River's booted foot connected with Bull's chest. The big man hit the ground hard, gasping for breath.

River swung from the saddle and walked the pinto to where Sarah and Amy were huddled. He pulled Sarah to her feet and helped her onto the pinto's back. He lifted the whimpering Amy up in front of her and handed Sarah the reins. "Take the girl back to her mama," he said softly.

Sarah nodded and turned the horse, afraid to look at Bull. Her spurless shoes didn't interest the pinto, but River's slap on his rump started him toward the ford. The women were scrambling up the bank, and Sarah could see Martha running toward them. Sarah waved, hoping to reassure the mother, as the child's soft crying turned to shrieks.

River turned back to Bull. He was gasping and cursing as he tried to roll to his feet. River pushed him back to the ground. "Let's get this straight this time. You will not bother the lady unless you want to find yourself left behind again. Do you understand?"

River glared at Bull for a full minute before he finally nodded. "Good," River said. He walked to

Bull's horse and gathered the reins. "You don't mind if I borrow your horse, do you? I've got work to do, and I think you could use the walk to cool down."

He caught up with Sarah in time to see Martha Williams hurrying toward the others with the crying child at her side. Sarah sat stone still for a moment, watching them go, before she turned toward him. Her face was composed, but she couldn't hide the tears forming in her eyes.

He brought Gaines's horse close beside the pinto and touched her cheek. "Are you all right?" he whispered.

Sarah nodded. "Where is he?"

"He'll be along." River studied the line of wagons and was satisfied that Eli had things under control. Gaines's oxen, led by Kirby and Nathan, had nearly reached the shore. River turned back to Sarah. "Do you want to join them?" He indicated the cluster of women and children.

Sarah shook her head.

"Rice's girlfriends are over there."

Sarah gave River a pleading look. Martha had been very upset when she had retrieved her daughter, and Sarah was sure she saw her as the cause of the little girl's fright. The other women would have heard all about it by the time she and River got there. She didn't want to wait with them. Yet she hated to ask River to let her stay with him; he had had enough trouble already.

River felt himself sink into deep brown eyes. For a moment, he wondered just what he would be willing to do to make those eyes smile at him again. He took a deep breath and came to a decision. "Bull will be catching up with us soon. Let's leave his horse with his nephew." He urged the horse into a walk and the pinto came obediently alongside.

Herman and Nathan led the oxen from the water. Nathan had been watching what he could see of his uncle's antics as he crossed the river. Now he caught Herman's attention, and they turned toward River and Sarah, leading the oxen out of the way of the approaching wagons.

River dismounted. "Hold your uncle's horse for him."

Nathan nodded. The ghost of a smile was in his eyes as he took the reins.

River turned to Sarah and indicated for her to scoot forward. He swung up behind her and took the reins from her hands. Without another word he turned the horse away.

Behind them Herman Kirby asked, "How did he come to have Bull's horse?"

"You want to ask him?" Nathan responded.

Sarah leaned back against River's strong chest and enjoyed his arms around her. She felt his breath against her temple just before he whispered, "If I wasn't afraid of wearing out my horse, I'd take you all the way to the coast like this."

She smiled but didn't answer. Eli in the lead wagon was only a few yards away.

Sarah grinned at Rice. "At least the scenery isn't monotonous anymore."

The day before, they had passed through strange sand formations known as O'Fallon's Bluffs before crossing the South Platte. Today they had traveled over a rugged, high prairie on a twisting trail with ravines on either side. The ravines had been littered with cedar trees and wrecked wagons. Now she and Rice looked down at nearly five hundred feet of steep grade that would take them into Ash Hollow.

Rice grinned back. "We'll set the brakes to keep the wagons from rolling over the teams. Everybody's supposed to have wheel shoes to keep from wearing down the iron tires. They'll lock the wheels in place in case the brakes fail. If everybody does what they're supposed to, it won't be too bad."

Sarah watched Rice head back for the wagon. Because there was some danger in the descent, River had ordered the women and children to walk down the hill ahead of the wagons and start for the spring two miles away. Each wagon would come down alone, allowing plenty of time in between for earlier wagons to get out of the way.

Since she rode in the second wagon, Sarah was getting a head start on the rest of the women. She couldn't help but wish River would come and let her ride with him. She had to laugh at herself. This wasn't dangerous as the river had been, and she didn't even mind the walk. She was just looking for an excuse to wrap her arms around River again.

She was a little uncomfortable about starting off so far ahead of the others, but surely Gaines wouldn't try anything again so soon. Besides, River had ordered the men to stay and help with all the wagons, even Gaines, who didn't have a wagon of his own.

She hadn't gotten halfway down the slope when she heard someone running and sliding behind her. Her first impulse was to walk faster without even looking back. She could hear the person gaining on her. Rice or River would have called her name, she was sure. She wanted to hurry, but she had to see who followed her.

She turned her head and regretted it immediately. She was moving too fast, and her foot slipped. As she felt herself start to slide, a hand caught her arm, pulling her up and giving her a chance at a sure footing again.

"Didn't mean to scare you."

Sarah looked into Nathan's intense stare. She righted herself as quickly as possible and pulled away. "I'm all right now," she mumbled, starting down the slope again.

Nathan walked beside her, keeping a respectful distance between them. After a moment he spoke, "If you don't want me to walk with you, I'll go away.

I don't want your River deciding to kick me down this hill."

Sarah frowned at him. It had been an attempt at a joke but even the boy wasn't laughing. His eyes held a mixture of question and hope. Sarah guessed he was looking for company but making it easy for her to refuse if she wanted to.

Under her scrutiny, his eyes dropped and he shrugged. "It's a wide hill. I'll walk someplace else, but I wanted to tell you I'm sorry about the other day. Uncle told me to get that kid away, and I usually do like he says. He said you'd be happy to be alone with him."

Sarah looked incredulous, and he gave her a lopsided grin. "Yeah, I know. I shoulda guessed. Not many women are happy to be alone with Uncle."

Sarah turned her attention to the hillside, and Nathan walked silently beside her for a minute. When he spoke again, his voice was softer. "I seen him bothering you yesterday. That River fella made him pure mad."

Sarah stopped in her tracks, and Nathan almost stumbled. "River didn't do anything to your uncle that he didn't deserve."

Nathan held up a hand to quiet her and glanced over his shoulder. "I ain't disagreeing. I'm warning." He eyed her again with that strange intensity she had noticed before. After a moment he turned and began walking again.

She caught up with him quickly. "Why bother?"

Nathan laughed but it wasn't a happy sound. "I'm just stupid, I guess."

They went on silently for a time. When Sarah lost her footing again, Nathan's hand shot out to catch her, but withdrew as soon as she regained her balance. Sarah knew she should be grateful he was making the descent with her, but he was a Gaines, and she wanted nothing to do with his uncle. Still, she couldn't help but feel sorry for the boy.

In the valley below, they could see a little cabin, and even at this distance, Sarah could tell it was deserted. It was the abandoned trappers' cabin Rice had told her about, where emigrants left letters they hoped would be taken to the nearest mail station by someone traveling in the other direction. The cabin looked so lonely Sarah shivered.

They had almost reached the bottom of the hill when Nathan broke the silence. "You gonna wait here for the wagons or go on to the spring?"

Sarah wanted to ask which he planned to do so she could say the opposite. She was ashamed of herself, but the boy, or her mixed feelings about him, made her uncomfortable. Looking in the direction they had come, she could see the first of the women and children starting down the slope. "Why aren't you helping the men with the wagons?" she asked.

Nathan shoved his hands in his pockets and shrugged. "I guess today I'm a child." At her puzzled frown he dropped his eyes to his toes. "River caught Uncle takin' a switch to me and sent me on ahead.''

Sarah didn't know what to say. She hated to think of River angering Gaines any more than he had already, but she wouldn't have wanted him to let Nathan be beaten, either.

After a moment he said, "Let's head for the spring.'' He glanced toward the travelers making their way down the hill, their voices already audible in the clear air. He reached out a hand as if to turn her but didn't quite touch her.

Sarah moved forward, and he fell in beside her again. "Uncle knows you spent time in prison.''

Sarah kept walking. She couldn't bring herself to look at Nathan. She had known Bull would find out sooner or later, and it didn't matter to her what he or his party thought, but something in the boy's tone made her uneasy. She had a feeling he had more to say.

Nathan's voice was soft again. "He heard this morning. Said in that case you had no business being uppity.''

From the corner of her eye Sarah could see him glancing over his shoulder again and knew he was worried about someone seeing them together. In spite of his earlier comment, she was sure it wasn't River he was afraid of.

"Miss Tanton.'' Sarah turned at the urgency in Nathan's voice. "Bull can be awful mean.''

Sarah looked away, not wanting him to see how frightened he was making her. Suddenly he announced, "You go on. I better wait at that old cabin." Before she could respond he turned and hurried away.

Sarah walked on, preoccupied with the things he had said. He was such a strange boy, but he had risked his uncle's anger to warn her. She wondered what he had done earlier to prompt Bull to take a switch to him, or if the man needed any prompting. There was a chance that River's interference would just make it harder on the boy.

At camp that night, Rice related the descent in exciting detail. Ernest Ortman had watched the first two wagons slide down the hill on their brake shoes and had come up with his own plan. He had insisted on unhitching and lowering both his and the doctor's wagons with ropes braced by the oxen at the top of the hill. He had borrowed all the ropes he could get his hands on and, with Prudence's encouragement, had started his brother's wagon down.

"It wasn't too bad an idea," River interjected with a grin.

Sarah could tell by the looks they were exchanging that something had gone wrong. All the wagons had come into camp in one piece so she knew it hadn't been too big a disaster.

Rice tried to look solemn. "He ain't too good at tying knots, I guess. I ain't never seen a wagon go so fast and not tip over. I thought it'd make it to the spring here before it stopped. Bet it's got a loose joint or two.''

Sarah tried to match the boy's look. "Too bad Prudence didn't ride. I overheard her complaining about how hard it was to walk down that hill.''

River got up to pour another cup of coffee. "Oh, she had wanted to ride. I don't think I could have stopped her, either, but Doc put his foot down, for once.''

River watched Sarah as she pictured the scene. When she laughed, it was soft and quiet, as if she hoped no one would hear. He had a sudden desire to hear the joyful laugh he remembered. What would it take? All it used to take was a spin in his arms or a new game of chance. A surprise of any kind used to delight her.

His thoughts were turning in a rather dangerous direction. Still, he couldn't pull his eyes away from her. After a moment, she gathered the dishes and took them to the tailboard.

Rice joined her, his expression serious. "Mr. von Schiller stayed to help, but he don't look like he's feeling good. His jaw's so swollen he hardly looks like himself.''

Eli spoke from across the fire. "If the old fool won't talk to the doctor, there ain't much else ya can do.''

River saw Rice look from the old man to Sarah. "Gretchen says her parents don't like American doctors. They had a little boy that died, and they blame the doctor. But Gretchen's awful worried."

"Maybe you could talk to the doctor and take his advice to Gretchen without her father knowing where it came from," Sarah suggested.

Eli grunted. "Ain't that like a woman to want to run everybody's lives?"

River frowned at Eli. Sarah and Rice ignored them both. She gave the boy an encouraging smile, and he left to find Dr. Carroll.

River was rather impressed with Sarah's advice to the boy. Only half-aware of his own change of attitude, he wanted to take the sting out of Eli's words. "Well, I think it's a good idea. Whether it does any good or not, Rice can feel like he's tried." He came to stand beside Sarah. "Besides," he said softly, "he'll have an excuse to call on Gretchen."

Sarah looked into the sparkling blue eyes and color rose to her cheeks. He had shaved again, even though it wasn't Saturday, and she had the distinct impression it had been entirely for her benefit. For a moment she forgot what she had been doing.

Eli's grunt brought her back to earth. "Will ya two get outta here? I don't wanna watch ya makin' calf eyes at each other all night."

Sarah's color deepened, and River laughed. "What a thoughtful suggestion, Eli. As a matter of fact, it is a nice night for a stroll. Don't you think so, Sarah? How about walking out with me?" He offered her his arm with an exaggerated air of chivalry.

Sarah fought back a giggle. "Why, thank you, sir, but I'm not sure it would be safe. Didn't the Sioux burn down a trading post near here a few years back?"

River's arm swept around her waist and pulled her against him. "I'll keep you safe," he murmured. There were other caravans in the valley now, and Indians weren't likely to attack so large a group. He didn't need to tell her that, however.

"But, sir," Sarah gasped, feeling her heart beat faster from the contact, "I'm not sure it would be proper."

River's eyebrows shot up. "Fair lady," he whispered, "I can assure you it won't be."

Sarah's eyes widened, but before she could speak, he propelled her away from the campfire. Eli's chuckle could be heard behind them.

Chapter Twelve

River walked Sarah toward a grove of ash trees and into their shadows. He pushed his hat to the back of his head and pulled her into his arms. She melted against him immediately, meeting his kiss with a hunger of her own. The response stunned as well as delighted him. Even after her teasing he had expected some resistance.

As her arms tightened around his neck, he realized he wasn't going to walk her back to the wagon, at least not anytime soon. He was strongly tempted to take her to the place he had chosen to spend the night. It was closer to where the livestock grazed than to the wagons and situated on a small rise. The blanket on the grass would be so much softer than the hard crates in the wagon.

He lifted his head and found himself almost breathless. "Damn, Sarah!" he whispered.

From his tone, Sarah might have worried that he was scolding her, that he didn't want her as much as she wanted him. But she was pressed against his body tightly enough to know better. She rubbed her cheek against the soft buckskin jacket and sighed.

"God, Sarah!" River wrenched her away from him. "If you want to see that wagon again before daylight you can't do this to me."

Sarah tried to move back into his arms, but he held her firmly. "What wagon?" she whispered, running her fingertips along the fringed sleeve of his jacket.

River regretted pulling her so far into the dark grove. He couldn't see her face to know if she understood what he was telling her. As he tried to decide, his hold loosened, and she slipped her arms around his waist, bringing her body against his again. In a moment her lips had found the opening at the throat of his shirt.

He drew her firmly away, having made his decision. "Walk," he choked out. After clearing his throat, he repeated, "Walk. I promised you a walk."

"I don't want to walk," Sarah protested, keeping one arm around his waist as he propelled her out of the grove.

River chuckled. "Doesn't that depend on where we're going?"

"Hmm." Sarah leaned her head against his shoulder as she walked. "Where are we going?"

"It's a surprise," he whispered.

"A surprise?" She giggled. "I used to love surprises."

River didn't miss her use of the past tense. He wanted to ignore it. For tonight he wanted to imagine she hadn't changed.

Halfway there Sarah turned in his arms, making it impossible for him to walk. He didn't have any inclination to scold her again. He lifted her face with his hand and kissed her warm lips, wanting to drink in her sweetness again before going any farther. God, it was starting to seem like an enormous journey to get her to his bedroll.

"Sarah?" he murmured against her lips.

She moaned softly in answer.

"Sarah, at this rate we'll never get there." He drew away from her and started forward again, momentarily afraid he had lost his direction.

"Maybe not, but it's fun." She pouted.

River laughed. *That's my Sarah.* He hesitated to say it aloud. He had a feeling the relationship was too fragile to handle many reminders of the past. She could slip back into the frightened young woman at any moment.

Finally he stopped her, turning her body slowly into his arms. He tried to kiss her gently, but she took his hat with one hand while the other slipped into his hair and pulled him toward her.

Sarah stood on the tips of her toes and kissed him until her ankles threatened to give out. When she sank to the ground again, releasing his neck, he drew back and studied her. She wondered if his vision was better than hers; she could barely make out his features in the twilight.

"You know something crazy, Sarah?" He had to swallow hard before he could continue. "I think I'm still in love with you."

Sarah smiled at the wonder in his voice. Could he possibly be feeling the same things she was? Or was he mistaking passion for love? But then, she had already decided that passion was enough.

When she didn't answer he took a deep breath. He felt as if he had been running all the way here instead of strolling leisurely. Sarah pressed against him, her face turned up, tempting him to kiss her again. He had to do it. He felt himself drawn toward her even as he tried to speak. "I love you, Sarah."

Sarah felt light-headed, as if River's strong arms were all that kept her from floating away. His words echoed in her mind; dare she trust them? If she loved him enough in return, could she make them true?

After a moment River drew reluctantly away, touching a fingertip to her moist lips before stepping beyond reach. "You have to stop so I can show you my surprise." He knelt and untied the string that bound his bedroll and spread the blanket on the ground. "Well, maybe it's not much, but it's the best room in the house. Granted, the bed's a little small, and since there's only one, we'll have to share."

"Daniel," Sarah said with a laugh, tossing his hat aside as she came to kneel on the blanket in front of him. "I wouldn't have it any other way."

Her laugh, her teasing tone were so close to what he remembered he felt his hands tremble. "I may hold you to those words," he murmured past the lump in his throat. He gently pushed her down onto the blanket and braced himself above her. "You won't have it—" he kissed her cheek "—any other way—" his lips trailed down her neck "—but with me." He captured her lips with his own.

Sarah arched against him, trying to tell him with her body what she was afraid to put into words—the vow he had made in jest, she had already made in her heart.

River savored the sweetness of her lips while one hand slid down her body, tracing the gentle curves. He could take his time tonight; there was no encroaching storm, no responsibilities to call him away.

When his hand reached her thigh, he began bunching the skirt and slip, slowly drawing the hems of the garments toward his hand. In a moment, he would be free to touch the smooth skin that hid beneath. He felt more than heard her soft moan against his mouth.

To Sarah it was slow torture. When she could stand it no longer, she wrapped her leg around his body, letting the skirt slide to her waist. The movement brought him more firmly against her and only added to her desire.

River freed his hand from the fabric and stroked the leg that held him a most willing captive. The miles of walking had made the muscles firm beneath the silky skin.

Sarah let her leg slowly slide across his backside and down his leg, causing River to end the kiss and gasp for air. When her ankle slipped off his calf, he rolled to his side, lifting himself away from her.

The moon rose over the sandy, wind-carved hills, giving him a chance to see her half-closed eyes and her reddened lips. He took in the disheveled dress and the long, bare leg, which almost glowed in the pale light.

Sarah didn't let him gaze at her for long. She ran hungry fingers down his chest, parting the fasteners of his jacket as if by magic. With a muttered oath, River tore the jacket from his shoulders and quickly removed his boots. His haste elicited a soft laugh from Sarah, and he glanced at her, remembering guiltily his earlier intention to move slowly.

He winked at her and reached for her feet, removing the shoes and stockings and massaging each small foot before lying again on his side next to her. He moved his body over hers, staring into the passion-filled eyes, and stopped.

The fingers of both her hands were tucked in his waistband, effectively keeping a space between them. At his surprised laugh, she whispered, "Just one more thing."

River kissed the smiling lips and rolled off her. "Anything you say, fair lady."

In a moment, he was lowering himself over her again. "Is this better?" he teased between kisses.

Sarah's hands slid along the cotton shirt, down his back, to find the warm flesh beneath. "Better," she murmured.

River playfully nipped an ear. "Your teasing's going to get you into trouble."

"It hasn't so far."

River found himself unable to play any longer. "Don't tease anyone but me," he pleaded in a choked whisper.

"I won't," she sighed, arching upward to meet him.

Suddenly her arms were wrapped tightly around his neck, and there was a different quality in her voice. "No one but you. Ever." Her voice was so soft he wasn't sure if he had heard her or only imagined it.

River was lost in the sweet softness of her body. "I love you," he whispered. "I love you." And everything else was forgotten.

Afterward, when she was sleeping in his arms, he stared up into the starry sky and tried to make sense of what had happened. He had told this woman he loved her, and he knew it was true. In fact, he was beginning to think it had always been true.

He had passed up a few chances to settle down during the last few years because he was still looking for something. Had he been looking for Sarah all this time, or at least for someone like her? He laughed at himself. Would someone *like* Sarah have been enough? He doubted it. He couldn't imagine his life if Sarah hadn't found him.

He clutched her closer and stroked her hair. "Sarah, Sarah," he murmured. "I didn't know I was unhappy till you came back and made me remember how to dream." He shifted his shoulders to a more comfortable position. Maybe it was time to rethink his future.

Nathan Gaines crawled into the bushes by the creek and rolled over. With one arm braced across his ribs, he tried to get his breathing back to normal. There was no use hiding if he was going to be gasping for breath.

Bull wouldn't find him; he didn't worry about that. He never came after him once he let him run away. He might send Herman, but Herman would look just long enough to let Bull cool down. Herman might be sort of stupid, but he knew how to avoid a beating.

Nathan stifled a groan as he scooted deeper into the bushes. He would sleep here tonight. In the morning, he would wash the blood off his face and stay out of sight at the back of the train. Maybe he would hide until the train pulled out, then follow along behind.

He hated himself for his weakness. If he was a man, he would stay here. It would be better to starve than go back to Bull. But he didn't want to starve.

He could survive his uncle's beatings, and one day he would get his chance. *There'll be a better time to run away,* he told himself. *Sometime when it won't mean starving.*

He stiffened at a sound nearby and gritted his teeth against the pain. It was probably Herman. He closed his eyes and tried to relax. His eyes flew open at the sound of a German accent so heavy he couldn't understand the words. All he knew was that the voice was sweet and filled with concern.

"I don't know," came a boy's reply. "But that old man Gaines was acting pretty strange."

"He know, he know! He lie!"

Nathan raised his eyes in a silent prayer. Rice and both von Schiller girls were standing not ten feet from where he hid, talking about his uncle and, in all likelihood, looking for him.

One of the girls began to cry, and the other tried to sooth her. Rice walked closer to his hiding place, and Nathan held his breath. "I'm sure he's all right. He just took a walk or something," he heard Rice say.

"He run away?" sobbed one of the girls.

"Why's she so upset, Gretchen?"

Nathan heard anger in the girl's voice when she answered. "Bull's hands ... uh ... bones here ... bloody. *Meine* Frieda, she vas looking ... seeing ... blue around eye on Nathan once."

Nathan felt tears come to his eyes and bit back a groan. He hadn't realized the girls would remember his black eye from way back at Fort Leavenworth. He hadn't even noticed the girls until his uncle had rejoined the train. His shame hurt more than his ribs and face. If they found him he would try his best to die on the spot. He was sure he could do it; he was already starting to feel light-headed from holding his breath.

"It's dark," Rice said. "We have to go back."

The girls protested, but Nathan heard them moving away. "I'll tell River. He'll know what to do."

Their footsteps faded, and Nathan gasped for air. He felt his head spin and swirl into a pool of darkness.

Something warm touched his face and his brain struggled through a thick mist. He tried to move, but he couldn't make his body work.

"How did you find him?" The voice seemed to be drifting closer to him from far away.

"The girls and I went to his uncle's camp to see if he could come for a walk with us, and his uncle chased us off, saying he wasn't there. The girls got worried, and we went looking for him."

Nathan tried to open his eyes but closed them again against a bright light.

Rice continued. "Frieda was crying so much I had to take them back, but I thought I'd heard something. I think I oughta try to find River."

"No, ya ain't gonna try to find River." Eli's voice was close after all and the fog seemed to be clearing. "Help me get him up. Don't drop the lantern."

Nathan could offer no resistance as they dragged him to his feet. His head spun, and he let it loll against his chest, but he managed to put one foot in front of the other. At the fire, they lowered him to the ground, and he wasn't entirely successful at stifling a groan.

"Fetch the doctor," Eli ordered.

Nathan watched Rice run away and eyed Eli suspiciously. The old man brought a bowl of water and dipped a cloth into it. "That low-down sorry excuse for an uncle did this to ya, didn't he?"

He touched the cloth to a cut over Nathan's eye, and the boy flinched. "Nah," he gasped. It was harder to talk than he expected. In a moment he went on slowly. "I was just trying to climb that cliff over there and fell."

"Is that right?"

Rice and Dr. Carroll arrived as Eli finished bathing Nathan's face. Carroll examined the cuts and bruises, poking here and there, while Eli and Rice looked on. "I don't think the jaw is broken," he said, sitting back to look at the boy's eyes from a distance. "But he might have a concussion. That would explain why he passed out."

"I fell asleep. My head's too hard to break." Nathan started to laugh but caught himself too late. They had seen him clutch his side and grimace at the pain.

"Let's check the ribs, son." The doctor began to unbutton his shirt.

Nathan tried to push his hands away and was alarmed at how weak he was. "They're just skinny ribs," he said, lying back in defeat.

Carroll opened the shirt and nearly whistled. "Somebody really laid into you."

"Nah, I fell off a horse."

"Cliff," Eli corrected.

"Yeah, right."

"Have you coughed up any blood?" Carroll asked.

Nathan's expression seemed to dare the doctor to touch him. "I ain't coughed at all."

Carroll turned to Eli. "We should wrap the ribs good and tight in case any are broken. If he takes it easy for a few days, he ought to be fine."

Eli grunted. "Does walkin' count as takin' it easy? I can't see jigglin' around in a wagon bein' any good for busted ribs."

"If he's strong enough, I suppose. Otherwise, we could rig up a litter."

"Whoa. Just a minute." Nathan struggled to a sitting position and closed his shirt. "You ain't gettin' me on no litter, and I ain't got a wagon. So I walk, or I stay. Them's the choices."

Eli shot Carroll a knowing look. "Rice, fetch something to wrap his ribs."

"Yes, sir. Shouldn't I go find River? And where's Sarah?"

"Don't worry none about them. We can take care of young Gaines, here. We'll hide him in the supply wagon and see how long it takes Uncle Bullhead to come lookin' for him.''

Nathan's expression held both humor and shock. ''You don't know what you're letting yourself in for.''

''Well, neither does he.'' Eli got up and busied himself at the fire. ''Beatin' a boy till he crawls away. Bustin' him up. Face all cut to pieces.'' The comments faded into mutterings, and Nathan turned his attention to the doctor.

''Has this happened before?'' Carroll asked gently.

Nathan's eyes narrowed. ''Yeah, I fall down a lot. You got a cure for that, Doc?''

When his chest was wrapped in the strips of cloth, and Eli had fed him broth and settled him inside the wagon, Nathan tried to relax. He wanted to believe this was better than hungry and cold under the bushes. He wanted to believe these people were willing to be his friends.

It was hard. How could they like him when he was too big a coward to stand up to Bull or even run away from him? How could they want to help someone like him? Nathan remembered the things the old man had said about Bull and caught himself before he laughed. It wasn't so much that they liked him; they hated his uncle. Well, that he could understand.

He closed his eyes, realizing how tired he was. He hurt all over, but it was worth it. Bull had seen him walking down the hill with Sarah and had demanded to know what they had said. But he had kept his mouth shut. He had warned the pretty lady, and River had hidden her away. Old Bull wouldn't get to her tonight. With that reassuring thought, he was finally able to sleep.

Before dawn, River woke Sarah with a kiss. She tried to pull him into her arms, but he resisted. "Time to get up, sweetheart."

Sarah groaned softly, rolling over and snuggling under the blanket. "It's not morning."

"No, but I thought you might want to get back before Eli has breakfast ready."

Sarah sat up with a start. She had been so lost in sweet dreams she had forgotten where she was! River was sitting back on his heels grinning at her. "Are you this pretty every morning, or did last night have something to do with it?" He touched her hair where it tumbled over her shoulder.

Sarah felt herself blush. "You see me every morning," she murmured.

"Not this early." *I'd sure as hell like to from now on.*

She watched his eyes, pale in the darkness, gaze at her for a long moment then turn away. She buttoned the front of her dress, remembering how it had come undone. She was grateful she had slept in her dress even though it would be sadly wrinkled now. *Not much worse than usual,* she thought, letting a smile touch her lips.

She heard River's sharp intake of breath and looked up to see him come to his feet. "We better get back before I decide you're too pretty to leave."

He grabbed the blanket that covered her, and she pulled her skirt down quickly. She needn't have bothered, she decided. He wasn't interested in her legs, just in the blanket. She took her shoes when he handed them to her. He barely looked at her now. As she put her shoes on quickly, she wondered what had changed his mood.

"Get up," he coaxed. "I need to roll up the rest of my bedroll."

She scowled at him. "Now you're in a terrible hurry to get rid of me. What happened to 'you're too pretty to leave'?"

River risked a glance at her. Several inches of ankle were exposed while she buttoned the shoe. It reminded him of the long pale legs hidden under the wrinkled skirt. He could almost feel them wrapped around his body. He turned away to look for his hat. "Nothing, yet. Make your trip to the bushes, then let me get you back to the wagon."

Sarah grinned and hurried to comply. River watched her go. "You're a temptation, Sarah," he whispered under his breath.

He had the blankets rolled before she got back. While he waited, he tried to decide how much he should tell her. He had made some decisions during the night that he longed to share with her, but he couldn't risk having her reject them.

It would be smarter, he decided, to wait until he was sure she had forgiven him. She didn't even trust him enough to tell him her story yet. Not that he could blame her; he hadn't encouraged her when she had tried. But now things would be different. When she felt safe, when she trusted him, she would tell him, and he would believe her.

He was standing with the bedroll over one shoulder and his rifle in hand when Sarah joined him. She watched him as she approached, wishing she could read what he was thinking in the way he stood. She had taken the few remaining pins from her hair, aware that several had been lost. She knew there was little chance of finding them in the dark even if River was inclined to wait, which she was sure he wasn't.

They set off immediately for the wagons, River keeping one hand on Sarah's arm to hurry her along. He tried not to notice how her loose hair flowed freely down her back. He tried to pretend he didn't know how soft it felt. Out of the corner of his eye he saw her rake her fingers through it, giving it a shake. He tried to look away.

Sarah was feeling completely confused by the time he stopped her. They were near the ash trees where he had stopped her the night before, and they could see the wagon and the small red glow of last night's coals. His hand was still on her arm when he whispered, "Walk in like you've just gone out the way you do each morning."

Sarah nodded, trying not to be embarrassed that he had paid attention to her personal habits.

He let go of her arm for an instant and caught it again. "Wait," he whispered.

She turned, a question in her eyes. He dropped the rifle and bedroll and with one sweep of his arm brought her up against him. While that arm held her fast, his other hand buried itself in her hair and his lips sought and found hers. He tasted her willing mouth greedily and ended the kiss as abruptly as he had started it.

While she struggled to catch her breath, he smiled down at her, whispering, "Go in as if nothing has happened."

Sarah caught herself before she laughed. "Oh, you make that sound so easy," she whispered back.

His grin broadened. "I want to make sure it isn't."

She turned around so she wouldn't have to look at his charming grin. Taking a deep breath, she started toward the wagon, trying to think how she usually walked, how she usually acted. *I'm just going back to the wagon,* she told herself. *Back to the wagon I left only a moment ago.*

It wasn't easy. She ought to kick River for that last kiss. Now she wanted to run and hide in the wagon, to be alone long enough to think about this delightful change in River... and in herself.

When she finally arrived at the wagon, she took one last look toward the place she had left River. He was nowhere in sight, but she knew he might be hidden in the shadows. She resisted the temptation to wave before she climbed into the wagon.

River watched her go, praying with each step that their secret wouldn't be discovered. For himself he wouldn't care, but he had a feeling Sarah would find discovery humiliating, perhaps to the point of refusing to spend another night with him. He chided himself for his less than noble outlook.

She turned back at the wagon, and his guilt increased. He should move slower with her, let her learn to trust him, give her time to believe he loved her. He should wait until she had told him her story and listened to his plans. Then he should ask her to marry him. And until they came that far, he shouldn't touch her.

She disappeared into the wagon, and he stared for a long moment at the spot where she had been. God, he felt lonely already. With a sigh, he retrieved his bedroll and rifle. He would make a round of the camp then turn up at Eli's fire. He took one step forward and paused to look back at the wagon. "You're a temptation, Sarah," he whispered again.

Sarah heard Eli muttering moments after she climbed into the wagon. She lit the lantern and went to her trunk to find her brush and more pins to fix her hair. Eli was returning to the fire when she stepped out of the lead wagon. He didn't give her a glance but walked directly to the supply wagon.

Sarah went to the fire to add more wood and jumped when she heard Eli swear. "Damn, worthless, fool boy."

Sarah's eyes darted to the blankets where Rice was just waking up. "What's wrong?" she asked warily.

"Fool's run off. Ungrateful brat."

Rice struggled to his feet. "He's gone?"

"Yes, he's gone. Gone back to his uncle, I reckon."

"Who are you talking about?" Sarah asked, but she had a feeling she knew.

Rice affirmed her suspicions. "Nathan Gaines."

Sarah was almost afraid to ask. "What was he doing here, hiding?"

"We fed the little whelp," Eli said, still angry. "Patched him up. Even brought the doctor. What does he do?"

Sarah interrupted. "Brought the doctor?" She felt chilled. This was somehow her fault.

It was Rice who answered. "His uncle beat him, but he was all right."

Eli was fuming. "I'll bet he went back to his uncle. Ain't that just like a dog? Ya kick him, and he'll still come home."

Sarah and Rice looked at Eli then at each other. Rice shrugged, and Sarah went back to tending the fire. Both were afraid to speak into the uneasy silence after Eli's words.

Walking into camp a few minutes later, River sensed the tension. His first thought was for Sarah,

and he went to her, whispering close to her ear,
"What's going on?"

She glanced at Eli. "I'm not sure but it has to do
with Nathan Gaines." Her whisper wasn't quite soft
enough.

"Don't even talk about him," Eli interrupted.
"He ain't got the sense God gave a possum."

River's questioning gaze went to Rice, whose only
answer was a wide-eyed shrug. They went about their
duties in preparation for departure, giving Eli as wide
a berth as possible. By the time they were ready to go,
Sarah was more than glad to climb onto the wagon
seat beside Rice.

Once they were under way, River rode beside their
wagon, and Rice related to both of them the events
of the night before. He ended in a bewildered tone,
"We were going to protect him from Bull. I don't
understand why he would go back."

"Maybe he wasn't sure he could trust us," River
suggested. "If Bull had to come get him, he would
have been in trouble again. At least going back, he
knew what to expect."

Sarah could see Rice wasn't convinced. "You were
right to try to help him, though," she said. "At least
he knows there are people who will be kind to him."

"But Eli's so mad," he protested. "If he comes to
us for help again, Eli will turn him away."

River laughed. "I don't think so. Eli'll cool down.
He always does." He smiled at Sarah. "Just be glad
he isn't mad at you."

"Aw, that don't bother me," Rice said, missing the look his companions had exchanged. "I know he don't mean nothin'."

"See," said River. "It'll be the same with Nathan. I better make sure everyone's coming along all right. The road's nothing but sand, and if anyone can get bogged down in it, Ortman will." He tipped his hat to Sarah and waved at Rice before turning the pinto away from their wagon.

Chapter Thirteen

River had been right about the road, and travel was slow. It seemed they had again left all trees behind except a few willows on little islands in the North Platte.

Sarah listened to Rice talk about the von Schiller girls, especially Gretchen. She had quite suddenly become his favorite. He hadn't noticed earlier, but Gretchen was prettier, sweeter and much smarter than her younger sister. In fact, he was beginning to wish Frieda would get lost.

"She cried last night, and that's why we had to stop looking for Nathan," he said. "If we had found him while she was there I would have had two people to look after."

Sarah would rather not have been reminded of Nathan and his troubles. "How's Mr. von Schiller's toothache?" she asked.

"It's bad," Rice answered. "I told Doc Carroll about it, and Doc said he oughta have the tooth

pulled. That's why I went to see him last night, you
remember, to tell him what the doctor said. I just
suggested it, but I didn't mention the doctor. I think
he's going to try to pull it himself or maybe see if his
wife can.

"I suppose that's probably why Frieda cries so
easy," Rice went on. "She's worried about her father. Anyhow, I wish she hadn't come last night. She
was the reason we went to the Gaines camp in the
first place, so she could walk with Nathan and leave
us alone."

Nathan again, Sarah thought. She wanted to know
if he was all right, but she wasn't about to go to the
Gaines camp to find out. She was tempted to ask
Rice to go or at least ask around, but she didn't want
to put him in any danger. She knew part of her mo-
tive was guilt, but even if his beating had nothing to
do with her, she hated to think of anyone at Bull
Gaines's mercy.

In the afternoon, they saw a great herd of buffalo, and toward evening, River took two of the men
hunting and came into camp with their horses loaded
with meat. They cooked what they could and jerked
the rest, decorating the wagons again. Sarah was sure
the clouds of sand would make the meat gritty, but
Eli seemed unconcerned. Because of the extra work
of cutting the meat for jerky, Sarah had little time to
worry about Nathan. River spent the evening in
camp, providing an additional distraction.

"By this time tomorrow, we should be able to see Chimney Rock," he told her, looking up from the rifle he was cleaning. "You can see it for more than thirty miles."

Rice had told her about this strange rock formation that towered over the prairie. To him, it meant they were getting close to the mountains. She looked at Rice and smiled at the excitement on his face.

"We're about a week from Fort Laramie, Miss Sarah. That right, River?" the boy asked.

River nodded, but whatever he was going to say was cut short by Eli's voice. "Ya oughta give Sarie a ride out to that old rock when we get close, River. It's off the road a piece but wouldn't seem like no trip a'tall on horseback. That's exactly what ya oughta do."

"Sounds like a good idea," River said, grinning at Sarah.

She turned to her work to hide the color she felt rising in her cheeks. She couldn't fault River for anything he had said or even how he had said it, but the look in his eyes had made his thoughts all too plain.

It didn't help that she was already remembering the last time she had cut up meat this way. She and River had worked together and, when they were done, had gone to wash their hands in the river. If he offered to go with her this time, things would be different. When he moved to kiss her, she wouldn't pull away, and she wouldn't say anything that would make him angry. Back then, she had still held some hope of explaining everything to him.

The following day they continued along the track that roughly followed the North Platte, even though part of the time they were several miles from the river. The road was sandy in places but better than the day before. The prairie was dotted more and more by yucca plants. It made Sarah think of a desert, and she mentioned this to Rice.

"Nah, this is a lot nicer than a desert," he said. "I've seen some rattlesnakes around here, though."

After these encouraging words, Sarah decided to ride most of the day. By evening she was glad to stretch her legs and offered to excuse Rice from his usual job of getting water. He eagerly agreed, and she set off with the buckets. After going a few yards, she wondered why she thought she wouldn't have to worry about snakes now, if they had worried her all day. She was watching her path so intently she was startled to see a pair of boots planted almost in front of her.

Taking an involuntary step backward, she looked up into Nathan's bruised face. "You shouldn't come out here alone," he said.

Sarah recovered quickly. "Were you in trouble for talking to me?" She went around him and began filling the buckets, not wanting him to be hurt again because of her.

"He's planning something. Don't wander around alone."

She looked up to ask what he meant and discovered him walking swiftly away from her. He changed direction abruptly, and she realized anyone who saw him now would never guess they had been together a moment before. As she walked back to the wagon, she had a feeling Nathan still watched her. She didn't turn to see. She was afraid the slightest glance in his direction would give him away.

Because she was preoccupied with Nathan and what he had said, she was well into the supper preparations before she realized something was wrong at the next wagon.

The Williams family had been next in line, and Sarah had seen the children playing near the wagon earlier. The team had been unhitched and, she assumed, watered and turned into the corral, but there was no supper fire burning. She saw no sign of either parent and realized the children's play was more subdued than usual.

"Eli, what do you make of that?" she asked softly, indicating the neighboring camp with a nod.

As Eli came to stand beside her, Tom Williams climbed from the wagon. He walked past his children without speaking and started around the circle. The smaller boy hollered and tried to crawl after his father, but Amy grabbed him. He sat crying while Albert and Amy tried to comfort him.

Eli's eyes narrowed. "Ya go hush the young'un. I'll see what his pa's up to."

Sarah approached the children with some trepidation. Since they had been told to stay away from her, her presence might make matters worse. "Amy?" she asked softly. All three heads turned in her direction. Even Allen gave up his crying, watching her as his body shook with silent sobs.

"Amy, where's your mama?"

The little girl stared at her before deciding to speak. "In the wagon."

Sarah took the last remaining steps separating her from the children and knelt on the ground beside them. "Is she all right?"

Albert turned his attention to Amy, but Allen continued to stare at Sarah, shuddering occasionally. Sarah could tell Amy wasn't sure she should answer. Finally the little girl stood, placing a hand on each of her brothers. "Papa's gone for help. You're bad. You're not suppose' to be here."

With a sigh, Sarah nodded her understanding and rose to her feet. "I'll be nearby if you need me, Amy." The little girl didn't answer, and Sarah went back to her own fire.

She couldn't help but watch the children as she went about her work. It wasn't long before Eli, Tom and Dr. Carroll were hurrying toward them. Tom and the doctor went into the wagon, and Eli joined Sarah.

He turned to look at the children before he spoke. "The missus is havin' her baby, but it ain't nearly time."

The von Schiller girls had been right behind the doctor. They went to the children, and Sarah could hear the girls coaxing them to follow. ''Food. Eat?'' When they understood, each girl lifted a little boy to her hip, and Amy, after a glance at Sarah, followed them away.

Rice and River came to the fire, and Eli filled them in. As they started to eat their supper, Tom came out of his wagon and lit a fire, putting water on to boil. Eli went to talk to him, reporting back that there was nothing yet to tell.

Sarah was cleaning up the dishes when the von Schiller girls and their mother brought the children back. Mrs. von Schiller went into the wagon while the girls played with the children. Rice went to join them, and Sarah made a guess which girl was Gretchen.

There was an outburst of German from the wagon, and Gretchen went to see what had happened. After a moment she came back for Rice. Sarah could hear her agitated chatter as she pulled Rice by his arm toward the wagon. ''My English dou know. Mama vill say...I vill say...dou vill say to doctor.''

They had no more than climbed into the wagon when Tom climbed out. Sarah heard Eli mumble something about a crowd and knew he was watching the other camp as intently as she.

Tom brought out blankets for the children but left it to Frieda to put them to bed. He sat by his fire, staring at the flames. River filled a cup with coffee and took it to him. He had to tap the man's shoulder twice before he looked up. River left the cup in his hand and returned.

When her chores were done, Sarah sat beside River. He put his arm around her and pulled her close. There were low moans from the other wagon now. Sarah turned her face into River's shoulder at the sorrowful sounds.

They watched the neighboring camp as their fire died. Sarah knew she should turn in, but she wanted to be up if there was anything she could do. She didn't think she would sleep, anyway. She kept thinking of Martha's dreamy expression when she had first told her about the baby. She prayed Tom had been wrong and both mother and child would be fine in the morning.

The children finally fell asleep with Frieda curled up beside them. Tom went to look into the back of the wagon but returned to his place by the fire without saying a word.

Sarah found River's strong arm around her more comforting than any words he might have spoken. She closed her eyes and felt sleep steal over her.

The moon had risen when a scream awakened Sarah, a long, anguished ''Nooo'' that dissolved into heartbreaking sobs. She sat up, and River's arm tightened around her.

After a few minutes, the four who had been at the woman's side climbed out of the wagon. As she watched, the doctor went to speak softly to Tom, and Rice said goodbye to Gretchen and her mother.

It was Rice who brought them the news. "The baby's dead," he said softly.

He was pale and shaken, and Sarah began to realize what the boy had been through. River brought a crate and nearly pushed Rice onto it. He sat silently for a moment.

"Gretchen was real good," he said finally. "Me and her would help her mother talk to the doctor. I was awful scared. They talked about what they might do, but it didn't seem like there was nothing that would save the baby."

Sarah laid a hand on his arm. He looked into her eyes and whispered, "It was awful, Miss Sarah."

Sarah knelt beside him, wanting to draw him into her arms but afraid to even offer. He took her hand and spoke again. "It's wrapped in a blanket in the wagon. It was just so tiny."

Sarah felt tears come to her eyes. She had never witnessed a birth, let alone the birth of a dead child. And Rice was only a boy.

In a moment, Rice turned to River and said in an even voice, "Doc says it would be best if we waited here a day."

River nodded. He watched Rice carefully, amazed at what he saw. After a moment he smiled sadly. "You did good, son," he said, giving Rice's shoulder a squeeze. "We better all try to get some sleep."

The next morning, Tom carried Martha out of the wagon and set her on a camp stool so she could attend her baby girl's funeral. Frieda and Gretchen had taken charge of the other children. The rest of the train gathered around the tiny grave, and Reverend Fleenor took the opportunity to preach a sermon on God's help in time of need. When it was over, Rice remained behind to fill in the grave, having declined all offers of help.

"The reverend knew we wouldn't stop again tomorrow," Eli grumbled. "He snuck a church service in on us today. Though he has mellowed, ain't he." He glanced over his shoulder at Sarah, walking with River. "Well, let's get that bread baked. If he wants to pretend it's Sunday, so can we."

River gave Sarah a quick kiss on her temple and murmured a goodbye before he left her to make the rounds of the wagons. Sarah helped Eli with the bread, then went to the river to wash the clothes, much as she did on Sundays.

She wanted to pay a visit to Martha or at least ask if there was anything she could do, but she knew her presence would upset the poor woman. Other families brought food to the wagon, and there seemed to be at least one woman with Martha nearly all the time.

When Rice came in to eat at noon, he asked Sarah if she had seen Chimney Rock. He pointed it out to her in the distance and Sarah had a feeling he would never look at it in quite the same way again.

* * *

River kept the pinto at a slow walk. Sarah knew he wanted this ride to last as much as she did. She was behind him, her arms wrapped tightly around his waist, her cheek against his back. The wagons were circled opposite Chimney Rock, and after supper, as Eli had suggested, River had taken Sarah over to see it. Now they were on their way back to the train.

Sarah searched for some topic of conversation, something that wouldn't recall painful memories and start them fighting. Finally she asked almost hesitantly, "Rice tells me the train will likely split up a few days out of Fort Hall. Will you be going to Oregon or California?"

River smiled. He would love to tell her just what he planned, but it was too soon. "That'll depend," he answered after a moment. "In the past, Milburn and I would split up and meet again in San Francisco. There are ships going down the coast. The train's so small this year, we'll try to get the families into other trains."

Sarah reflected on this. She had been counting on his company all the way to California. When Rice told her about the split past Fort Hall, she had toyed with the idea of waiting to choose her own direction until she knew which group River would be leading. But he wasn't giving her any answers.

"There are a few old trappers that will guide caravans," River went on. "Some will be waiting at Fort Laramie, in fact."

Sarah was silent for the rest of the ride, afraid her voice would reflect her disappointment. She closed her eyes and tried to relax against River's strong back. Their time together was running out far too quickly.

"What in the hell's going on?"

At River's question, Sarah opened her eyes. It was almost dark now, but she could see the wagons lit by campfires. It looked as if everyone in the train were gathered at Eli's fire. As they approached, they could hear the angry voices.

The crowd fell silent as River rode in. He dismounted and helped Sarah down. Rice stepped forward and, as he took the reins, spoke softly to River. "Mrs. Hess says a watch and some coins turned up missing."

River glanced at Mrs. Hess, who stood bolstered by Prudence Carroll. He gave Rice a pat on the shoulder and urged Sarah forward as Rice led the horse away.

Eli came to meet them. "Am I glad to see ya. Shore took yer time getting back."

River looked from Eli to the women and the crowd behind them. Everyone was glaring at Sarah. He could feel her apprehension and spared a glance at her before he said, "Tell me what I missed."

Suddenly everyone was talking at once. He raised a hand and all but Prudence fell silent. "And I demand that that woman's wagon be searched!"

River glared at her, but she was too sure of herself to back down. "You can't expect anything less when you shelter a convict. It's a wonder she's waited this long. Why, I think we should all check our valuables, right now. There could be things she stole we haven't missed yet."

She turned to Ernest. "You wait here and see that both these wagons are searched." With one last sniff in Sarah's direction, she spun and helped Mr. Hess lead his wife away.

River took a deep breath and turned to Sarah. She had to be upset, but she was doing an admirable job of hiding it. The easiest way to satisfy these people would be to search the wagon, but saying so to Sarah would ruin any trust she might have in him. He had to let her know he didn't believe the accusations.

While he was trying to decide how best to do that, she said, "Search the wagons, River."

She knew Eli and Ernest were both standing nearby watching her, but all she saw was River's eyes searching hers. Was he trying to decide if she was a thief? He already believed that; she was surprised he was looking for the truth in her eyes. He had never believed her.

When he answered, his voice was just above a whisper. "I'm sorry, Sarah." He pulled his eyes away and looked for Ernest. "You want to witness this?" he asked. "You too, Sarah."

He helped her into the wagon. While River and Ernest followed her inside, she moved to the front of the wagon and loosened the pucker string as far as it would go. The wagon was too tiny for three people, and she knew she could have a sudden need for more air.

River lit the lantern and eyed Ernest. "You want to go through all these crates?"

The other man looked flustered and River noticed he avoided looking in Sarah's direction. "Just her own personal boxes and such and boxes what she uses stuff out of... for cookin' and the like."

River nodded. After a long look at Sarah, he indicated her trunk. "Do you have anything besides this?" When she shook her head, he moved to open it.

Ernest took a step closer. "What if she's lying?" The look on River's face made him back away.

River sat beside the trunk and hesitated before lifting the lid. He made one last effort to think of another way, but he saw none. He felt Ernest lean closer to see as he opened the trunk.

He handed the blanket on top to Ernest and shook his head in disgust as Ernest felt over it carefully. He looked back into the trunk and paused in surprise. Resting on the garments was a walnut jewelry box. He lifted it slowly, remembering. He had gone to her grandmother's house on Christmas morning, angering his parents more than usual. He had stood in the snow and watched while she opened it. "It's for all the pretty things I'll buy for you," he had said.

River shook off the memory. Afraid to look at Sarah, he opened the box. Inside were a few coins and hairpins. Beneath lay an envelope. He started to close the lid.

Ernest stopped him. "How do we know those ain't the coins?"

"No watch," River said, placing the box on the floor beside him and starting his search of the rest of the trunk.

"That don't mean nothin'. Suppose the watch is hid somewhere's else. I think we need to tell Mr. Hess about these coins."

"Do you think he'll recognize his own coins?" River lifted the Sunday dress and laid it on the trunk's open lid.

"Well, how do we know unless we ask him?"

River glared at Ernest. "How do we know Hess is even missing a watch and coins? How do we know you're not here trying to see what you want to steal from Miss Tanton? And for that matter, if we found a watch and coins, how would we know your sister didn't put them here?"

Ernest drew back in amazement. He sputtered a moment, unable to speak. River went back to lifting items out of the trunk. When he stopped, Ernest leaned forward to peer inside and seemed relieved that it was empty.

River turned to Sarah. Her face was still, her body almost stiff. He cursed inwardly. He would like to strangle Prudence Carroll for what she put Sarah through.

Her voice was steady when she spoke. "I'll put my things away, if you don't mind."

River nodded and glared at Ernest, daring him to disagree. After a moment he said, "Let's check the cooking supplies." They turned to the back of the wagon and went through Eli's cupboard and boxes, while Sarah smoothed each piece of fabric and put it back into her trunk.

They were still searching through the cooking utensils when she closed the lid. She didn't want to watch them. She returned to her place at the front of the wagon and turned her back on them. There was very little to see out the opening except the back of the next wagon. Several minutes later, when she heard River and Ernest leaving to continue their search, she pulled the pucker string closed. River had left her the lantern. She stared at it for a moment before moving to put it out.

Eli met River and Ernest at the back of the supply wagon. "Ya really went through that poor gal's things, didn't ya?" the old man grumbled. "Now yer gonna go through everything she ever touched, is that it? Ya should be ashamed. Both a ya!"

River tried to ignore him, but he moved to block their way. "Ya won't find no stolen watch, nor money, neither."

"Eli," River warned.

"Well, yer just bein' mean to Sarie, just as mean as ya was afore. Believin' she'd take somethin'. If ya found a watch, ya'd turn right around and say she was a thief and not give her a chance to say nothin'. Is that what happened afore?"

River grabbed Eli by the shoulders. "Will you shut up?" he hissed between his teeth. "I know there's no stolen watch here. I'm trying to show Ortman there's no stolen watch here. Now will you get out of my way?"

Eli shook his hands off and snorted. Reluctantly he stomped back to his fire, grumbling to himself. Ernest watched him go before climbing into the wagon after River. They had barely started their search when Eli was pounding on the side of the wagon. "Ya better get out here and see this."

"What now?" River mumbled, jumping from the wagon.

Tom Williams was standing by Eli's fire, a small bag in one hand and a watch dangling from the other. "My Amy took them," he said. "She was playing at the Hess wagon while Martha rested. She didn't know she shouldn't."

Eli was nearly crowing with glee. He hurried to the lead wagon. "You hear that, Sarie?" he called, knocking on the side.

River watched Tom eye the old man with a little dismay. He could hear Ernest behind him shuffling his feet. "You better return them to Hess," River said. "I'm sure he and his wife'll understand."

Tom nodded and turned to go. Ernest made to follow but River stopped him. "Tell your sister she owes Miss Tanton an apology."

Ernest swallowed audibly. "I can't tell her that."

"Sure you can." River smiled coldly at him.

Ernest looked from River to Eli before he hurried away.

Eli let out another gleeful laugh and pounded on the wagon again. "You hearin' all this, Sarie?"

River pushed past him. "Leave her alone," he advised. He climbed into the dark wagon and could hear the old man's chuckle as he let the canvas fall into place.

"Sarah?" he whispered. He knew she was in here, but he couldn't see anything. He waited, hoping his eyes would adjust, and heard a tiny muffled sound. He took a match from his pocket and struck it. In the feeble light he found her sitting on the floor, her head resting on her drawn-up knees.

He knelt beside her, shaking out the match. "Sarah?" He touched her shoulder, and she tried to turn away. He pulled her into his arms, his strength competing with her resistance until she gave in. He settled her comfortably against him and stroked her hair. He felt silent sobs rack her body and wrench his heart. "I'm sorry, sweetheart," he whispered. He rocked her gently. "Shh, don't cry."

Sarah couldn't believe she was crying, let alone crying in River's arms. An accumulation of things had opened the floodgates, which now seemed impossible to close. River was holding her, and River would soon be out of her life. She clung to him as if she could keep him from leaving by her strength alone.

She wished she could be angry with him; she wished she could hate him. That had been impossible six years ago even with ample justification. It was certainly impossible now. His tender words and gentle touch comforted her against her will. The floodgates finally closed, her strength ran out, and she slept.

River continued to cradle her like a child. He listened to her soft, even breathing and berated himself for hurting her again. He dozed awhile then woke to stroke her hair and whisper his love to her sleep-filled ears. He left her just before dawn.

Chapter Fourteen

Sarah squinted at the young man beside her. "You're quiet this morning," she said.

Rice watched the team as he spoke. "Mr. von Schiller's awful sick, Sarah. They finally asked Doc to look at that tooth. I guess the missus decided she could trust him after all. It don't seem possible a body could be so sick from a toothache."

"What did the doctor say?"

"The poison's got in his body, and he's gotta do nothin' but rest. All the work'll fall to the girls and their ma, and he thinks it'll be too much for 'em. He wants to stop and winter at Fort Laramie."

He shook his head slowly, and Sarah tried to comfort him. "Rice, I'm sorry. But surely he'll be all right if he does what the doctor says."

After a moment Rice continued. "Yeah, I guess, but they're leaving the train!"

"And you're missing Gretchen already," she whispered.

He turned to her, his expression a mixture of sorrow and anger. "I should be thinking about the poor man that's so sick. I should be thinking about his wife and daughters that'll have to find work at the fort so they can afford to go on next spring. But all I can think about is Gretchen and how I'll never see her again."

"Don't be too hard on yourself, Rice. It's human nature to think of ourselves. This girl is special to you. Of course you'll miss her." She watched him stare at the team, his lips set in a grim line, and added softly, "If it's meant to be, Rice, you'll meet again."

He gave her a skeptical glance. *You're probably right,* she thought. But she couldn't tell him he would forget Gretchen; she had never forgotten Daniel. Though she understood Rice's feelings of loneliness all too well, she had no comfort to offer.

Rice was pensive the rest of the day, and soon after camping, he headed for the von Schiller wagon. Eli made more food than usual and reported that until Martha was well the others were taking turns cooking for the family. "It's my turn tonight," he told Sarah when she had dipped up a portion for herself and River. He left a plateful for Rice before gathering the pot and bread and hurrying away.

Sarah stared after him in open amazement, causing River to laugh. "I think you let Eli's grouchy disposition influence your opinion of him," he said, taking the plate from her hand.

"Maybe so," Sarah conceded, following him to the crate seats. "Have you heard about Mr. von Schiller?"

River nodded. "I think the doctor's being overly cautious, but the man doesn't look well."

Sarah wondered how much River knew of Rice's personal sorrow. She would leave it to Rice to tell him if he chose.

They ate in silence, both thinking more about the other than about von Schiller. Finally River set his plate aside and turned his full attention to Sarah. "Has Mrs. Carroll been around to talk to you?"

Sarah stared at him wide-eyed and shook her head.

River's eyes narrowed for a second, then his face relaxed into his easy smile. "Much as I'd like to sit here with you all evening, I have an errand to run." He rose to his feet, and her eyes followed him warily. He took the plate from her hand and set it aside. With a gentle tug, he pulled her to her feet and into his arms. "Kiss me goodbye."

A smile spread across Sarah's face as she wrapped her arms around his neck. "Am I kissing you goodbye, or good-night?" she murmured.

"Certainly not good-night." He lowered his head to claim his kiss, pulling her against his lean frame. When he gradually drew away from her, she was breathless, her eyes closed. He saw her eyelashes flutter up to reveal those deep brown eyes. His voice was hoarse when he whispered, "Just goodbye and only for a little while."

Sarah watched him walk away, a little stunned by how weak he could make her feel. She was falling more deeply in love with him each time he touched her. Was the pleasure she received now worth the pain their eventual separation would cause?

She sighed and gathered up the plates. If it wasn't, it was too late now. She felt powerless to deny him anything.

She turned toward the tailboard and gasped, letting the plates clatter to the ground. Bull Gaines stood beside the wagon, and before she could move, he grabbed her shoulders, pulling her hard against him.

"I know what you are," he growled. "Don't go pretending you're better'n me."

Sarah tried to push away from him, but his arms had locked around her. His hold was so tight she could barely breathe. She struggled to draw enough air into her lungs to scream, but all she could manage was a whimper. He tried to stifle even that with his mouth, and she gagged.

"I can make it nice for you if you make it nice for me," he said near her ear. "Unless you want to play rough. That's just fine, too."

She tried to kick at his legs but was too close to him. He laughed and held her tighter. She felt her head spin from fear and lack of oxygen. A black haze swirled at the edge of her vision.

She heard a strange pop and thought her ribs had broken. The next instant Bull's grip was gone, and she crumpled to the ground, gasping for air while her vision cleared. In front of her, Bull was pulling himself to a sitting position while blood ran down the side of his face. River stood over him, holding his rifle like a club.

Sarah scrambled to her feet and backed away. She didn't want to look at Bull and fastened her eyes on River.

"You're off this train," River said through clenched teeth. "Tomorrow morning, pull out of line and give us at least thirty minutes before you follow."

Bull glared at him with open hatred. He looked as if he would speak but changed his mind. He came slowly to his feet.

River stepped back enough to give Bull room to leave, keeping himself between the man and Sarah. He gripped the rifle in frustration and didn't take his eyes off Bull until he was out of their camp. He wished the man had put up a fight. Right now he could kill him with his bare hands.

He looked around for Sarah and saw her leaning against the wagon, watching him intently. He took a deep breath, remembering his original errand. "Mrs. Carroll," he said. "You have something to say to Miss Tanton?"

Sarah's eyes followed River's. Prudence was staring at the rifle stock, her hand at her mouth. She glanced at Sarah, but her eyes went back to the rifle. "I...I...I..." she stammered.

Then her chin went up, and she squared her shoulders. "No. Not after what I just saw. She's a tramp!" She puffed herself up, her indignation giving her courage to face even River's angry glare. "Letting that man kiss her! The two of you fighting over her! I will not apologize for calling her a thief. For all we know, she planted those stolen items to let the child take the blame."

River exploded. "Not one more word!" He took a step toward Prudence, and she turned and bustled away.

River swore under his breath. He put the rifle down with exaggerated care and walked to Sarah. "I'm sorry. That's not what I intended her to say." He folded Sarah into his arms, and she buried her face in his shoulder. "Forget about that old witch. Did he hurt you, sweetheart?"

She shook her head and wrapped her arms around his waist. She tried to take slow, even breaths to calm herself. She didn't want to cry again. River's arms made her feel safe, and in a moment, she felt her control returning. He must have sensed her relax because he drew away slightly.

"You were making it hard for him," he said with a slight smile. "I'm glad you like my advances better."

"Don't compare the two," she whispered.

"You mean if I try to kiss you, you won't kick me in the shin?"

The glint in his eye was infectious. "You could try and see," she teased.

His smile broadened, and he leaned slowly toward her. When his lips were an inch from hers, he drew back. "I wouldn't ever treat you like he did, Sarah. You know that, don't you?"

Sarah had been anticipating the kiss and was startled when he spoke so seriously. Closing her eyes and leaning toward him, she whispered, "I know."

River walked into the Gaines camp early the next morning. He stood for a moment, studying the three sleeping figures, before stepping up to Bull Gaines and nudging him in the ribs with his booted toe.

Gaines came awake reaching for the pistol beside his head. River's foot was on Bull's hand before it touched the handle.

"I just came to remind you to leave the train this morning."

River bent and lifted the pistol before he removed his foot from Gaines's hand. Gaines made a show of flexing his fingers and rubbing his injured wrist. "You can't leave us unprotected. I hear Injuns pick off stragglers, and Nathan there's only a boy."

"I thought of that," River said. "That's why I'm offering Nathan and Kirby the chance to stay with the train."

Herman and Nathan had both awakened moments after Bull. Nathan was already on his feet, but

Herman was rubbing his eyes as if he couldn't understand what he was seeing.

"What about it?" River asked, turning from one to the other. "You can go with him or continue on with the train."

Nathan spoke first. "I'll go with you." He glanced at his uncle and looked away quickly.

"It seems one of those oxen ought to belong to the boy," River said. "And a third of your provisions."

Bull snorted, raising himself to a sitting position. "If that ungrateful brat leaves me, he's goin' empty-handed." Laughing, he turned to Nathan. "Ask again, Nothin'. See if he's still eager to take you if you come without supplies, you worthless little bastard."

River watched Nathan's eyes register a fear that was quickly masked. He wanted to kick Gaines in the teeth, and he was standing in a perfect position to do it. He smiled coldly down at him. "Do you enjoy cheating your brother's boy?"

"Hell!" Gaines laughed. "His ma said he was my brother's boy, but she was a whore, so who knows?"

Barely restraining himself, River pushed Gaines back to the ground with the toe of his boot. "Nathan, get what's yours together, and go to Eli's wagons." As the boy hurriedly complied, River turned to Kirby. "How about you? You coming with us?"

Herman looked from Bull to Nathan in bewilderment. Finally he said, "I reckon I should go with Bull."

"Suit yourself." River stepped back. Gaines glared at him, making no further effort to rise. Nathan was already walking away. River tossed the pistol as far as he could from Bull and turned, catching up with the boy.

Sarah made her way back to camp from her morning walk, as Eli had decided to call it. She had overslept a little, but Eli had barely started breakfast when she left. She took her time returning, wanting to savor the memories of the night before. River had taken the first watch, and, early in the morning, he had come to her wagon. He had stayed with her, loving her gently, and hadn't left her until almost dawn.

She knew there was a dreamy look on her face she ought to lose before she got too near the light of the fire. Somehow this morning, she hardly cared. River had become more likely to kiss her in front of the others, and she doubted if they fooled Eli at all. Still, it wasn't something she wanted Eli openly discussing. She could just imagine him saying something that would turn her face bright red.

As she came into camp from one direction, River and Nathan came in from the other. At the sight of the Gaines boy Sarah paused. River had effectively wiped out all thoughts of Gaines, but the boy refreshed her memory.

Nathan stopped at the edge of the camp, uncertain of his welcome. River glanced back at him as he went to greet Sarah. He gave her a very possessive kiss for Nathan's benefit as much as his own. He had a feeling the boy had a crush on his woman.

Sarah's cheeks burned when he drew away. He was ready to tease her when Eli swore. He turned with Sarah to watch the old man. Rice was crawling out from under the wagon, rubbing his eyes. He looked around at the others and kept quiet.

Eli glared at Nathan. "I see ya've come crawlin' back."

"No, sir," Nathan said.

The startled look on Eli's face made River chuckle. Eli said, "Ya left here without so much as a thank ya kindly and now—"

"Thank ya kindly," the boy interrupted. River read a faint smile in his eyes, but he still looked uncomfortable. The small bundle he had carried into camp lay at his feet, and his hands were shoved into his pockets.

"Well, what makes ya think ya can just come waltzin' back?"

This time it was River who interrupted. "I invited him." He walked to Nathan and retrieved the bundle, taking his arm to urge him forward. "Don't let Eli bother you, his bark is worse than his bite." He tossed the bundle to Rice, who caught it handily. "Stow his stuff, and show him what to do."

Rice smiled. "I'm glad you're not leaving with your uncle."

Nathan's only reply was a raised eyebrow. He glanced at Sarah before following Rice to the back of the lead wagon. The full weight of the decision he had made was settling on him. It left his knees weak and his stomach trembling. He was running away from Bull! People he didn't know and who probably didn't like him were taking him in, at least for a time.

The old man's disapproving look and harsh words made him wonder if he had jumped from the frying pan into the fire. Memories of the night Rice had found him hiding in the bushes helped him dismiss the notion.

Free! Could he really be free of Bull? The man had always hated him, enjoyed hating him. Bull would welcome a chance to get his hands on him again. *One last time,* he thought with a shiver. After this his uncle wouldn't hesitate to kill him.

Rice was explaining about the wagons, and Nathan tried to listen. He wasn't safe yet. Bull would be following behind, waiting for a chance to get him and the pretty Miss Tanton, as well. He wasn't the kind of man to give up meekly after River had taken that much from him.

He sat on the barrel where Rice directed him, aware that the other boy eyed him curiously. Eli and Miss Tanton were fixing breakfast. It smelled good, and he was always hungry. He worried this would end at any moment. Did River have any idea the danger he had put them in by defying Bull Gaines?

No, not River, he corrected himself. *I put them in danger. I shouldn't have agreed to leave.*

While Nathan agonized over his decision, Sarah watched one of the von Schiller girls come shyly toward the camp. Rice went to meet her. "How's your father this morning, Gretchen?" Rice asked.

The girl shook her head sadly. "He no like restink ven us vorkink." She looked around a moment as if searching for words. "I not vant in Laramie to stay. I vant to California go. I go!"

Rice reached out and took her hand. "Won't they need you, to earn money, I mean?"

"I askt the Villiams if I go. I eat no supplies. They buy for me no supplies. I go! I their children I . . . play . . . feed . . . ?"

"Care for?" Rice provided.

She nodded, smiling shyly. "They say yes."

Rice squeezed her hand, and they looked at each other for a long moment.

Eli interrupted the young people. "Every time I turn around there's another young 'un showin' up. Am I expected to feed her, too?" Sarah scowled at the old man, but he didn't notice.

"No, sir," answered Rice without taking his eyes off Gretchen. Suddenly, the girl turned and ran for her wagon.

"Might as well come eat, then," Eli said.

"Yes, sir." Rice, grinning, took his plate to the fire.

Nathan hesitated before following his example. He held the plate as if he expected to be hit with the spoon.

It touched off a stream of Eli's mutterings. Nathan took his full plate and returned to his seat, watching the old man warily. After the meal was over, he showed obvious relief when he followed Rice to bring in the teams.

When the train left camp that morning, Sarah sat beside Rice, and Nathan walked beside the wagon, having turned down their offer of a ride. He was used to walking, he said. He didn't tell them he felt safer on the ground, where he could keep track of his uncle. As the train uncoiled, Nathan could see the wagons pull around his uncle's camp. The two men watched the lead wagons, and Nathan felt his skin crawl.

Bull told Herman to take his time loading the supplies. "We got to wait that half hour, anyhow. Might as well take it easy."

Herman nodded.

"They're stealing our boy," Bull said after a few minutes. "I don't think we ought to let them do that, do you?"

Herman shook his head.

"And that little gal, they stole her, too."

Herman looked surprised. "They did?"

Bull sat down beside the fire. "They didn't never give her a chance to make up her own mind about me. That River'd come along and chase me away every time we got friendly. She would be my woman, but for that. Don't that sound like stealin'?''

Bull liked to watch Herman's face when he tried to figure something out. He twisted his brows together as if he were trying to squeeze information from his brain. The most convoluted logic would convince him.

''We ought to get to take the woman in exchange for the boy,'' he said when he thought Herman was ready. ''We'll follow along behind, and when we see our chance, we'll go in and . . . rescue her.''

Herman nodded. ''How we gonna do that?''

''We'll find a way,'' Bull said. Already a plan was starting to form. He would like to teach that boy a lesson. Had he forgotten how they were each going to claim a piece of land? The boy owed him that much. He had fed and sheltered him for three years. Did the whelp think he had done it because he wanted to? Hell, he was glad to be rid of the little bastard but for the land.

And the woman, how dare she turn him down! Acting like she was better than him! She would be his, and he would make her sorry she had caused him so much trouble. When he was done, she would do whatever he said. It would be nice having a woman to cook and clean and warm his bed.

If he planned it right, he would take what should have been his and get his revenge on River, as well. He was absolutely certain River would follow.

He smiled to himself and saw Herman smile back. "The first thing we need to do is trade our oxen for some horses. There's a train not far behind us."

Herman looked over his shoulder, expecting to see the train coming up on them. It made Bull laugh. "You know, Herman," he said slowly, "I might not be able to get both of them out of there. Which one should we leave behind, do you think?"

Herman answered, "Leave the woman. I'm gonna miss Nathan."

Bull laughed even harder. In a moment Herman laughed, too.

River had promised to join Sarah once he had checked the night guards and the others had fallen asleep. While she waited, she sat near the back of the wagon, the walnut jewelry box on her lap, and listened to the night sounds. They were familiar to her now, the nocturnal insects and birds, the soft sounds of the oxen as they settled in to rest, the occasional howl of a coyote. Through all the quiet noises she listened for the sound of River's footsteps. When he came, she would go with him to whatever spot he had chosen and love him.

Her body tingled in anticipation even as her heart seemed to crumble a little. She closed her eyes and sighed. River's treatment of her could only be described as tender. He had even told her he loved her, and part of her was ready to believe him. She wanted desperately to think they had a chance.

Recently it had occurred to her that she might become pregnant. At first she had dismissed the idea, not wanting to think about it and, she knew, not wanting to deny herself her lover's touch. But Martha's miscarriage had reminded her that a baby was a possibility.

Martha's grief had stirred something else, as well—her own maternal instinct. What if River left her with a baby? Raising a child alone would be far harder than anything she had ever done, but wouldn't having River's baby to love be worth the hardship?

Still, she wanted to believe there was a chance for them to be together. He had said he loved her, she reminded herself firmly. Tonight she would swallow her pride and show him the contents of the envelope she kept in the bottom of the box. Her hands trembled as she ran her fingers over the carved surface. What if all he felt was guilt or pity?

She set the box aside as her determination weakened. If he loved her, wouldn't he know she was innocent? Wouldn't he trust her without proof?

The sound of a twig snapping under a boot brought her out of her reverie. Uncertain, she climbed out of the wagon, snatching up the box at the last moment. She found herself caught by hard rough arms. A hand was clamped firmly over her mouth, and Bull's voice whispered, "Hurry up, Herman. Get her hands tied, like I said."

Sarah fought down the panic that rose like bile to her throat. Bull Gaines held her locked against him! Her struggles only made him hold her tighter. She couldn't scream; she could barely breathe.

The box tumbled to the ground forgotten as Herman forced her arms behind her back. Her wrists were tied quickly but clumsily, and she felt a spark of hope. She could pull them loose when the time was right! Not yet, though. Now they would only be tied again.

"Hold her, now," Bull whispered, and a different set of hands clasped her shoulders. She tried to kick at Bull, but he rewarded her with a kick of his own, sending pain up her leg and making her knees buckle.

Bull removed his hand from her mouth and shoved a handkerchief inside in the same movement. "You got a hold of her, Herman?" The grip on Sarah's shoulders tightened painfully. "Get her to the horses and wait there."

Sarah felt herself being led away and decided this was her chance. She twisted her wrists, but they were tied more tightly than they had seemed. Surely a little noise would wake Eli. She tried to scream around the handkerchief and gagged. They were getting farther from Eli with every step. She tried again to pull away from Herman, hoping to slow him down, but Herman simply lifted her off her feet when she stumbled.

Sarah had no idea how far Herman dragged her before they came to a ravine. Herman helped her down the crumbling slope to where three horses waited. Sarah knew Bull only had one horse and wondered fleetingly if the other two were stolen.

"We're supposed to wait here for Bull," Herman offered politely. "Then you're gonna ride with Nathan."

Sarah shook her head and tried to make a sound, hoping Herman would remove the handkerchief. She continued to twist at the ropes, knowing her best hope of escape was before Bull joined them.

Herman seemed surprised that she would disagree with him. "You don't need to worry, little gal. Bull's just rescuin' you from River."

With one quick jerk, Sarah pulled her arm from his grip, and the ropes slipped off her wrists. She reached up to remove the handkerchief, barely catching hold of it when Herman's fist connected with her jaw. She saw dancing stars and hit the ground before she knew she was falling. She was conscious of pain and disappointment before she passed out.

Nathan wasn't breathing. He tried to force himself to take a slow, careful breath and trembled inside.

He had spread his blanket near Sarah's wagon, imagining he could protect her if he was nearby. He cursed himself. When had he ever protected anybody? Here he had lain while Bull and Herman grabbed Sarah, too paralyzed with fear to act even as Herman led the poor woman away.

Now Bull was in the wagon taking God alone knew what, and he was still unable to move. This was his chance, he told himself. He should wake Eli and Rice. Together they could stop Bull. He finally forced leaden muscles to work and fought his way out of his blankets. *Eli! Eli!* his mind screamed, but his choked breath was all that came past his throat.

He found himself huddled in a ball under a nearby wagon. Instead of heading for Eli, he had crawled to the darkest shadow away from Bull. God help him, he wanted to save Sarah, but something in his mind believed Bull was unstoppable.

From his hiding place, he watched Bull climb out of the wagon and bend to lift something from the ground. He felt a tear slip from the corner of his eye. Even now there was time to stop him! He couldn't make his body work, he couldn't even breathe properly.

He watched Bull approach his discarded blankets. He thought he saw the glint of a knife in his uncle's hand and felt his body quake. Bull nudged the bedroll with his toe, and Nathan imagined he heard him swear. The man looked hastily around, and Nathan was certain he had seen him. But the shadows were deep, and Bull turned away. Without wasting any more time, Bull left the way Herman had gone.

Nathan felt a flood of relief that was quickly replaced by shame. *Move!* his mind screamed. *It's not too late to stop them!* But all he could do was tremble while tears trickled down his face.

He had no idea how much time passed, but he was beginning to regain control of his limbs when he heard stealthy footsteps. He thought Bull was returning and his insides turned to ice.

"Sarah?" came a whispered voice.

River! It was River, not Bull! Nathan's body shuddered as he scrambled from his hiding place. "River!" he croaked.

River heard the strange sound behind him. He turned to find Nathan stumbling toward him. His first thought was the boy had been lying awake, waiting to defend Sarah's honor. He looked around quickly to see if he had awakened the others.

Nathan was gasping for breath. "They took Sarah," he managed to say at last. "Took her away."

River grabbed a handful of the boy's shirt. "What are you talking about? Who took Sarah?"

Nathan struggled for control. *He'll hate me for not saving her,* he thought. *I deserve whatever he does to me.* "Bull," he whispered. "Bull took her."

"When?" River demanded.

Nathan shook his head. "I don't know. I wanted to stop him. I couldn't." He fought back a sob and was only partially successful. "I wanted to..." He wished with all his heart he had confronted Bull, even if it had meant his life. Death would be better than this horrible regret.

It was dark now, and River could barely make out the boy's face. He wouldn't find any tracks until the moon came up. He heard a string of oaths from under the next wagon and knew they had awakened Eli. He felt Nathan stiffen. The boy was terrified.

So am I, he thought. *Sarah's in the hands of Bull Gaines.*

Chapter Fifteen

It was the shaking that roused Sarah, a steady shaking that made her head vibrate with pain. She became conscious of the movement of a horse beneath her and realized she was lying across a saddle. Ropes tied her wrists and rubbed the bare flesh of her legs below her tangled skirt. She stifled a groan as memory of Bull and Herman brought her fully awake.

Sarah remained limp as she tried to understand what was happening. They were traveling fast and, as near as she could tell from the horse's gait, over rougher terrain than the wagons had traveled.

Herman spoke in front of her. "Why didn't you bring Nathan?"

"I told you to forget about Nathan. There weren't no time to go lookin' for him," Bull answered.

Herman mumbled, "Well, I miss Nathan."

Bull didn't respond, and Sarah stole a glance at him. They hadn't noticed yet that she was awake, and she hoped they would ignore her long enough for her to see a way of escape. Her hope died when the horse's plunge up a slope elicited a groan she couldn't stifle.

"Decided to wake up, did you?" Bull pulled his horse to a walk, and Sarah's mount followed suit.

At first, Sarah was grateful the jarring had stopped. She raised her head to look around and saw Bull leering at her. With a show of courage she didn't feel, she demanded, "Where are you taking me?"

"Just on here a ways," Bull replied casually. "Country gets a little rough, but I hear tell it's awful pretty. Too bad you can't see none of it."

"River will come after us."

Bull laughed at that and in a moment Herman joined in. "That's what I'm counting on, little Miss Prim-and-Proper. But the nice thing about rough country is the places you can hide."

"He'll find you." Sarah heard the confidence go out of her voice. There would indeed be plenty of places to hide.

Bull laughed again. "Now, missy, I didn't say I didn't want him to find us, did I?"

Sarah felt a shiver along her spine. Fear for herself was replaced with fear for River. Bull gave her only a moment to think before he kicked his horse into the bone-jarring pace he had set before.

River halted the pinto by a little trickle of water, and Milburn's black came alongside to drink, as well.

He would let them drink and rest for a moment, then trade mounts and press on. The tracks were easy to follow, even by moonlight. Either Bull was a fool, or he wanted to be followed.

River dismounted and stretched, knowing he should rest if he hoped to stay alert enough to avoid a trap. At the same time, he felt a need to follow the trail as long as he could. If he lost the tracks, he would rest until daylight. He knew sleep would be impossible in any case.

He unfastened the lead rope from the black's halter and fastened it to the pinto's before checking the cinches on both saddles. He knew the gear was tied securely, but he checked it just the same. Eli had packed enough food for a week, it seemed, and had evenly divided it between the two horses. River prayed it wouldn't take anything like a week to get his Sarah back.

Just the same, he had instructed Eli to take the train to Fort Laramie. After a few days' rest, he was to continue on. He hoped he would be able to catch up before they got to Fort Hall, but if not, Eli was to leave word there of what he planned to do. The train had to get over the mountains before winter, and they couldn't afford to wait for him.

He hadn't told Eli the rest of his plans. If he didn't bring Sarah back with him, he would no longer have the heart for them, anyway.

He rubbed a hand across his forehead as if to wipe away the thought. It produced the same sinking

feeling inside he had had when he checked the wagon
for Sarah. Until he had entered the empty wagon, he
hadn't been able to bring himself to believe Nathan.

River swung onto the back of the black and led the
pinto away from the stream. If he let his mind dwell
on Sarah, he would go crazy with worry.

The tracks River followed led south and east toward Wildcat Ridge. He wondered if Bull had any
idea where he was going. It wouldn't matter. River
would find him.

Less than an hour later, River was having trouble
seeing. At first he thought it was fatigue but soon
realized the soft moonlight was becoming unreliable
as more and more clouds drifted across the sky.
Losing the tracks now would mean wasted time
backtracking in the morning. Reluctantly, River
looked for a place to camp.

Sarah couldn't be sure, but she guessed it was a
couple of hours until dawn. Bull had called a halt
and, while Herman held the horse, untied the ropes
that bound her to the saddle. He took the opportunity to run his hand far up her thigh. Sarah could
manage barely a whimper in protest. Bull laughed
and dragged her from the saddle. He let her slide
down the length of his body, her skirt bunching at
her waist and her bare legs brushing the fabric of his
trousers until her feet touched the ground.

Sarah's stomach heaved, and she instinctively
fought it down. She wished she hadn't. She wanted

nothing more than to turn and throw up in the man's face. The fact that he would retaliate with violence entered her mind. Choosing a different tact, she went limp. Far better for him to think she was completely exhausted. It wasn't far from the truth, anyway. Perhaps he wouldn't bother to tie her if he thought she was too weak to escape.

Bull lifted her, and she resisted the temptation to struggle. Sarah pretended to be asleep as he laid her on the ground and knelt above her. He ran a rough finger down her cheek, and she flinched away.

She heard Bull laugh as his hand settled on her mouth, but she didn't open her eyes. "I'll wait till you're feeling a little stronger, missy," he said in a hoarse whisper. "But I want to give you something to think about tonight." His hand moved downward to caress her breast, massaging it gently.

Sarah was revolted by the intimate touch but tried not to pull away from him. She prayed he would stop if he thought she was beyond caring. His fingers found the tip of her breast, and he pinched it hard, causing her to cry out.

"Bull?" Herman's voice came from the darkness.

Bull leaned close to Sarah's ear. "Don't be putting on airs no more, missy. Your River ain't here to push me around. I'm the boss now, and you'll do as I say."

"Bull?" Herman persisted. "Where should I tie the horses? I can't see nothin' in the dark."

"You just think on it tonight," he murmured, giving her breast another squeeze. A sob escaped Sarah's throat, and Bull chuckled.

She felt him leave her side and fought back the tears. *Don't panic,* she told herself. *Wait for your chance and escape!* But part of her mind was already withdrawing. She felt her own sobs with almost a detached interest.

Bull returned with the rope and bound her hands and feet. "You get some sleep, missy," he said in an imitation of friendliness. "We'll talk more in the morning." He emphasized "talk" with another squeeze to her sore breast.

Sarah rolled to her side and brought her knees up to her chest. It seemed to still the shuddering. In the distance she could hear Herman and Bull talking. Sometime later Herman brought a blanket and spread it over her. They didn't light a fire, and Sarah's shudders turned to shivers.

Breathing in the cold air seemed to clear her mind, though. She realized River would have missed her immediately and would be following close behind. Bull seemed to think she wouldn't be missed until morning. She needed to let him continue to believe that. If she could stall them in the morning, River would catch up before they had a chance to lay their trap.

Unfortunately, she could think of only one way to stall. As revolting as it seemed, she would have to pretend to warm up to Bull. Perhaps with Herman around, Bull wouldn't do anything. She didn't really believe that. Bull would probably simply tell Herman to go wait elsewhere. The thought brought on the return of the sobbing. She tried to control it by relaxing and found herself drifting off to sleep.

She shook herself, wanting to think of another plan. The way she was tied allowed her hands to reach the ropes at her ankles. She had no hope of getting away from Bull, but if she could sneak out of camp and hide, the time it took them to find her might be the time River needed. She cringed when she thought of what Bull would do when he found her. It was still better than her first plan.

She tried to listen to the men's breathing to determine if they were asleep and had to shake herself awake again. Perhaps it would be better to wait until closer to morning. She needed rest to regain her strength. But she also needed to stay awake, she told herself. In the end her mind lost, and her tired body won.

She awoke to shaking again. For a moment she thought she had fallen asleep on the horse and dreamed that Bull had made camp. Herman's voice brought her fully awake. "Bull said I was to wake you. He wants you should fix us some breakfast." He shook her again for good measure.

Sarah rolled over and groaned. Her body was sore from last night's punishing ride and cramped from sleeping on the cold ground, restricted by the ropes. Blinking up at Herman, she realized it was almost fully light. Her plan came back to her like a splash of cold water. Her chance to hide was gone, but fixing breakfast might work to gain time for River.

She sat up slowly, and Herman moved back as if he were a little afraid of her. She glared at him a moment before offering her wrists for him to untie.

"Bull says I'm to untie your feet so's you can walk, but you can cook with your hands tied, he says."

Sarah didn't respond. Herman seemed to be waiting for something, and Sarah was glad to let him wait. She looked around the camp. A fire had been started, but Bull was nowhere in sight.

Herman cleared his throat. She took her time turning to him. He reached toward her twice and drew away. "I'm gonna untie your feet now," he said.

She glanced down to where the blanket covered the lower half of her body. He was too shy to remove the blanket, and there was nothing to be gained by making it easy for him. She had once felt sorry for the poor simpleton, but he had made the choice to follow Bull. She had to defeat him if she was going to save River. She simply glared at him and let him squirm.

Herman swallowed hard and knelt beside her. He gingerly lifted the tip of the blanket that trailed on the ground. He brought it up slowly until he could see her shoes and sighed with relief. He laid the blanket across her legs and grinned at her. "I'm gonna untie your feet now," he repeated.

Bull's nasty laugh brought their attention to the other side of the camp. "Quit drooling on the woman, Herman, and get the job done."

Herman grinned sheepishly at Sarah and began to work on the knots. Bull's presence in the camp made her doubt all her plans. She could feel his eyes on her and remembered his crude touch. Fear washed over her, and she wasn't sure she would have the courage to get to her feet, let alone try to stall them.

Herman stepped back. "You can get up now." His head bobbed up and down as encouragement.

River, she told herself. *I have to do it for River.* She came slowly to her feet. Her legs were sore, and she didn't fake the stumble that brought Herman's hand out to steady her.

"You all right, Miss Sarah?" he asked with real concern.

Bull laughed again. As he came forward, Herman backed away. "She's just fine," he said, uncoiling a length of rope. "See, missy, I told Herman he could have you after me." He ran a finger down her bruised cheek, and she drew away. "But he's gonna have to watch to see how it's done."

Panic overruled rational thought, and Sarah turned to run. Bull caught her easily, laughing as he slipped the rope around her neck. "Did you think I'd let you get away? I want my breakfast, and I want my fun." He led her by the arm toward the fire. "And then I want to kill River. I reckon he's been on our trail about an hour by now."

He left her at the fire and, holding the end of the rope, went to sit on his blanket. He gave the rope a little shake, and Sarah's bound hands went to her neck. "Everything you'll need is right there. We got a hankerin' for some female cookin'. Haven't we, Herman?"

Sarah didn't turn to see Herman's reaction. Her eyes went to the fire and supplies. Part of her wanted to crumple to the ground and give in to the sobs that constricted her throat. In prison she had learned to do what needed to be done while she kept her feelings inside where they were safe. She could do that again. She knelt and shook the coffeepot. It was full of water. As she fumbled through the bag of supplies to find the coffee, Bull gave the rope another shake.

She did her best to ignore it, but her hands trembled as she put the coffee into the grinder, spilling some of the beans on the ground. She was rewarded with another tug on the rope.

"Watch it there," Bull warned. "See, Herman, I told you she could do it. You can tie a dog to a stake, and he'll still keep the coons outta the corn." They laughed. Bull howled like a dog and laughed even harder.

As Sarah ground the roasted beans, she tried to ignore Bull. There had to be a weapon. She reached for the coffeepot and her eyes settled on the fire. She added the grounds to the hot water with shaking hands, while she studied the individual sticks that protruded from the blaze.

''Let's see what the gal keeps in this cute little box here,'' she heard Bull say. She glanced at him to see him open her carved walnut box. The fury at seeing him touch her most precious possession put an end to thoughtful consideration. With a savage cry, she grabbed up a burning branch and hurled it at Bull.

Bull scrambled to his feet, screaming obscenities as he brushed at his burning clothes. Sarah didn't take time to retrieve the box. She slipped the rope from her neck and headed for the horses as Bull, in a panic, ran blindly around the camp.

Sarah had almost reached the trees when an Indian, moving like a ghost, appeared in front of her. She froze. Unlike the Pawnee she had seen earlier, this man wore a blue army coat and buckskin leggings. His hair hung in two long braids, tied with strips of leather. He stared straight at her, and she wondered why he wasn't afraid of Gaines and Herman. Oh God! If Gaines was on fire, she had only Herman to protect her from this Indian.

At that moment, Gaines's screams ended abruptly. Sarah felt the hairs on her neck prickle. She turned slowly to discover Indians all around. Her initial horror was slowly replaced with an odd feeling of relief. *If they kill us, River will be safe.*

Bull's pistol was lying on the ground beside Herman. He seemed to take a second to consider before lifting it and firing. His hands were shaking, and the shot went wild. Sarah jumped at the sound, thinking too late that she should have used that second to run. She started to back away from the blue-coated Indian but a strange vibrating sound brought her around in time to see Herman topple backward, an arrow in his throat. He made strange gurgling sounds that were so horrible Sarah found herself sinking to the ground.

River judged he had been riding for two and a half, maybe three hours since dawn when the pinto pricked his ears. He pulled to a stop, and the black danced sideways. Sitting still, he listened to the sounds around him. After a moment, birds that had been startled by his presence resumed their conversations. But something was bothering the horses.

He swung from the pinto's back, rifle in hand. He looked ahead where the trail would lead him into a thin stand of pine and tried to guess where Bull might be waiting.

It seemed odd. Ahead a few miles the country turned to rocks and cliffs that would surely suit Bull's purposes better than this. But perhaps Bull didn't know that, or was counting on catching River before he became wary of an ambush.

He tied the horses and walked cautiously into the trees, keeping himself far to the right of the trail. Ten yards into the trees he stopped short. In front of him was a perfect moccasin print.

Fear for Sarah seemed to stop his heart. What dangers had Bull put her in? He cursed himself for not leaving Bull and his companions with their broken wagon on the riverbank.

He moved in the direction the Indian had gone, though he didn't see a second track. Within minutes he found the camp... and the bodies.

"Sarah," he breathed, his grip tightening on the rifle. But in an instant, he knew she wasn't there. He recognized the two bodies as Bull and Herman. He walked swiftly around the perimeter of the camp, checking for signs of a flight into the trees, terrified that he would find her body away from the others.

He found a spot where horses had been tied and where they had been led away, the same horses whose trail he had been following. He found several places where moccasined feet had stepped into the clearing but only one where they had left. The Indians had taken Sarah!

He went back to the bodies. Both men were missing their boots. Herman's coat and pants had been taken, as well. Herman had an arrow in his throat, and Bull had been cut several times, and his clothes were burned. Near Herman's hand was a pistol. River lifted it and could smell the powder. There had been no time to reload for a second shot.

The campfire had burned itself out. Stirring the ashes, River found a few sparks; the fire hadn't been out for long. The metal blades and gears of a coffee grinder turned up in the ashes. A few feet away lay a smashed wooden box.

Curious how only part of the coffee grinder would have ended up in the fire, River lifted a piece of the box. Turning it in his hand, he saw the corner of a carved leaf. This was no coffee grinder; this was Sarah's jewelry box. He knelt and lifted the rest carefully. Pieces fell away as he turned it over. A dirty white envelope was wedged between the splintered sides. He stuck the envelope in his pocket before dropping the pieces to the ground.

He came swiftly to his feet. There was nothing else to be learned here. He knew their direction, and he knew he had no choice but to follow. There was no time to bury the bodies, he decided quickly. Sarah was more important.

He walked quickly to his horses, mounted the black and rode through the camp, past the bodies and onto the trail the Indians had followed. The sight of the two dead men bothered him very little, but the memory of Sarah's jewelry box, smashed to pieces, haunted him.

River lay on his stomach in the tall grass and watched the Sioux village. An hour ago, when he had found where the braves had stopped to prepare for their entrance into the village, he had left his horses and crawled to the top of a nearby rise. He was too far away to see much, but he couldn't get closer without being seen.

For three days he had followed the trail. He was certain the Sioux hadn't been aware they were followed or they would have hidden their trail more carefully. Among the tracks he had often seen the print of Sarah's small shoes. That sign of her continued health had always been enough to restore his hope and energy.

He slid back down the rise to the horses. He didn't have many choices. Gathering up the lead rope, he swung onto the black. The pinto, he reasoned, would be more likely to behave, but he would need to ride the black to control him. In a moment, he was on the trail again. The ground was torn by horses' hooves, probably from the braves' last headlong dash into the village.

He kept the horses to a steady walk. Riding in would be relatively easy; riding out would be difficult. Sudden activity told him the alarm had been sounded, and women and children had been sent to safety.

All Indians, especially Sioux, admire bravery, he reminded himself. "Perhaps they'll sing songs about me," he mumbled. "After they kill me."

Dead, he would do Sarah no good, but he could find no other choice. If he went to the army for help, this village would move, or Sarah would be traded long before he got back. No, he had to handle this alone, as best he could.

Close to the village, four young men on horseback came at a run to meet him. They screamed at him, controlling their mounts with their knees as they shook their feathered lances. They circled him twice, and River nodded his approval, keeping a tight rein on the black as he kept his horses moving at a steady pace. The riders took up positions around him and escorted him into the village.

River dismounted and raised his hand as a sign of peace to the three elders who waited to meet him. "I am Saves Child from River," he said in broken Sioux and sign language. "I come as a friend of the People."

The elders watched him for a long moment. River stood relaxed as if he were merely visiting some neighbors. He was aware that several braves were looking over the horses and the supplies on their backs. Finally, one elder spoke in English. "Deer Tracks has heard of Saves Child from River."

The man didn't seem inclined to say anything more. River hoped his smile looked friendly; any sign of impatience would be understood as nervousness.

Deer Tracks spoke again. "What has brought you here?"

"I'm looking for a woman, one of my people." River spoke in English but used sign language, as well, not wanting anyone to feel left out of the conversation. "One of my people," he repeated in Sioux.

"She is here."

River smiled. "Good. I thank my friends for taking care of her."

"I heard the story of the girl child who fell into the river and the bluecoat who pulled her out and pushed life back into her body. We will give you the life of this woman as payment for the child."

A brave wearing a cavalry coat stepped forward. River couldn't help but wonder about the coat's previous owner. Of course, many a mountain man wore buckskins he had taken off a dead Indian.

The brave spoke quickly in his own tongue, obviously objecting to Deer Tracks' words.

Deer Tracks considered for a moment, then spoke to River. "Running Elk says the woman belongs to him. He saved her from bad men, and now she is his."

River watched Deer Tracks and Running Elk for a moment, keeping his poker face firmly in place. Deer Tracks had shared this news without any comment of his own, and River guessed that no decision had been made yet. He had a feeling the outcome hinged on what he did.

"I agree with Running Elk," he said, directing his signs to the brave. "They were bad men. I thank him for taking her from them." He paused, turning his attention to Deer Tracks. "Sarah is already my woman, my wife."

Running Elk turned to him, anger in his eyes. "You no protect her," he declared in English. "Running Elk protect her!" He folded his arms and stuck out his chin. In his mind, the matter was settled.

River tried to keep his expression bland while he considered his next move. The elder could advise the villagers, but his word wasn't the law. River would have to deal with the young brave.

He had opened his mouth to speak when a commotion at the far end of the village attracted everyone's attention. River moved forward to see and found his arms caught on either side by strong men. Running Elk headed into the middle of the activity while the elders looked on with mild curiosity.

When the warriors brought Sarah into camp, she was so tired she barely knew what was happening. They had marched for days, eating only at dawn and dusk, and sleeping but a few hours. Before they reached the village, they had stopped and painted themselves and the horses. Sarah had been afraid they were about to raid another tribe, and she would find herself in the middle of a battle. Instead, they had made a noisy entrance into their own village, where they were greeted as heroes.

The warrior with the blue coat seemed to claim her. He had kept a close eye on her and had been the one to give her food. She was uncertain if he was the leader. He may have been in charge of her because he spoke a little English. Running Elk, he called himself.

At the village, he took her to a hide-covered structure and turned her over to two women. They were dressed in long buckskin skirts and wore braids just like the men. They pointed out a pile of furs, indicating that she should sleep there. The place smelled of smoke and animal hides, but Sarah was too tired to care. After the last few days, she probably smelled even worse.

She didn't know how long she slept before the women woke her. They had some kind of mush they wanted her to eat. She was hungry and took it eagerly. With the rest and the food, the numbness that had settled on her brain began to lift. Bull and Herman were dead, but she was in as much trouble as ever—and so was River. He would follow. When he did, he would face an entire tribe instead of two men.

She discovered her hands were no longer tied and rubbed the rope burns as she looked around, trying to think of a way to escape. Could she possibly run away and stop River before he got to the Indian camp?

The older of the women was chattering at her, and Sarah looked up in mild surprise. The woman held a small pottery jar out to her as she knelt on the hides. It smelled foul, and Sarah drew away. The women laughed.

As Sarah eyed the jar suspiciously, the woman pretended to dip her fingers into it, rubbed them on her own wrist, then held the jar out to Sarah again. Understanding, Sarah took it and rubbed the greasy unguent on the scraped skin.

As she started to hand the jar back, the grinning woman touched the neckline of Sarah's dress. Sarah

drew away, but the woman persisted, touching a
tender spot. She remembered then the rope Bull had
put around her neck days ago. Most of the soreness
had disappeared. She took the woman's advice anyway and smeared the salve on her neck, as well.

"Thank you," she said, handing the jar back to
the woman.

"Thank you," the woman repeated, haltingly.
Both women giggled. Instead of taking the jar, the
woman touched two fingers to her own nose and
cheeks, indicating that Sarah should put the salve on
her sunburned face. Sarah wrinkled her nose and
shook her head, pushing the jar into the woman's
hands.

A distant shout caught the younger woman's attention. She lifted the flap that covered the doorway
and went outside. Soon she was back, chattering excitedly to her companion. They both eyed Sarah and
fell silent, listening. After a moment, the young
woman went to look outside again but was pulled
back by the other.

The camp became unnaturally quiet, and the
women waited expectantly. There was a last burst of
noise, the yells of braves similar to those at her own
arrival, then silence. Sarah tried to imagine what
might be happening. If another tribe was attacking,
surely they would do more than hide in their tents. If
more warriors were returning, why weren't these
women greeting them?

Suddenly Sarah knew. River had come! She was on her feet and out of the lodge before the women could stop her. She saw a group of men across the village and ran toward them. She heard shouts behind her, and Indians were running from all directions. Slipping by one after another, she ran across the village. She caught a glimpse of River, captured securely between two warriors.

"River!" The scream escaped from her burning throat.

She ran headlong into Running Elk. He grabbed her around the waist, lifting her with one arm. Sarah thought she was going to be returned to his lodge, and she kicked furiously, trying to break his hold. He set her down in front of him, her back pinned against his chest by a hand on each arm. She swung her head to get her tangled hair out of her face and found herself standing only a few feet from River.

She stopped struggling to stare at the face she had thought she might never see again. "River," she whispered. His arms were gripped by two fearful-looking warriors, but his face was composed. His eyes seemed to reach out to her, and she knew he wanted to hold her as much as she wanted to run to him. He nodded slightly, as if to reassure her.

"My woman!" announced the man who held her.

Sarah resumed her struggles immediately, trying to bang her head against the hard chest behind her.

"Calm down, Sarah!"

"I'm not your woman!" she growled through gritted teeth. Her efforts hurt her own arms more than her captor.

"Calm down, Sarah!"

This time River's words penetrated the panic. She went limp, her head hanging as she gasped for breath.

With a wave from Deer Tracks, the warriors that held River stepped away. Running Elk's grip didn't loosen, however. Sarah watched River, glad the Indians seemed to trust him but still frightened for him.

Deer Tracks spoke. "Prairie Fire thinks she is woman to Saves Child from River."

"No!" Running Elk responded. He talked emphatically in his own tongue.

Deer Tracks nodded and turned to River. "Running Elk says she belongs to him now. He does not choose to return her. You are free to leave."

River smiled at Running Elk, intentionally avoiding Sarah's eyes. There was no way to make her understand. He spoke slowly, choosing his words carefully. "I can understand Running Elk's claim. It is true, as he said, that I did not protect her. I know a Sioux will not take a woman that belongs to another Sioux brave. I am not Sioux by blood but some of your people have called me brother. And remember, Prairie Fire did not leave me by her own choosing."

Sarah saw the flicker of amusement in River's eyes as he used the name Running Elk had given her. She felt a surge of anger; there was nothing funny about their situation. Judging by the grip Running Elk kept on her arms, River's words were having very little effect on him.

River took a casual step toward Sarah and Running Elk before he continued. "I am willing to trade," he said. "A horse for the woman."

River saw Running Elk look past him at the horses. He thought he saw a glint of interest in the dark eyes, but the resolve quickly returned. He would have to take another tack.

"Perhaps you would like to prove that you can protect her better than I can. I will fight you for her." He heard Sarah gasp, but his eyes remained locked with the young man's. He watched him slowly nod.

Sarah found the hands gradually releasing her. The instant she was free she propelled herself toward River. He wrapped his arms around her and held her as tightly as he dared. She was trembling, and he wanted nothing more than to comfort her and promise that she was safe. But she wasn't. Not yet.

As gently as he could, he drew her away. "I love you, Sarah," he whispered.

She raised her eyes to meet his and held them there. "I love you, River," she choked. She could read a silent plea to trust him, and she wanted to be strong for him. But wouldn't it be better for him to ride away and leave her here than for him to *die* and leave her here?

"No," she murmured. Taking a deep breath, she spoke more forcefully. "No. You won't fight for me. I'll stay. I want to stay." Tears betrayed her at the last, and she brushed them away, the smell of the salve making her eyes water even more.

River removed his jacket, smiling gently at Sarah as he handed it to her. "No one believes you, sweetheart. And you could show a little more confidence in my ability to fight."

Frustration completely overruled caution. She threw the jacket on the ground. "This is stupid! I won't let you two fight over me! Don't I get any say in this at all?" She stomped her foot and turned to Running Elk, fear nourishing her fury. "You! You saved my life, and I'm grateful, but that doesn't mean I belong to you!"

She swung back to face River. "How dare you try to trade for me!"

River's eyes took in the men's reactions to her outburst. Deer Tracks and the other elders watched with amused interest. Running Elk looked completely stunned.

Aware that it would do nothing to cool Sarah's anger, River grinned at his adversary. "You're the one who named her Prairie Fire. Would you care to reconsider my offer?"

He watched the young man struggle for a second before staring at him with his former determination.

River slowly turned toward his horses and then leveled his gaze on the warrior again.

Running Elk shook his head. "We fight. You die. I get woman and both horses."

Chapter Sixteen

Sarah stood between the two women, clutching River's jacket to her heart. The fight hadn't taken place immediately as she had assumed. It seemed it was to be the day's entertainment. A place was chosen, and everyone came to watch the sport. *Some sport,* Sarah thought in horror. *One of these two men will die.* She was praying with all her heart that it wouldn't be River.

She looked around at the circle of eager faces and shuddered. If River killed the young warrior, would he have to fight the rest in order to leave? She searched her mind for some way to stop the fight, but she had already tried. No one, not even River, had paid much attention to her.

Finally River and Running Elk stepped forward. Running Elk had removed his coat, as well, leaving his bronze chest bare. River rolled up the sleeves of his shirt, circling away from Running Elk until he was ready. He pulled the bone-handled knife from its sheath at his thigh and advanced on the Indian.

Tears clouded Sarah's vision as she watched them circle each other. Sunlight glinted off Running Elk's blade as it flashed dangerously close to River's chest. She muffled a scream in the jacket, afraid any distraction could get her lover killed. The crowd around her had no such concern and yelled encouragement to their favorite.

River's knife slashed toward the warrior in the same manner, then they circled again. Sarah buried her face in the jacket for a moment, but she had to know what was happening. She tried to blink away the tears.

River watched his opponent spring to avoid his knife. They were still measuring each other, testing the other's reflexes. In weight and strength they were evenly matched; it was speed and skill that would determine the outcome.

River didn't look at the crowd; he didn't dare think of Sarah. Without warning he lunged forward, catching Running Elk's knife hand in his left and thrusting with his right. Running Elk caught his hand and they struggled, each trying to draw first blood with one hand while keeping the opponent's knife away with the other.

River twisted closer, bringing his knee up hard against the Sioux's right elbow, and the knife fell. As he brought his leg down, he hooked it around the warrior's knee and pulled him off-balance. They fell to the ground, Running Elk still keeping River's knife away.

Running Elk brought his knees up and planted his feet in River's stomach. River was thrown backward, and a whoop went up from the crowd. While River fell back against spectators who thrust him forward, Running Elk scrambled for the knife.

Again they circled. River moved in closer and tossed his knife to his left hand. While the Indian's eyes followed the blade, River surprised him with a hard blow, low in his left side.

Running Elk staggered but recovered quickly. Angry now, he lunged. River sidestepped out of harm's way. Running Elk turned and lunged again. This time, River caught his right hand and twisted. The knife fell, and River kicked it away.

Running Elk broke free and watched him warily. River grinned and threw his own knife after the Indian's. He read surprise but no pleasure in the other's face; Running Elk wasn't happy about the prospect of a fist fight. *Good!* he thought. *Let's do this on my terms now.*

River moved in, delivering several hard blows. Running Elk got in several hits himself. River knew he was trying to work his way toward the edge of the crowd where the knives lay. River hooked his leg around Running Elk's again and tried to knock him off-balance. It didn't work a second time; Running Elk twisted away and tried to edge around River, glancing at the knives.

River saw his eyes leave him for an instant and feinted with his right, then followed hard and fast with a left-handed blow to the man's face. Running Elk fell backward, and River was on him, pinning his hands to the ground. While Running Elk tried to shake him loose, he planted his left knee on the warrior's forearm. His free hand went to his boot and pulled out the smaller knife.

Running Elk paled when he saw the blade gleaming in the white man's hand. He went still, gauging his chances. He saw none and decided to die bravely.

River read the decision on his face and brought the knife slowly toward his throat. He waited a moment, catching his breath, then spoke softly. "I think I can protect her."

Running Elk only glared at him.

River let the tip of the knife touch the brown skin then drew it away. He came swiftly to his feet but kept the knife poised in case Running Elk doubted that the fight was over.

"Why do you not kill me?" Running Elk made no move to rise.

"Your people need you to protect them, to help feed them."

Running Elk shook his head.

River slid the knife into his boot. He reached out to Running Elk to help him rise. "You saved my woman's life. I have no wish to ride away to the sound of your women weeping."

After a moment of hesitation, Running Elk clasped the offered arm just below the elbow and came to his feet. "Besides," River said, "I may need you for a friend someday."

Running Elk rose to his full height. "I will never be a white man's friend."

River grinned. "Suit yourself." He walked to the knives, slipping his own into the sheath on his thigh and tossing the other to Running Elk. The villagers were talking and smiling, obviously pleased with the show. River supposed, however, that they would have been at least as happy to see Running Elk kill him.

He met Sarah coming slowly toward him. She touched a shaking finger to his bloody face. He gathered her into his arms and held her. "You're safe now," he whispered, not knowing Sarah had been about to whisper the same thing.

The sun was dipping low in the sky when River helped Sarah onto the pinto and mounted the black. Deer Tracks had invited them to eat and stay the night in the village, but River had declined, knowing Sarah would be happier away from the Indians. Besides, after three days and nights of constant worry, he felt a need to have his Sarah to himself.

The Sioux village was situated at a bend in a little creek, which River followed upstream, looking almost immediately for a place to camp. He watched Sarah as he rode, aware by now that the straight back and calm face could hide exhaustion. "We'll stop soon," he said softly.

Sarah nodded slightly. "I knew you would come."

River was amazed at how good that simple statement made him feel. He couldn't help but grin at her. "You did?"

Sarah turned to him. "I don't know how I knew it when you didn't come the last time."

"Last time?" River prompted.

Sarah swallowed. She hadn't meant to talk about the past. She didn't want River upset with her, not now when she needed him so badly. When she spoke, she heard the tremor in her voice. "When I was in jail."

"Sarah, you refused to see me. I went to that jail every day..." He froze as his memory revealed things he hadn't understood at the time. "Father."

Sarah watched him curiously. "You did come?" she whispered, almost afraid to believe it.

River let out a slow breath and mumbled, "I wonder what else the old man managed to interfere with." He turned to her, studying the deep brown eyes that held a mixture of hope and bewilderment. "How did you know I would come this time?"

She shrugged, deciding not to answer directly. "I thought you would come, and die because of me." She turned away as her eyes filled with tears.

River wanted to pull her into his arms and kiss away the tears. There would be time for that when they found a place to camp, he reminded himself. And serious conversation could wait until they had had a rest. He nodded his understanding. "Then I guess you would have made Running Elk a good second wife."

"Second wife?"

River shrugged. "I don't know. Maybe third."

Sarah remembered the two women in the lodge and wondered if either was Running Elk's wife. Maybe both were! They hadn't seemed jealous of her; in fact they had been quite kind. She decided River must be teasing her. At least her eyes were dry now.

When River found a spot to his liking, he dismounted and helped Sarah to the ground. His hands on her waist and the nearness of her body made him want to hold her again. He kept thinking about how close he had come to losing her, and holding her seemed the best way to chase away the awful feeling. Instead, he bent and placed a quick kiss on her lips before releasing her. She needed food and rest, and his own needs would have to wait. "Start a fire," he said. "I'll take care of the horses."

Sarah nodded, watching him go, relieved that he didn't go far. There was plenty of wood, and she had it arranged inside a circle of rocks in short order. River was still rubbing down the horses, and she went to join him. She glanced at the packs on the ground before speaking. "I'm not going to look for flint and steel when I know you carry matches in your pocket."

River found the match and held it out to her. "Before you start supper, how about a swim?"

The suggestion made Sarah feel too shy to take the match from his fingers. A bath would feel wonderful, and it wasn't as if their bodies were strangers. But it had always been dark before.

The heat in River's eyes brought a warm glow to Sarah's face. She took the match, nodding slowly, and River grinned. "There's soap in that smaller pack. Feel free to start without me."

Sarah took the pack he had indicated and returned to start the fire, knowing the heat would be welcome after a swim in the cold stream. She found the soap and glanced toward River. He seemed to be more interested in the pinto than in her.

At the bank, she removed her dress. Kneeling in her chemise at the edge of the stream, she wet the old dress and rubbed it with soap. She discovered several small tears and one large one. It wouldn't take much more mending; sun and soap had faded most of the print from its original blue to a dull white.

She was hanging it on a pine branch near the fire when River joined her. He brought the other packs with him and, rummaging through one, came up with blankets and two clean shirts. "I personally would prefer that you wear only a blanket," he said. "But there's a shirt if you'd like."

She smiled her thanks, leaning toward him invitingly.

River chuckled. "Don't tempt me, Prairie Fire." Her eyes narrowed at the use of the Indian name, and he laughed, turning her toward the stream. "The cool water'll be good for your sunburn and cuts and bruises, not to mention mine." He touched his cheekbone where a cut had swollen enough to keep it from closing. His fingers came away sticky. "But let's do it before it gets too cool."

Sarah turned her back on River, removed her shoes and stockings and finally the chemise. She picked up the soap and self-consciously waded into the water. It was cool as River had predicted, but it felt good to her feet, sore from days of walking. In a moment, River was behind her, the warmth of his body contrasting sharply with the chill of the water.

"We can't exactly swim," he said, noting how the water barely came to his knees.

"It's too cold, anyway." Sarah knew there was more than one reason for the quiver in her voice.

"At least it's clear." River bent and dipped a small square of cloth in the water and held it out to her. "I thought you might not be too eager to lie here and soak."

She reached for the cloth, recognizing it as a piece of one of the rough gray blankets.

"On second thought," he said, pulling it away, "I'll keep this so I can wash your back." He bent to kiss her lips as he took the soap from her hand.

She laughed and turned around, holding her chestnut hair off her shoulders with both hands. The shock of the water made her gasp. The cold, rough cloth and his strong, gentle hands seemed to be two kinds of torture.

And he didn't stop with her back. She protested once that she could manage, but he ignored her, planting occasional kisses that made her knees tremble. Finally he stood in front of her and lifted her chin. He worked the cloth carefully over the sunburned face. He noticed the rope burns on her neck and planted a soft kiss there.

"The Indians?" he questioned gently.

"Gaines."

His eyes narrowed, but she shook her head. She didn't want to talk about any of it. She could feel a warmth reach across the space between her chilled body and his still-dry frame. She rested her hands against his chest as he washed her face. He felt warm, strong and safe. In a moment her head was against his chest and his arms were wrapped protectively around her.

He kissed the top of her head. "You better get back to the fire before you freeze."

She nodded, feeling slightly disappointed. River had left a blanket near the bank, and she dried herself quickly, leaving it for him to use. She scurried to the fire and donned one of the clean shirts before wrapping another blanket around her shoulders.

She added more wood to the fire and tried to warm her feet, hopping from one to the other while she clutched the blanket around her. She heard River laugh and turned to scowl at him. He had obviously been less hesitant to submerse himself in the cold stream. Water dripped from his hair to his sleek shoulders, and the last of the sunlight glistened in the hair on his body. He walked out of the water, and Sarah thought she shouldn't look but did anyway. He picked up the damp blanket, and she realized he was watching her with that easy grin of his.

"See if you can find something for us to eat," he said. She turned away but knew he was still grinning at her.

She rigged the blanket around her waist to serve as a skirt and knelt by the packs. Two canteens were lying nearby, their wet leather coverings indicating they had been recently filled. She found the utensils first and put water on to boil. In the packs she found coffee, salt pork, rice, beans and a variety of staples. There was even one of Eli's precious cans of peaches.

"How long did you expect to be looking for me?" she asked over her shoulder. "There's a lot of food here."

It was a moment before River spoke. "Eli believes in being prepared."

She didn't know what was taking him so long to dress and come to the fire, but she was afraid to look and see. She knew she was being foolish, but it embarrassed her when he caught her watching him. Her feet were cold, and she wished she had her shoes and stockings, but they were by the stream with her chemise—with River.

She busied herself with supper preparations. Finally she heard him approaching and looked up. And swallowed. He was dry now but still naked. In his hands he carried a bundle of wet clothes, which he proceeded to hang on branches near her dress. She was staring again, watching the muscles play across his shoulders, his legs, his buttocks.

He shook out one of her stockings. The intimacy of him washing her stocking was almost as startling as his nakedness. "I about lost one of these little bitty things," he said. "It would have washed right down to the Indian village. Wonder what they'd make of that." He glanced over his shoulder at her, grinning. "What's the matter? Don't you strip down naked to wash your clothes?"

All she could do was stare.

"There's a certain efficiency to it," he concluded, turning back to his work.

Sarah tried to return her attention to supper but failed. The rice was going to stick if she didn't stir it. She realized she was staring at River again when she felt the edge of the pot burn her hand. She jerked away, nearly knocking the rice into the fire. She brought the wound to her mouth and hoped River hadn't seen her. It did at least give her the determination to stop watching him.

After a few minutes he dropped her shoes near her and strolled to the packs. She set the rice and pork off the fire, near the plates, before reaching for the shoes.

She was pulling them on when he spoke. "In the morning we ought to go back to the Indian village and see what we can trade for a pair of moccasins for you.''

Sarah gave him a withering look, and he laughed. He had pulled on a pair of clean pants and was sliding his arms into the sleeves of a shirt. ''We'll be in Fort Laramie soon.''

Then what? she thought.

She watched him search the pockets of his jacket. He withdrew an envelope and something that looked like a wad of paper. He uttered a surprised laugh and turned to watch her a moment before approaching the fire. ''This belongs to you,'' he said, holding out the envelope. ''Bull must have taken the jewelry box. I found it near . . .'' He didn't finish.

She set the envelope aside as if it were unimportant, brushing away the memory of Bull and Herman. She was relieved River had seen the clippings. It had been foolish not to show them to him in the beginning. Wanting him to believe *her,* trust *her,* not some newspaper, had been a childish dream. ''The box?'' she asked, trying to sound unconcerned.

''Broken to splinters.'' He saw the disappointment in her eyes before she turned away. Did his gift from so long ago mean something to her? He found himself wanting to grin.

Sarah reached for a plate to fill, but he stopped her. ''This is yours, too.''

The tiny paper-wrapped parcel didn't seem familiar. She looked into his eyes as she took it from his outstretched hand. A gift, she realized. In a moment, she lifted the red satin ribbon from its wrappings and eyed him curiously.

"I got it for you at the Hollenberg Ranch." At her startled look he nodded. "Yeah, way back then. I didn't get around to giving it to you and forgot about it."

Sarah smiled. Now that he knew the truth, perhaps it was safe to recall the old days. "Red, Daniel?"

River looked at her sharply as his memory flashed a picture of the younger Sarah holding the red dress he had just given her. "Of course, red," he said softly.

Their eyes held each other's for a long moment. It was River who broke the spell. "Is that food for us?"

Sarah laughed, dropping the ribbon in her lap. She dipped up his supper and handed him his plate. Before she dipped up her own, she used the ribbon to tie her hair at the back of her neck.

"Thank you, River," she said.

River found himself disappointed she hadn't called him Daniel. He was sure she had deliberately reminded him of the past. He had hoped it meant she was beginning to trust him, but now he wasn't sure.

She had known he would come for her; surely that was a good sign.

He set his empty plate on the ground and cleared his throat. It was now or never. "Sarah, what do you plan to do?"

Sarah started to shrug, then squared her shoulders. "I plan to open a dressmaker's shop. I can take in mending and laundry until it gets going." She had a feeling her words sounded rehearsed.

"Does it matter where you do that?"

Sarah looked up from the plate she had been carefully studying. "What do you mean?"

River leaned forward, resting his arms on his knees. "Do you remember what we used to talk about doing?"

Sarah laughed. "You mean the branch of your father's store we were going to set up somewhere that would include gambling tables and a dance floor?"

River acknowledged the description with a rueful grin but turned serious quickly. "It wasn't all crazy, Sarah. There are little mining towns all over California where folks'll pay a lot for the simplest supplies. We won't be in partnership with my father, of course, but I remember some of what he tried to teach me, and I know how to get the supplies across the mountains."

Sarah wasn't sure what he was saying. He was looking at her expectantly, as if her approval were somehow important. "We?" was all she could manage to ask.

"I wouldn't expect you to go back east for supplies every year. You could mind the store and sew your dresses. Rice could drive a wagon, and we could hire the rest. Maybe Nathan will stick around."

"We?"

River stopped. His plans had come so far in his own mind that he was springing them all on Sarah too quickly. "Do you think you might want to cast your lot in with me?"

Sarah didn't know what to make of the things he was saying. Part of her was screaming, *You won't have to leave him!* But he had said nothing of marriage. This was a partnership he was discussing. "You could mind the store," he had said.

At her hesitation, he spoke again, afraid to hear her objections. "It wouldn't have to be California, Sarah. I'd go anywhere you wanted."

Sarah's eyes widened. "River—" she started.

He interrupted. "Sarah, I love you. I'm sure you love me. I can't lose you again."

She stared at him, her plate forgotten on her lap. Was he only offering this because he knew he had made a mistake six years ago? Was he suggesting this partnership out of guilt? She had decided she would take whatever he offered, but somehow this hurt too much. She started to shake her head, but he raised his hands to stop her.

"Don't answer now," he said softly as he stood. He lifted the plate from her lap and set it on the ground. A tug on her hand brought her to her feet in front of him. "Don't answer now," he whispered, bringing his lips toward hers. "Not if the answer's no."

River's shirt was still open, and Sarah's hands found their way around his waist. She raised herself on her toes and leaned into his kiss. She had been waiting for this since he washed her in the stream. No, since he helped her from the horse, or maybe even longer. But that was before she knew he had read the papers in the envelope, before guilt had driven him to come up with some way to take care of her.

River easily slipped the blanket from around Sarah's waist. With a flick of a wrist he tossed it away. While his mouth tasted the soft flesh of her neck, his hands splayed against her thighs and traveled upward, under the shirt. Her skin was soft and warm, and he felt a stab of pain when he thought of how close he had come to losing her. His lips returned to hers with a new sense of urgency. He wouldn't lose her again! If she wanted to walk away, he would let her, but he would follow. Every time she turned around he would be waiting.

Sarah's body trembled as he caressed her bare skin. His hands found the swell of her breasts, and she moaned against his lips. When his thumbs began to circle the hardened tips, she felt her knees go weak with longing.

River gathered her into his arms and set her down on the blanket, spreading it haphazardly as he laid her upon it. In a moment he had shed his clothes and lay beside her, undoing the buttons on her shirt while her fingers drew trails of fire on his chest.

He loved her then, knowing her passion was as great as his, believing she loved him. She had to love him. But there was something almost sad about the way she touched him. Much later, he rose to add more wood to the fire and find another blanket. She was watching him when he returned, and he knew he hadn't imagined her sadness.

"Sarah," he whispered, lying beside her and drawing her into his arms. "I know you don't trust me. I can understand that. But someday..." He sighed. There had to be some way to make her understand. "I know you didn't rob my father's store. I think I knew it at the time, at first anyway. When they told me you wouldn't see me, I had to convince myself I'd never loved you. It was the only way to save my sanity."

Sarah stirred, and he looked down at her. Her voice quavered. "And I had to cling to my love for you for the same reason."

River held her more tightly. "Maybe someday you'll trust me enough to tell me what really happened, what I really saw that night."

Sarah wondered if she had jumped. She was about to ask River to repeat what he had said, but she knew she had heard. He must have felt her reaction because he pulled away from her a little, trying to get more light on her face. "What's wrong?" he asked.

It took her a moment to find her voice. "Didn't you read the article in that envelope?"

"No. It wasn't mine to open. I didn't really think about it."

"But, I thought... How did you... You said you knew I was innocent."

"Sarah," River said patiently, "I loved you six years ago. I love you still. I know you couldn't have robbed the store. I don't know *how* I know, I just do." He waited a moment before asking, "Do you want to tell me what's in the envelope?"

"Six years ago..." Sarah stopped, uncertain how to explain. Finally she said simply, "Linda stole my red dress."

River drew in a sharp breath. Of course it had been Linda, Linda who had suddenly become so eager to please. He had let himself be fooled by a dress! Six years! And now the story was painfully clear. His arms tightened around her, and he buried his face in her hair, a low moan escaping his lips.

Sarah went on softly. "They found her body a few months ago. Most of the money was still in her little shack. According to the article, one of her friends said she went a little crazy. She meant for me to take the blame. I think she was after you more than the money. Alcohol killed her, I guess. Anyway, that's why they let me out of prison."

River raised his head and kissed her warm lips. "I'm sorry, sweetheart. I should have figured it out. She really pursued me when you were in jail, but I didn't make the connection."

"It's over now," she said.

River was quiet for a moment. "When I made my offer before, did I leave out marriage?"

Sarah had to giggle. "Yes, you left out marriage."

"I don't think I explained it very well. Marriage was always part of the deal. Would it have made any difference?"

"Not then," Sarah said. "I thought you had read the article and were feeling guilty."

"Well, I am feeling guilty, but that's only part of it. If I renew my offer and include marriage this time, do you think you might consider it?"

Sarah couldn't hide the smile in her voice. "Yes," she said.

He grinned, feeling unimaginably happy. "Is that a yes, you'll marry me, or yes, you'll consider my offer?"

She laughed, and he bent to kiss her before pulling back to look into her eyes. "You know, six years ago our love seemed so fragile, but look how it's lasted."

She brought her hand around his neck and whispered as she drew him toward her, "Maybe now it's a different kind of love."

* * * * *

WOMEN OF THE WEST

Exciting stories of the old West and the women whose dreams
and passions shaped a new land!

Join Harlequin Historicals every month as we bring you
these unforgettable tales.

Don't miss any of our **Women of the West!**

RUGGED. SEXY. HEROIC.

OUTLAWS *and* HEROES

Stony Carlton—A lone wolf determined never to be tied down.

Gabriel Taylor—Accused and found guilty by small-town gossip.

Clay Barker—At Revenge Unlimited, he *is* the law.

JOAN JOHNSTON, DALLAS SCHULZE and **MALLORY RUSH**, three of romance fiction's biggest names, have created three unforgettable men—modern heroes who have the courage to fight for what is right....

OUTLAWS AND HEROES—available in September wherever Harlequin books are sold.

HARLEQUIN ®

PRIZE SURPRISE SWEEPSTAKES!

This month's prize:

BEAUTIFUL WEDGWOOD CHINA!

This month, as a special surprise, we're giving away a bone china dinner service for eight by Wedgwood**, one of England's most prestigious manufacturers!

Think how beautiful your table will look, set with lovely Wedgwood china in the casual Countryware pattern! Each five-piece place setting includes dinner plate, salad plate, soup bowl and cup and saucer.

The facing page contains two Entry Coupons (as does every book you received this shipment). Complete and return *all* the entry coupons; **the more times you enter, the better your chances of winning!**

Then keep your fingers crossed, because you'll find out by September 15, 1995 if you're the winner!

Remember: The more times you enter, the better your chances of winning!*

PRIZE SURPRISE
SWEEPSTAKES

OFFICIAL ENTRY COUPON

This entry must be received by: AUGUST 30, 1995
This month's winner will be notified by: SEPTEMBER 15, 1995

YES, I want to win the Wedgwood china service for eight! Please enter me in the drawing and let me know if I've won!

Name_____

Address _____ Apt. _____

City   State/Prov.   Zip/Postal Code

Account #_____

Return entry with invoice in reply envelope.

© 1995 HARLEQUIN ENTERPRISES LTD.   CWW KAL

PRIZE SURPRISE
SWEEPSTAKES

OFFICIAL ENTRY COUPON

This entry must be received by: AUGUST 30, 1995
This month's winner will be notified by: SEPTEMBER 15, 1995

YES, I want to win the Wedgwood china service for eight! Please enter me in the drawing and let me know if I've won!

Name_____

Address _____ Apt. _____

City   State/Prov.   Zip/Postal Code

Account #_____

Return entry with invoice in reply envelope.

© 1995 HARLEQUIN ENTERPRISES LTD.   CWW KAL

OFFICIAL RULES
PRIZE SURPRISE SWEEPSTAKES 3448
NO PURCHASE OR OBLIGATION NECESSARY

Three Harlequin Reader Service 1995 shipments will contain respectively, coupons for entry into three different prize drawings, one for a Panasonic 31" wide-screen TV, another for a 5-piece Wedgwood china service for eight and the third for a Sharp ViewCam camcorder. To enter any drawing using an Entry Coupon, simply complete and mail according to directions.

There is no obligation to continue using the Reader Service to enter and be eligible for any prize drawing. You may also enter any drawing by hand printing the words "Prize Surprise," your name and address on a 3"x5" card and the name of the prize you wish that entry to be considered for (i.e., Panasonic wide-screen TV, Wedgwood china or Sharp ViewCam). Send your 3"x5" entries via first-class mail (limit: one per envelope) to: Prize Surprise Sweepstakes 3448, c/o the prize you wish that entry to be considered for, P.O. Box 1315, Buffalo, NY 14269-1315, USA or P.O. Box 610, Fort Erie, Ontario L2A 5X3, Canada.

To be eligible for the Panasonic wide-screen TV, entries must be received by 6/30/95; for the Wedgwood china, 8/30/95; and for the Sharp ViewCam, 10/30/95.

Winners will be determined in random drawings conducted under the supervision of D.L. Blair, Inc., an independent judging organization whose decisions are final, from among all eligible entries received for that drawing. Approximate prize values are as follows: Panasonic wide-screen TV ($1,800); Wedgwood china ($840) and Sharp ViewCam ($2,000). Sweepstakes open to residents of the U.S. (except Puerto Rico) and Canada, 18 years of age or older. Employees and immediate family members of Harlequin Enterprises, Ltd., D.L. Blair, Inc., their affiliates, subsidiaries and all other agencies, entities and persons connected with the use, marketing or conduct of this sweepstakes are not eligible. Odds of winning a prize are dependent upon the number of eligible entries received for that drawing. Prize drawing and winner notification for each drawing will occur no later than 15 days after deadline for entry eligibility for that drawing. Limit: one prize to an individual, family or organization. All applicable laws and regulations apply. Sweepstakes offer void wherever prohibited by law. Any litigation within the province of Quebec respecting the conduct and awarding of the prizes in this sweepstakes must be submitted to the Regies des loteries et Courses du Quebec. In order to win a prize, residents of Canada will be required to correctly answer a time-limited arithmetical skill-testing question. Value of prizes are in U.S. currency.

Winners will be obligated to sign and return an Affidavit of Eligibility within 30 days of notification. In the event of noncompliance within this time period, prize may not be awarded. If any prize or prize notification is returned as undeliverable, that prize will not be awarded. By acceptance of a prize, winner consents to use of his/her name, photograph or other likeness for purposes of advertising, trade and promotion on behalf of Harlequin Enterprises, Ltd., without further compensation, unless prohibited by law.

For the names of prizewinners (available after 12/31/95), send a self-addressed, stamped envelope to: Prize Surprise Sweepstakes 3448 Winners, P.O. Box 4200, Blair, NE 68009.

RPZ KAL